The Second Girl

The Second Girl

David Swinson

MULHOLLAND BOOKS

LITTLE, BROWN AND COMPANY
NEW YORK BOSTON LONDON

Copyright © 2016 by David Swinson

Mulholland Books/Little, Brown and Company
Hachette Book Group
1290 Avenue of the Americas, New York, NY 10104
mulhollandbooks.com

First Edition: June 2016

Mulholland Books is an imprint of Little, Brown and Company, a division of Hachette Book Group, Inc. The Mulholland Books name and logo are trademarks of Hachette Book Group, Inc.

The publisher is not responsible for websites (or their content) that are not owned by the publisher.

The Hachette Speakers Bureau provides a wide range of authors for speaking events. To find out more, go to hachettespeakersbureau.com or call (866) 376-6591.

ISBN 978-0-316-26417-4
Library of Congress Control Number: 2015942054

10 9 8 7 6 5 4 3 2 1

RRD-C

Printed in the United States of America

For my wife, Catherine,
and my daughter, Vivienne

Keep your eyes open to your mercies. The man who forgets to be thankful has fallen asleep in life.

—*Robert Louis Stevenson*

The light shines in the darkness, and the darkness has not overcome it.

—*John 1:5 NIV*

PART ONE

ONE

I've been sitting on the run-down two-story row house on Kenyon Street Northwest off and on for eight days. That's the longest I've had to surveil a location, but it's worth the effort. I know it'll be a good hit.

Lord knows I need a good hit.

At least five Salvadoran boys are living in the house on a regular basis; all of them nothing but little big men, aspiring to be hard, slingin' their shit in the area of 16th and Park. Mostly weed, crack cocaine, and heroin, but they recently got into powder, which is what interests me most. Powder cocaine is getting harder to find nowadays. Crack is still the drug of choice on the street, and of course heroin. Then there's PCP, but that's a whole different monster. It made a comeback a few years ago. Kids're walking around in the open, smoking dippers like they're regular cigarettes. The Salvadoran boys won't mess with that shit. But I've seen them hanging with someone who will.

Cordell Holm.

I had dealings with Cordell back in the day, when I was on the job and working narcotics. He's the leader of a crew that controls most of the corners in the Adams Morgan area, and one of that area's main distributors. Cordell's crew usually works south of Columbia Road. Park Road is north of Columbia, so when I saw him with the Salvadorans like they were talking business, I figured Cordell was expanding his horizons, maybe got himself into bed with one of the bigger Latino gangs that control Columbia to Park.

I don't know if the Salvadorans are affiliated with one of those gangs or if they're just a bunch of orphans who got themselves adopted by the Holm family. Doesn't matter to me which scenario it is. All I know for sure is that Cordell Holm deals in weight, and that means I have a chance of getting a piece of that today.

Like I've done all the other days I've been sitting on this spot, I watch them as they make their way out the door, usually by ten hundred hours. They slide into an older model, mostly primed-out, four-door gray Toyota with chromed-out wheels, an oversize metallic-red spoiler, and home-tinted windows. A little El Salvadoran flag, fringed in gold, hangs from the rearview mirror.

They head west, like they always do, toward 16th Street and Park Road. I've tailed them enough times to know they'll park at a spot another Latino kid reserves for them, a young boy, twelve to fourteen years old, just another kid trying to get his foot in the door and working up to something more.

The driver, an older-looking boy who keeps his hair slicked back and shiny, will stay with the car. The other four will split up by twos and cover the area that spans east on Park from 16th to 14th Street.

The boy with the shiny hair takes care of the stash. He keeps it in a crumpled up Doritos bag, which he drops in the gutter at the rear of their vehicle as if it were trash. He keeps a thick wad of cash rolled up and stuffed in the sock on his left foot.

Another boy, who always wears an oversize Wizards jersey and black Jordan Super Fly sneakers, returns to the car when they're low on merchandise, usually after a couple of hours. He drives the car back to the house to re-up, then returns it to Shiny.

I should be long gone by the time they need to re-up. But then I know all too well what can happen. Shit, just about anything can happen. Shiny might get lucky and hook up, bring her back to the house on Kenyon. Or maybe it'll be a busy day and Super Fly'll need to re-up sooner. You can never predict; you can only prepare. I'm prepared. But I also do my best to eliminate the possibility of an encounter—no more than fifteen minutes inside. You'd be surprised what an experienced person like me can find in fifteen minutes.

These boys have been running free on the streets, as if they own that real estate they're working. It wouldn't be difficult for even a mediocre cop to figure out what they're doing. But I haven't seen any of them try. Third District's short on manpower. The whole police department's short on manpower. All the smart ones are leaving and most of the old-timers are on their way out or already gone. The few that remain are getting themselves pulled from their regular assignments by the chief for one ridiculous thing or another—some detail with a fancy acronym. By the time those officers get off from working that shit, they're either too tired to work regular or they just don't give a damn. Hate to say it, 'cause I like most of them, but their fatigue or sloppiness works to my benefit.

I sit on the house for another ten minutes after the Salvadorans pull out.

When it feels right I step out of my Volvo, and slip on my suit coat, and tighten the knot of my tie. I shoulder my nearly empty backpack, which contains only a few items I might need once I get inside—a small Streamlight, a stun gun, a crowbar, a screwdriver, pliers, a box cutter, zip ties, and an extra pair of handcuffs.

I look both ways and cross the street.

It's about half a block to the house.

I walk like I belong.

Two

Most of the leaves have fallen from the few trees that hang tough on this block. The largest one, an old oak, with roots like fat, arthritic fingers reaching over the median, stands tall, anchored defiantly in front of their house.

The sidewalk and the walkway leading to the front porch are littered with dead leaves, crunching under my feet.

If I'm walking like I belong, why try to walk quietly? That wouldn't be natural. It's the way I look and dress, the way I carry myself, that means the most. Those years on the job stay with you, and I learned well. A commanding exterior presence. The inside, well, maybe not so much.

An empty bottle of Cuervo 1800, spent containers of sports drinks, cigarette butts, and scrunched-up red plastic cups are piled in a corner of the patio, in front of a couple of fold-up chairs. The black security gate is aluminum; the front door's wooden, and there's one dead bolt above the doorknob. Old, just like the house. You'd think based on what they do for a living they'd have more sense and give the front door an upgrade, invest in a steel door with a stronger frame. Maybe they're just too fucking confident. They'll know better soon.

I pull a pair of latex gloves out of the front pocket of my pants, put them on. I ring the doorbell a couple of times. I hear it chime, muffled through the wooden door, wait a few seconds and ring again. No answer. No barking dog, but I never saw them with a dog, so I don't expect one.

I look behind me, scan the block, unshoulder the backpack, unzip one of the pockets, and grab a large screwdriver.

I wedge the tip between the door and the frame to the right of the dead bolt, find the spot where the bolt meets the metal, then slam the screwdriver with the heel of my palm. It doesn't take more than a couple of hits.

Another quick glance behind me, and I pry the door open and enter, closing it behind me. It swings open a bit 'cause it won't latch. I notice a single tennis shoe on the floor, grab it, and push it against the door so it stays partly open. Push back my suit jacket and remove my Glock from its holster. I tuck it to my side.

The smell inside the house is like ripe armpit mixed with cheap old liquor. I've been in worse places, though. More shoes on the floor, discarded shirts on two stained sofas, empty bottles of liquor, beer, cigarette butts falling out of ashtrays, beer cans replacing ashtrays, brand-new flat screen on an old coffee table against a wall.

It doesn't matter how much preparation you put into a spot before you go in. Unless you can see through walls, you never know what you're going to find. Fortunately, this is a small house, so there are not a lot of rooms to clear. No basement either, so one of the upstairs bedrooms is more than likely the spot I'm looking for. I've got a feeling Shiny likes to keep the stash close, so after I clear the house, the room I believe he beds down in is the one I'll tear up.

The kitchen is littered with pizza boxes, more empty beer and liquor bottles. There are a few power tools—circular saw, drills, tile cutter, and so on—lined up against a wall near the rear door. Doesn't look like they do much cooking. There are a couple of nearly full bottles of Cuervo on the counter. I'll give it a more thorough search after I check the rooms on the second floor.

The wooden staircase leading to the second floor is narrow and creaky, the railing flimsy. I grip my gun with two hands and keep it at the ready.

Move up the steps.

An equally narrow hallway with wood floors, an open door to a bedroom straight ahead. Two other rooms, one of the doors open, separated by a bathroom. A linen closet with a slightly open door is across from the bathroom, past the flimsy metal banister rails.

I clear the room ahead of me first and then the next one. I'll make my way back to search both rooms after I clear and search the master bedroom.

The closed door should be the main bedroom. Probably Shiny's. I swing it open.

It's the master bedroom. One window with drawn blackout curtains and a large king-size bed against a wall. A soccer ball's in the middle of the floor, surrounded by dirty laundry and a black garbage bag stuffed with more dirty laundry. A portrait representing Christ, eyes toward heaven, hangs on the wall over the bed. Graffiti, as if they've been practicing their craft, on the other walls. There's a small walk-in closet and another closed door with a latch and a padlock on the outside. I like padlocked doors.

I pull the curtain open enough to peek out. The old oak directly ahead. My Volvo across the street half a block down. Same cars that were parked there earlier. An old black man walking along the sidewalk on the other side of the street.

The padlocked door has to be a bathroom. It's an obvious first choice to search.

I position myself to the side of the door and put my ear against it, give it a bit of a push, then turn the knob. I hear what sounds like a chain or a leash scooting on the floor. Sounds like I might have gotten the dog ownership thing all wrong. The last thing I want is an underfed pit bull jumping out at me after I open the door. All the time I've been sitting on this place I've never seen them with one. Sometimes they'll keep them locked up and secured inside where they keep the stash. The dogs get meaner being confined like that. If it is a dog, it might think I'm its master and won't attack until after I break off the latch and it suddenly realizes I'm not. Dogs don't scare me, but that doesn't mean I want to deal with one right now. I put my ear against the door again, push at it. Nothing this time, not even a low growl. But there's definitely something in there. If it's a dog, I'm hoping it'll be crated.

I set my backpack on the floor, grip my weapon with my right hand, and pull out the crowbar from the backpack. It's a tool that's not only good for busting out a padlock on a latched door, but for teaching a bad dog a valuable lesson. Last thing I want to do is shoot the damn thing. Putting one through the head's not only messy, but will attract attention. I holster my weapon, then wedge the crowbar in the latch where it meets the screws, and give it a yank. The screws tear out, splintering the wood. The latch and locked padlock fall to the floor.

I grip the crowbar tight like I mean business, then stand quiet and listen. Nothing. A dog would have reacted. Maybe. You never know with some of those gunpowder-fed psycho breeds, so I open the bathroom door slowly, while stepping back to a more defensive position.

"Damn," I say, but it sounds more like a sudden release of breath.

A young girl, mouth duct-taped, in nothing but her underwear, sits cowering on the tile floor, snug against the wall below the sink and next to the corner of the bathtub. Her hands handcuffed in front, secured to a chain that's fastened to a large eyebolt, which is screwed into the floor. Her shoulder-length blond hair in a ponytail. Bruises on her legs. Her face mostly hidden, tucked down to cradle herself, as if she's afraid of what I might do to her.

THREE

For an instant I want to turn around and hightail it the hell outta here. I want to pretend like I never saw this shit. I'll just find a new spot to hit—quickly. This nature of mine is all about fight or flight, and right now it's all flight. What the hell am I supposed to do with this? Fuck. Despite the desperation and need that overwhelms me after I'm coming down from a long binge, I have a stronger old self that knows better.

I can't run.

She's still huddled there, whimpering, ninety pounds of serious living shit.

"I'm not gonna hurt you, girl," I try, in my most comforting tone.

I grab my key ring out of my pants pocket.

"I'm gonna take those off you, okay?"

I lean down on one knee, reach for her hands. She resists at first, still unsure. The handcuff key I carry on my key ring works for the ones that bind her. She tries to scoot away, like a feral child in chains, but the wall stops her.

"I'm not gonna hurt you," I say again. "See, look."

I slowly pull my wallet out of my back pants pocket and unfold it to show her the police badge. My thumb hides the portion of the badge that reads "Retired." "See, it says 'Detective.'"

I reach for her cuffed hands again, and this time she doesn't resist. They're sturdy handcuffs, like the ones I have, not something you can buy just anywhere. Cops, or maybe security guards, carry cuffs like this. I slip them in my left front pants pocket.

After I release her, I realize I should've peeled the duct tape off first. I notice a few track marks on her right inner arm, but not like someone who's been using for a long time—just a few new bruises. Her small breasts are also bruised. She can't be more than fifteen. She covers her breasts with her arms. I almost want to say I'm not looking at her like that, but I take off my jacket instead to offer to her. I can see she notices the holstered gun I carry on the right side of my waist.

She grabs the jacket, drapes it around her shoulders, and grips it tight to cover her body. It's large enough to cover her down to her knees. I slide the wallet back into my pants pocket. "Let me take that off your face."

She shakes her head no and starts to pull off the duct tape on her own. She whimpers as it tugs and pulls at the corner of her thin lip, but she manages to get it off. The area around her mouth is blotchy, scaly. It's been pulled from her mouth more than once.

"What's your name?" I ask.

It takes her a moment to say, "Amanda."

"Amanda, I'm Frank, but my friends call me Frankie or just Marr. Where do you live, Amanda?"

"Burke, Virginia."

"That's in Fairfax County, right?"

"Yes. My family, are they okay?" She begins to weep.

"Your family?" I ask, wondering if I somehow missed finding them when I cleared the house. "Are they here?"

She looks at me, confused now.

"No, they're home. They're home, aren't they?"

"I'm sure they're home. I need to get you out of here now. You'll be with them soon enough."

"No. No. I thought you were here because they're safe. I thought you came here to get me. No, I can't go home," she says, tears now streaming.

"Why can't you go home?"

"Because he said they'd kill my family if I ever went home," she cries. "You said you are a policeman. Have you seen them, my mom . . . my dad?"

"I came here because of something else and found you."

"I can't go, then. They'll kill them! They know where I live. They'll kill my mom and my dad."

"No they won't. I'll make sure of that. I gotta take you outta here now, all right? Trust me when I say they're not gonna touch your family, or you. Okay?"

I can tell she's afraid to leave and why she was cuffed in front instead of in the back. She wasn't about to escape. Those boys knew that. They've had enough time to brainwash the shit out of this kid. Judging by the tracks and the bruises, I'd say a few days. That's more than enough time for a child like this.

"They been putting that shit in your arm, or have you?" I ask, and realize afterward that I'm talking to a little girl, not the junkies or crackheads I'm used to talking to.

"He has," she says, with a firmness that suggests anger. Her lip quivers.

And I wonder if "he" is Shiny.

"Heroin?"

"Yes, and something else once, but it kept me up for almost two days so they didn't anymore."

"What else they got you using?" I ask, realizing how my mind is working now.

"Just weed. I want to go now."

"I need to know first. The stuff they shot you up with, which made you stay up for two days, do you know where they keep that?"

"I don't know. Why are you asking me this? Please, I want my mom now."

I'm such an asshole. Who thinks like this?

"Where do they keep their stash?"

She looks at me, eyes wide, like she remembers when I said I didn't come here for her.

"Is it someplace in the room there?"

"I don't know," she says, fear in her voice now. "Please take me home." She breaks down and sobs.

I'm kicked back to reality. Her fucking reality.

"Are you hurt anywhere? I mean, can you move?"

"I can move."

I maneuver myself calmly toward her and offer my hand.

She accepts.

"Let's get outta here," I say.

I help her up, but her knees buckle after she stands.

"Button up the jacket. I'll have to carry you."

She does.

I grab around her with my left arm, over my jacket where it falls below her rear. I lift her, and it's like lifting nothing at all. She wraps her frail arms around my neck. I slip the crowbar into my backpack with my free hand on the way out and shoulder the backpack. She doesn't say a word.

I pull the living room curtain and peek out before I exit. It looks clear, so I kick away the shoe that props the door. Once outside, I try to pull it shut the best I can. With my luck, some crackhead burglar's going to roll up on the spot and find the stash, along with who knows what else. Damn, I can't even think about it. Here I am, cradling this little girl, who's been through hell, and this is what I think about.

I got just enough of my own to get me through tonight at least, but I don't like the prospect of what tomorrow might bring if I don't get the job finished today. I got a few necessities to help me through in the event of a total crash—Valium, Klonopin, Oxy, a good amount of weed, and a lot of liquor. But I like my life on the ups, not the downs.

I walk quickly to my car and around to the rear passenger's side. I set my backpack on the sidewalk and push the button on the key fob, unlocking the door. I gently put her in, sit her on the seat. I buckle the seat belt for her.

"This is a funny-looking car for a policeman," she says.

"It's a specialized car, for cops who don't want to be made as cops," I return with a smile.

I close the door and walk around to the driver's side, open the door and set the backpack on the front seat, peel off my latex gloves, and shove them in my pants pocket. I start the car.

Before I pull out I look at her through the rearview mirror and I realize I can't go to the cops. It doesn't matter that I'm a former cop turned PI and still have a couple of friends I can trust. And seriously, there's only two.

Yeah, I can make up a good story. I'm not worried about that. Hell, I rescued a little girl. Exigent circumstances. Those words alone allowed me to kick in plenty of doors back in the day. But the fact is, if I take her somewhere like the Third District, which is the closest station, I'll be there most of the day answering questions and making up stories. I don't have the time for that shit.

And I can't just take her home. Cops would still get involved, and Fairfax County PD would be slow-cooking my ass for even more hours than DC. Whatever choice I make, cops are going to get involved. I just have to do it in a way that minimizes my exposure and allows me to get back out here and do what I gotta do before they move on it first.

Then it comes to me.

Costello.

I'll take her to Costello's office downtown. She'll know how to handle it. She retains me as an investigator for some of her bigger defense cases. All this other shit I do, well, that's just sustaining a lifestyle I couldn't afford otherwise.

I look at my wristwatch. If I hurry, I might have enough time after I drop off the kid to come back and make a quick run through before those Salvadoran mopes return. I'll just have to give Costello the condensed version of a story I haven't thought of yet.

Four

I take Georgia Avenue south until it turns into 7th. Howard Hospital is behind me. I think about turning around to take her there. I look at the rearview again, notice her wrapped in my suit jacket, unexpressive and gazing out the window.

My mind's been racing, but like I said, taking her to Costello's might buy me the time I need to finish up what I spent days planning so I stay the course.

"How old are you, Amanda?"

I see her break away from the window as if something jarred her.

"Sixteen."

"You look a little young for sixteen. When's your birthday?"

She doesn't answer. It's like she forgot.

"Amanda, can you tell me your birthday?"

"October eleventh."

"That was like a couple days ago, huh?"

"Yeah."

Damn, what a way to spend your birthday.

"Did they kidnap you, Amanda?" I ask directly.

She disappears again, somewhere in her head or out the window.

"Did they kidnap you?"

"No," she says, just as directly.

"Tell me what happened. I need you to focus now because I'll need to explain it later."

She is looking at me watching her through the rearview mirror.

It takes a moment, but she says, "There's a boy," then pauses, thinks. "He goes to my school, Edgar. He took me there once. He said they were his brothers and I should meet them because he wanted me to be his girl."

"So you dated Edgar before that?"

"Yeah, I guess. He has a car, and we'd drive around sometimes, maybe go to the mall."

"The first time you were there, is that when they kidnapped you?"

"No. They took me to a mall and bought me stuff."

"Your parents ever say anything about that?"

"They never knew. Don't tell my parents," she adds desperately.

"I won't tell them."

I can guess the rest. Shit like this has been going on for a while. It even hit the news recently, how some of the gangs are moving to the suburbs to recruit impressionable high school kids, especially teenage girls. Cute young gangbangers wooing them, buying them shit, taking them places, and giving them the kind of attention they crave at that age. Next thing they know, they got them smoking weed and moving up the chain, to harder drugs. The bigger gangs around here are notorious for this shit. After that they either put them to work at a brothel or on the streets.

"What school you go to?"

"Lake Braddock."

"This is important, Amanda, so I need you to listen carefully, okay?"

"Okay?"

"What I do is very sensitive, so I can't just drive you up to a police district and drop you off."

"So you're going to take me straight home?"

"Someone else is going to take care of that."

"What, why? Why can't you just take me home now?"

"It's not that simple. There's a lady I know. She's a lawyer—"

"I don't want to go there. I just want you to take me home."

"You are going home. This lady works with the police all the time, not just me. She's a very nice lady, and I gotta take you to her office. She'll take care of you and call your parents."

I'm telling her all of this assuming Costello's going to do it. For all I know she's going to tell me to go to hell and take her to headquarters, which is not even a block from her office. I'm hoping if that happens I can convince her otherwise.

"It's how things like this work, Amanda," I lie.

"I can go home today?"

"Yes. You'll see your parents very soon, and either they'll take you home or the police will."

"Okay." She looks out the window again.

"The police will ask you a bunch of questions, like how long you've been held there against your will, what they did to you, how they made you do drugs. They'll have some tough questions."

"Okay."

"They'll even ask about me and how I got you outta there. You just tell them what you know, and if and when there comes a time they have to talk to me, I'll fill in the rest, all right?"

"Okay."

I can tell she's in shock, so I leave it at that. I pull out my cell phone to call Leslie's office. It kicks into her voicemail. I let her know I'm on my way and that it's extremely important.

Traffic is heavy once I hit downtown DC. I look at my watch again. I still have time, but I gotta make my way through all of this. I hate this city, hate this damn traffic. I usually avoid having to come downtown as much as possible. The only time I'm down this way is when I have to meet up with Costello for a job she has for me, or sometimes for a sandwich at Jack's Deli with my old partners Luna and McGuire.

I hang a left onto F Street. Traffic eases up a bit.

At 5th, I swing right and try to find parking, which is usually next to impossible, but it's better than 6th. You got the U.S. Attorney's Office, the mayor's building, police headquarters, the Office of the Corporation Counsel, Superior Court, and District Court all located within a short walking distance of one another. And this city doesn't have one public parking structure to ease the pain. There are a couple of private underground ones if you want to pay up the ass, but that's it. I manage to hit a curb spot just as someone is pulling out. It's only half a block from Costello's building on Indiana Avenue, near 6th. A moment of grace.

After I take off my seat belt, I untuck my shirt so that it'll conceal my holstered weapon. I pick up my backpack from the front seat and place it on the floor behind my seat. I exit the car and walk around to open the door for Amanda.

"Do you think you can walk now?" I ask, but then look at her bare feet. "Maybe I should carry you."

"I can walk."

I take her hand as she steps out of the car and close the door behind her, then let go of her hand to lock the doors.

She grabs my other hand and holds tight.

We walk toward Costello's office, and I think about how tight her grip is, as if she's afraid that if she lets go I'll lose her. I feel uncomfortable and sad, two feelings I don't usually surrender to.

"Watch where you're walking," I tell her.

Costello's office is located in one of the older buildings on the south side of Indiana Avenue. It's connected to another large redbrick building that takes up half the block. Most of the offices in the buildings on either side of the street are occupied by attorneys who work in private practice. Some of them have big names and even bigger clients. And many of them, like Costello, used to work for the U.S. Attorney's Office, but chose the dark side after they realized the hours they were working for the government didn't justify the paychecks they were getting.

Costello's an unusual breed, though. She began her career in law as a police officer. That's how we met. We were in the academy together. Developing a friendship with someone while going through the academy strengthens the bond, makes the relationship more like family. She already had an undergrad degree from George Washington University. She worked hard for seven years to obtain her graduate degree, and after that she resigned from the department, passed the bar, and worked for one of the larger corporate attorneys here in DC for a couple of years. Now she has her own practice. She is like a Swiss Army knife. Now she does a lot of pro bono work, takes on cases for the "less fortunate."

Amanda's still squeezing my hand when we step out of the elevator and walk down the hall to a corner office. There's a plaque affixed to the wall to the left of the door; it reads "Law Office of Leslie Costello."

The receptionist shoots me a sweet smile when I open the

door, then furrows her brow when she notices Amanda, wearing my large suit jacket like a dress, walk in after me.

"Morning, Leah." I smile.

"Good morning, Mr. Marr." She smiles again and looks down toward Amanda.

"This is Amanda. I need to see Leslie right away."

FIVE

Costello shoots me the same kind of look Leah did when I walked into her office holding the girl's hand. Must be an effect little girls have on people, or maybe it's the effect I have, being seen holding the hand of a little girl with nothing but a suit jacket on.

Costello lifts herself out of the expensive ergonomic chair behind her desk, walks to the front of the desk, and leans her butt on the edge. She's wearing a solid gray pencil skirt and a matching two-button blazer with a red button-down shirt. The skirt shows off her long legs, and if I weren't on the verge of a mental crash, and holding this poor girl's hand, I might feel my blood pumping itself in the right direction. The shirt she wears is one of her "go to" power shirts, usually reserved for an important court appearance. That's probably why she didn't answer the phone when I called. I'm crossing my fingers and hoping it was a matter she already took care of and not something she's on standby for.

"You can let go of my hand now, Amanda."

She does, but reluctantly. I can see her studying Costello,

maybe feeling a bit more comfortable because of the comfortable office setting and Costello's pleasant demeanor.

"Hi, Amanda," she says.

"Hi."

Costello gives me that same look, obviously waiting for an explanation.

I look at my wristwatch again. It'll have to be the seriously condensed version.

I nod my head sideways and downward toward Amanda, a signal that it might be best to talk in private. We've worked together long enough that she gets it immediately.

"Amanda, do you like orange soda?"

She nods.

"I have another room here that I use for meetings. It has a television with cable. I'd like to take you there to wait with Miss Leah if that's all right. I think we can find something good for you to watch on TV while Mr. Marr and I talk."

She stands from her leaning position on the desk and offers Amanda her hand.

Amanda takes it.

Amanda looks at me, then turns to Costello. "Can Frankie come, too?"

"Yes, Frankie can, but he'll have to leave you with Miss Leah while we talk in private."

Amanda nods.

We walk out of her office and down a little hallway to the conference room.

A large rectangular mahogany table is in the center of the room. A conference phone sits at the left end. Three chairs are tucked under the table on each side, and one at each end. Other than a nineteen-inch flat screen affixed to a bracket in the right corner of the room and a large whiteboard with nothing written on it centered on the opposite wall to the left of the door, the room is devoid of anything that might be overly distracting.

"You can sit anywhere you want," Costello tells her.

She doesn't decide, so I walk in and pull out the chair at the end of the table closest to the TV.

"This one has the best view," I say.

She walks toward me slowly and sits down.

Costello pushes a button on the phone.

"Yes, Miss Costello," says Leah over the speaker.

"Would you come to the conference room, please? Oh, and bring an orange soda and whatever snacks you can find."

"Be right there."

I find the controller for the TV and push the power button. CNN pops on, with a panel discussion about the latest terrorist threat. I hit the channel button and stop on the Discovery Channel.

I hand the controller to Amanda.

"Here. You can watch what you want."

She takes it and tucks it in both hands on her lap.

Leah arrives shortly thereafter carrying a medium-size wicker basket that contains assorted snacks—Snickers bars, granola bars, small bags of pretzels, potato chips, and Wheat Thins. Amanda grabs a bag of potato chips. I tell her I'll be right back, then exit and walk to Costello's office.

"What the hell's with the little girl, Frankie, and who is she? And why does it look like your suit coat is the only item of clothing she's wearing?"

"I've been working on this case I picked up couple of weeks ago. I was conducting a bit of surveillance on this house and there were exigent circumstances, so I had to go in. That's when I found her."

"Exigent circumstances? Don't try to con me with that 'exigent circumstances' shit, Frankie. You know me better. What the hell is this about?"

"Damn, Leslie, I got in because it was necessary, and now there's a little girl who's been through all kinds of shit and has to get back to her family."

"Okay, okay, tell me what's going on."

"I found her in this house on Kenyon Street. She was being held against her will, handcuffed to a chain in a bathroom. They shot her up with heroin, some other shit, raped her, I'm sure, although she won't talk about that right now. I'm certain it's some sort of gang-related thing, but she's not a part of the gang. They were just trying to make her a part of it and probably would have had their way if I hadn't gotten there. She's scared to death. Didn't even want to leave at first because they convinced her they'd kill her family if she ever escaped."

"That poor girl. So why didn't you call 911 and take her to a hospital? I don't get why you'd bring her here."

"I wasn't thinking straight. This case has got me running circles in my head."

"This is not good, Frankie. I don't know what you're thinking, but this is not how it's done and you know that."

She's right, I'm whacked out right now 'cause I'm starting to crash. I got to get myself back up so I can think straight. I'm starting to feel like the room's shrinking, the air thick. Next, I'll be spinning.

"I've got to use your bathroom," I say.

"What? What the hell's wrong with you? Have you gone mad?"

"I really have to use your bathroom," I say, and turn and walk quickly toward the bathroom down the hall.

"I'm calling the police, Frankie," she advises as I open the door to the bathroom and walk in.

I lock the door. I pull a prescription pill container out of my front pants pocket and twist it open.

I don't have any more than a couple of grams in the container. My heart pounds, mostly because the thought of soon being without anything is terrifying. I turn on the water. I pull out two capsules and set the container on a shelf above the sink. I twist one of the capsules open and carefully squeeze the powder out of each half and onto the back of my hand. I close one nostril with my finger and snort it up through the other. I do the same with the other one. I straighten up, lick the residue from the back of my hand, then wipe the residue from my nose and upper lip, and rub it on my gums. I pinch my left nostril shut again and sniff quietly one more time.

A sudden, beautiful wave across my brain mixes everything together perfectly, lighting me up and releasing the neurotransmitters. Everything is clear. I put the capsules back together and drop them in the container, then slip it back in my pocket.

"Shit," I say, as if I suddenly realize how stupid I am.

But that's all right.

I walk out of the bathroom with a new lift and find Leslie walking out of the conference room holding my jacket.

"Leah found something more suitable for her to wear. And I called 911. I'm sure they'll be here any minute now."

"She said they know her address, and you know damn well the police won't act on it fast enough. Once these boys find her gone, her home will be the first stop they make. I got her to leave with me 'cause I promised her I'd keep her family safe. I'm going back to the house I got her out of."

I take my jacket from her hands. "I'll call you within an hour and give you the address. I'm pretty damn sure that Amanda doesn't know it. Tell the police what you have to, but I got to do what I got to do."

I walk toward the exit. She follows behind with quick steps. I slip on my jacket without stopping.

"Frank! You can't just drop off a kidnapped teenage girl who's probably been gang-raped and expect me to try to keep you out of it! You can't just walk out of here!"

I open the door and turn to her and say, "I gotta take care of this, Leslie. And notify Fairfax County police too, because she lives in Burke."

I let the door shut itself and choose the stairs instead of the elevator.

"Man, am I fucked," I mumble to myself on my way down.

Six

When I get to Kenyon Street, I find a parking spot across from the house, near where I parked before. I don't see the Salvadoran boys' vehicle anywhere. I grab the palm-size binoculars from a zippered compartment of my backpack, cup them between both hands, and peer through them at the house.

The door looks the same as when we left. I zip the binos back into the compartment, then look at the dashboard clock.

Thirteen-twenty hours.

I took too much time taking care of the girl. I'm wondering if the kid, Super Fly, already returned to re-up, but hightailed it out of there after he noticed the door had been pried open. I grab the pill container out of my pocket and twist off the cap.

"Fuck," I say after I see how many full capsules are left.

What I have here, it won't last long for me. I twist the cap back on and slip the container back in my pocket.

I open the backpack's main compartment and pull out six zip-tie handcuffs and a small but very effective stun gun. I clip the zip ties to a small carabiner key chain on the left side of my belt, opposite the gun. My jacket will hide everything well enough. I also put on my Kevlar tactical gloves this time. It's a bit chilly outside, so they're less conspicuous than latex and better on my knuckles if I have to go to blows. But first I power down my cell, because I know Leslie will start burning it up with calls soon.

I step out of the car.

I'm more conscious of my surroundings as I walk to the front door of the house. The last thing I want is one of those mopes pulling up while I'm entering. Before I do, I ring the doorbell, wait a few seconds, and ring it again. After that, I knock hard on the door, pushing it halfway open.

I step inside and close the door behind me, sliding the tennis shoe against it with my foot.

"*Policía,*" I call out.

I don't hear anything.

I have my thumb on the switch that'll activate the stun gun while I quickly but quietly make my way to the master bedroom. Nothing else matters right now. Just focus: find the drugs and then move on. I'm going on too much adrenaline to know any better. I clear the kitchen. There's nothing there, so I continue, clearing the same bedrooms before the master.

The master bedroom looks the same, the bed and the blacked-out window and the nasty clothes. I move to the bathroom and everything is just as I'd left it.

I look out the bedroom window, scan the block. I unlock the window latches and slide it up halfway so I can hear better what's outside.

The first thing I do after that is lift the bed's mattress. Nothing but a few porn magazines. I look under the bed. A mess of shit under there—shoe boxes, old socks, underwear, assorted clothing, two thin clear plastic storage containers. I reach under and pull those out first. It looks like there are more magazines inside, but I open them and toss them in the middle of the floor. I pull out the shoe boxes and do the same thing. A couple of them are empty, and the other three contain expensive Jordans. I toss the contents along with the boxes in the middle of the floor.

I look out the window again. No car. The block is quiet.

Back to the room again. I do a slow survey: a cluttered night-stand with a single drawer beside the bed next to me, the door to the closet, the bathroom, a dresser on the left side of the window, black construction-type trash bags that appear to be stuffed with dirty laundry, on the floor near the center of the room, dirty car-pet; a large stuffed teddy bear with a red ribbon, likely a gift from one of his girls, sits in the corner to the left of the dresser. I hear a car with a heavy, familiar engine outside.

My heart races for a moment, and I peer through the curtains. Nothing but a UPS truck passing the house and heading east. I fo-cus my attention outside for a moment, then back to the room.

I like teddy bears, so I grab it by the ear and squeeze the fat belly. Doesn't feel like anything's in there, but you never know. I pull out my knife, flick it open with my thumb, and gut the thing. I was hoping drugs would spill out, but there's only white stuff-ing. I pull it all out until the teddy bear looks like a bear puppet with sad, fallen eyes. I toss it in the middle of the room, then go back to the nightstand, where I pull out the drawer.

A small .38 with duct-taped grip. I like that, so I put it in my backpack, along with a box of live rounds. Always good to have another throwaway gun. You never know. The drawer also contains assorted packaged condoms, two prescription pill containers, and several other loose live rounds that look like 9mm. I take one of the pill containers, look at the label; it reads "OxyContin." It was prescribed to a "Marianne Oliver," a name I don't believe is associated with anyone in this house-hold. I pick up the other one and it also reads "OxyContin" and is prescribed to the same person. More than likely pulled in a robbery, or traded in exchange for crack by someone who burglarized her home. Looks like fifty-plus pills from both containers combined.

"Nice," I say to myself, and drop them in the backpack.

I hear a car door slam shut.

Looking through the window, I see Jordan Super Fly strolling leisurely toward the house.

I shoulder my backpack, grip the stun gun, and run as fast as I can downstairs to the living room.

I make it to the door just as I hear him shuffling on the porch and saying, "¡*Cabrón!*"

I quietly set my backpack on the floor and position myself so I'll be behind the door as he opens it. But he doesn't; he just pushes at it, and it barely opens. I hear more shuffling. I get the feeling he won't come in, and might just call for that backup. I gotta assume they can get another ride from 16th and Park if they have to. I don't even think about it. I pull out my wallet to reveal my retired detective's badge, 'cause I'm not worried if he can read. I hold it in my left hand and tuck the stun gun against my thigh with my right.

"¡*Cabrón!*" I hear again outside.

I step to the other side of the door, can barely make him out, but I can see enough of him to see that he's about to tap in some numbers on his cell. I swing the door open, holding my badge in the air.

"¡*Policía!*" I command, but not loud enough for the whole neighborhood to come to alert.

He's right next to the door, about a foot from me. The cell phone he's holding drops to the ground, and I know he's about to bolt, so I flip the switch and stun the shit outta his belly.

"¡*Aiyee!*" he cries, and slumps forward into my arms.

I manage to catch him while still holding my wallet and the stun gun. He's thin and no more than a buck fifty, so I easily drag him in and let him drop to the floor under the window to the left of the door. I kick his feet away so I can shut the door.

He's moaning, and I'm pretty sure he shat himself.

SEVEN

I zip-tie his hands behind his back, duct-tape his mouth, and prop him against a wall in a sitting position. The front window beside the door is to his right, giving me a good vantage point. I remember the cell phone he dropped. I reach out the door from a leaning position and pick it up. It looks like a cheap pay-as-you-go phone. I look at the screen. He only had time to find the contact he was about to call—Angelo. I'm assuming this is Shiny. I close the door and drop the phone into my backpack.

I lean down next to the boy. The stench coming from his lower body is bad. I've smelled it before, but not enough times to get used to it. He moans, eyes glazed but open. The stun wasn't enough to knock him out. He's small, though, so it whacked out his system pretty good. I lightly slap the right side of his cheek several times with the tips of my fingers. His eyes widen when he comprehends the situation.

He struggles and puffs unintelligible words that are muffled by the duct tape. I stand up and pull my suit jacket open so he can see my sidearm. Then I pull out my wallet and show him my badge. I lean back down beside him, press my index finger against my lips as a warning to be quiet, and slowly peel the duct tape halfway off so he can speak. He's scared, breathing fast. I pat him on the right shoulder a couple of times.

"*Cálmate,*" with my best accent.

He nods.

"You speak English?" I ask.

Shakes his head no.

I show him the stun gun again and flick it on so he gets a little zap, crackle, and spark show.

"No! No!"

"Do you speak English?"

"*Sí,* a little."

"You make this easy by just telling me where you keep the stash."

"I no understand what you mean."

I shove the stun gun to his crotch, but don't zap him. He still belts out a yelp in anticipation of it. I push harder.

"One more time—*uno más,*" I begin. "*¿Dónde está* the drugs?"

"Please, I know nothing here. Nothing, Officer," he pleads.

"Yes you do, and I warned you, just *uno más.* One more chance."

I seal his mouth with the duct tape. He struggles, but I push him tight against the wall with my left hand, let go, flip the switch, then give him a good one right on the hip bone. It's enough to convulse his body and send a violent push of breath that almost rips the duct tape off his mouth; watery mucus shoots out of his nostrils, nearly hitting me. I hold the stun gun in front of him so he can see it. His body goes limp, but he's far from out. His eyes stream tears now.

I pull the duct tape halfway again.

"The drugs," is all I have to say.

He motions his head up, like he's telling me upstairs, and, nearly breathless, he says, *"Arriba. Arriba."*

I nod like he did okay and give him a few seconds to recover.

"You show me."

"Por favor. Please, I go to jail now."

I show him the zap and spark again.

"No. You show me where exactly. *Exactamente.*"

His eyes close briefly, then he simply nods. I stand up, grab him under the arm, and lift him to a standing position. His legs are weak, so I have to hold him steady.

I wrap the duct tape along his mouth again.

"You show me. No lies or I fuck you up bad, *comprende?*"

He nods.

His cell phone rings from inside my backpack.

I lean him against the wall, wobbly legs and all, and grab the strap to pull it out.

The screen on the cover reveals the caller as "Angelo."

I shoulder my backpack, put the stun gun in the outer pocket of my suit jacket. I grab the kid from under the arm with my left hand before he can slide all the way down to a sitting position. I remove my gun from its holster and place the barrel against his forehead.

"I'm not fucking around."

He nods like he understands.

I help him walk up the stairs.

EIGHT

He leads me to the master bedroom. I pull away the duct
tape. It's like he can't help himself from looking toward the
bathroom. I set my backpack on the floor near the bed.

"Is that where you keep the drugs, in the bathroom?"

He shakes his head no, nervously.

"I didn't think so. You make an addict out of a little *chica,* you
can't trust her being near the drugs, right?"

He doesn't answer. I lead him by the arm to the bathroom,
show him inside.

"*Sí,* she's not here. *No aquí.* You can't hurt her no more."

I pull him back to the middle of the bedroom, with a bit of
force this time.

"Show me."

"There," he says, his head indicating the closet.

"The closet?" I ask with disbelief. "Only stupid people keep
their stash in the closet."

I pull him there.

"*¿Dónde?*"

"*Caja de zapatos.*"

"You gotta be kidding. That's too easy."

"*Sí*. It's there."

I push him up against the wall.

His cell phone in my backpack rings again.

"Shit," I say, then take it out.

"Angelo."

I show it to him and say, "You tell him you'll be there soon, that you're taking a shit or something. You damn well better make him believe it. *¿Claro?*"

"*Sí.*"

"*¿Entiendes lo que digo?*" I ask, so he knows I understand.

I place the phone against his ear and mouth.

"*Sí,*" he speaks into the phone.

I put my ear close so I can hear a bit.

Angelo asks him why he didn't answer.

"*Tengo que cagar,*" he advises Angelo.

Angelo laughs and tells him to use the hallway toilet and then something about the girl.

"*Sí, claro.*"

Angelo says to hurry back and something about the girl again, like "Don't fuck around." And then something about "No more bruises."

"*¡Claro que sí! Hasta pronto.*"

Angelo says good-bye, and I take the phone, disconnect, and toss it back in the backpack.

"Good job. Now *siéntate*," I tell him.

When he does, I make him stretch out his legs and cross them. I grab the shoe box out of the closet, move toward the bed to examine the contents. When I do, I find several zips, mostly tens and twenties and maybe fifty grams. But it's fucking crack. What am I gonna do with this shit? I close the box, set it on the floor next to my backpack, and then look directly at the boy.

"I never asked before. What's your name?"

"Andrés."

"Well, my little friend, you're full of shit. I mean, not including what you already filled your underpants with. You do wear underpants, right?"

He doesn't know what to say.

I move toward him, take him under the arms, and pull him up to a standing position.

"No. Wait, please!"

I grab him by the jersey close to his neck and toss him over so he falls on the bed.

"Wait, *señor*. It's all in the box."

"Cocaine, powder!" I demand then, "Heroin and money too. Show me now. No more playing around."

"Only crack. That is all."

"Wanna be a big man, huh?"

"No, no..."

"Cállate, little big man."

"Por favor, señor," he pleads.

I slap the tape back over his mouth and roll him over onto his belly.

He's trying hard to say something, but it's only mumbling and too late anyway. I don't have much time here before his boys return. Not to mention Leslie. For all I know, I really messed up and Amanda does know the address. Police might already be on the way. I move toward the window and look out.

Looks clear.

I go back to what I have to do. I take Andrés's left hand and grip his pinkie tight with the whole of my hand. He struggles more after he realizes what is next. I yank his pinkie hard, all the way back and then to the side. I hear it pop out of the socket with a rip. His squeal of a scream is filtered through the duct tape. I roll him back over so he's on his back.

He's crying. I slap him hard on the cheek.

"Cocaine, heroin, *dinero*," I demand.

I slap him hard again so he knows.

He gives several short nods.

I have no pity for this piece of shit. All I gotta do is think about the girl first, my needs second, and that's enough. You'd be surprised what most of us are capable of.

I already know what I'm capable of, and it's a lot more than bustin' little fingers.

I pull back the tape. Don't have to say anything this time.

He catches his breath. A few snivels. He looks toward the corner of the room, over the foot of the bed.

"Under . . . pull up."

I look in that direction, but don't know what he means.

"*Tapete,*" he says.

I don't know that word, so I repeat, "What is *tapete?*"

"Floor."

"You mean carpet?"

He nods.

I move to the corner of the room, tapping the carpet with my foot. I notice the edge of the carpet near the corner is slightly shredded, not enough to draw attention unless you were looking. Eventually, with time, I would have looked. I've torn up more carpets, busted holes in more drywall than I can count.

I lean down and pull it up and then toward me. The floorboard has been cut and replaced with hinges. I lift it.

There are three shoe boxes inside, one bulky kitchen garbage bag more than half full with who knows what, and a

9mm Taurus semiauto with a clip in the butt and two clips resting near it.

I pull out the bag first and open it.

"Okay, my friend. You did good."

He doesn't reply, only whimpers.

Inside is a shitload of money, rolled up real tight and secured with a green rubber band looped around several times. I toss the bag to the center of the room near my backpack.

I open the shoe boxes to find more than I bargained for. Everything nicely sealed in extra large freezer ziplock bags. The box containing the cocaine has to be half a kilo, and it's mostly rock. Doesn't look stepped on. I almost belt out a laugh. I open it up, take a healthy pinch, and sniff it up my nose. It's immediate.

I'm alive.

I hear the boy cry, probably having realized "the cop" just sniffed some of the evidence. I zip it back up, make sure it's sealed tight, and put it back in.

The other two shoe boxes contain heroin and crack. Looks like about two ounces of heroin and even more crack.

I look in the closet again. I notice one duffel bag and one large suitcase on rollers. I pull out the suitcase and open it.

Nothing but dirty clothing.

"You boys never do your laundry?" I ask, but don't expect an answer.

He's nothing but a rapist, a little piece of shit who'd probably be the one to put the 9mm I just found against the head of Amanda's dad and pull the trigger. If he goes to jail, he'll just come out stronger, smarter. I know I can't leave him here, let him agonize and slowly boil over to seethe with vengeance. He'll turn into nothin' but a weapon, a bomb.

No, I can't do that, so I drag him off the bed to the middle of the floor near the dirty laundry.

"Pedazo de mierda," I tell him.

He curls up in a fetal position like he's expecting a serious beatdown. That'll happen, but not just yet.

"Roll on your stomach. Facedown," I command.

"Please," he begs.

"Now."

I grab him by the arm and help him roll over, then I tell him, *"No te muevas."*

I turn back to the suitcase and empty the contents onto the floor next to the bathroom door. I search through everything to make sure there's nothing hidden. After that I grab my backpack and stuff the cocaine in the large compartment and zip it closed. I take the 9mm and drop it in the suitcase, but then I remember something. I take the bag of money and put it next to my back-pack instead of the suitcase.

That's when I notice that the limber fuckwad managed to slip his butt under his zip-tied hands and get his legs through so his hands are now in front. He slipped out of his left shoe in the process.

By the time I react he's already on his feet and hobbling toward the bedroom door. I'm quick to stand and draw my weapon, but I decide not to shoot 'cause it'll attract too much attention.

He's making his way around the flimsy banister rails toward the top of the stairs when I get out the bedroom door. I won't get to him in time so I kick at the top of the rail with force, like I'm kicking open a locked door. The rails split from the floorboard just enough to fall out and hit his shoulder as he's running down the top of the stairs. It stuns him and he stops, but only for a second. He pushes up at the banister rail with his tied hands, but by that time I'm close behind. Close enough to send him a swift kick to his lower back. He can do nothing but tumble down the stairs to hit the floor, headfirst, and all bent up.

NINE

I make no apologies.

I lift the suitcase, slide it into the back of the Cross Country, and close the hatch. When I open the driver's side door, I toss the bag of money to the passenger's side floor and set the backpack stuffed with goodies on the passenger seat.

I remember their vehicle, the one the kid drove back to the house. I turn and see it parked along the curb.

"Damn," I say to myself.

It doesn't take me long to mull over all the scenarios and realize nothing will really come of leaving the car here. I'll give the vehicle information to the police. Once the police roll onto the scene and hopefully snatch up Shiny and the rest of his crew, Shiny will figure his boy Andrés made a run for it after he learns Andrés wasn't arrested. He'll figure he made off with the coke, one of the guns, and the money. Obviously, if Shiny is arrested, he'll get a defense attorney and the police will have to provide discovery, everything that was seized from the home. Those items won't be on the list.

Another possibility—Shiny manages to elude capture; then he'll just figure Andrés got himself locked up and all that stuff was seized by the cops. He'll never know otherwise. It's a win-win.

Disposing of the vehicle is not an option.

Disposing of Andrés is a necessity. It keeps whoever these boys owe for what I took away from me, because my name will probably be included in that discovery package. After all, I did rescue the girl, as unintentional as that was.

I hop in my car. I power on the cell. I know all too well the number of missed calls from Leslie and Lord knows who else that'll pop up on the screen.

Eight.

Not as bad as I thought. Seven of them from Leslie and one a number that belongs to DC police; I recognize the prefix.

I call Leslie.

She picks up after the first ring. "What the fuck, Frankie!"

"I've got the information you need."

"The police are still here. Fairfax County is sending a couple of their detectives and the girl's parents should be here any second, so where in the hell are you?"

"Tell me when you're ready to copy."

"Whatever information you have related to this poor girl here you need to give directly to the police, not me."

"Who are the DC detectives there?"

"I don't know. They're Youth Division, and I stay away from juvenile cases."

"Let me talk to the detective who looks like he's got the most time on."

"Frankie," she says, and I can only imagine how she looks when she says it, "you really put me in a situation here. Hold the line." Instead of being put on hold, I hear what sounds like the phone receiver hit a desk.

Seconds later: "Detective Davidson here."

I know Davidson. He's good people. A fucking hard worker.

"What's up, Scott? This is Frank Marr."

"Yeah, I know. Your new boss told me."

"She ain't my boss. I do some work for her on the side, 'cause forty percent doesn't cut it."

"This one of the cases you did on the side?"

"Not for her, no."

"You need to come in, Frank, so we can talk and get whatever information you have."

"I can do that, but not for a couple hours. I'm outta the DC area right now." And before he can answer I say, "Tell me when you're ready to copy what I have."

"Hold on." A bit of shuffling, then, "Go ahead."

I give him the address on Kenyon along with the vehicle info.

"I was there not even forty minutes ago," I say, while looking at the car, but I don't mention seeing the car. "The house was unoc-cupied when I was there. Wouldn't be surprised if you find some drugs in there, too, at least according to a reliable source I have."

I made sure they will, because I left the crack and the heroin under the bed. Those drugs are useless to me. Don't want any-thing to do with that shit. Good blow, some weed, and a few pills are what I care about most. I don't go and try to make money off this shit.

I also straightened things up a bit so it wouldn't look like there was a struggle, and I left a little bonus—the .38 I put back in the nightstand's drawer. I'm sure it'll be traced back to a shooting or two.

"You might want to get Luna and McGuire in on the hit with you. I'm sure they'll take the narcotics off your hands, unless it's something you want to handle."

"What the heck kinda case you working there, Frank?"

"You know I can't talk about that, Scott. Needless to say, it got that girl the hell outta there, right?"

"Yeah, amen to that, brother, but we still need to talk. And I mean soon."

"Understood. You need to act on this right away, though. Get a couple of unmarked units on the house. Oh, I almost forgot. I also have information they might be armed."

"You have any names for me?"

"Just one. Angelo. His crew works selling their shit in the area of Sixteenth and Park."

"I'll get on this right away. You call me first thing when you get back, all right?"

"Yeah, no problem."

"You still have my cell?"

"Of course I do."

"Frank, seriously, I need you to call me ASAP, right when you get back. I don't know what you were thinking, because you went about this all wrong. I mean, you should know better, brother."

"Yeah, I can't argue with you but I didn't have a choice at the time. I'll explain what I can when I get back. Don't worry yourself."

"I'm not worried, but you'll have to if you don't call me."

"Don't start with that kinda talk now. You know better."

"You need to talk to your boss again?"

"No, not at the moment."

"I'll talk to you soon, then."

"Later," I say, and disconnect.

I pull the car out and head north, the opposite direction from where the unmarked units should be coming.

TEN

I bought the two-story connected row house on 12th Street Northwest back when a working cop could afford to buy in DC. I had finished my probationary period and figured the minimal investment was worth the risk. It was a fixer-upper in an area that wasn't quite up-and-coming yet. I gutted most of it. It took several years because I was on the job then and working my ass off.

I've always been handy that way, able to fix most everything. Started out working for a landscaping company based out of DC when I was still in high school. They did most of their jobs in Upper Northwest, where the homes had real backyards. I moved from that job to working for a small general contractor. That's where I learned how to work with drywall, basic electrical and plumbing, and just about everything else you might need to know to get things done yourself.

My home is south of Cardozo High School's football field. I take Florida Avenue to the narrow alley west of 12th and hang a left, then drive a short distance to the back of my house on the east side of the alley. I squeeze close to the tiny cut at the back of my house and the privacy fence of my backyard. The alley's so narrow a bicycle would have a tough time getting around me.

It's quiet around this time of the afternoon. Only a few old-timers live on this block, some new families, too, mostly white, who bought up a lot of the homes in this area. Then you got 12th Place, at the rear of the homes on the east side of this alley. Most of them are good people. Some of the kids in the homes on that block are not so good. I even locked up a few back in the day. It's all about business, so no hard feelings. As far as they know, I'm still a working cop, so they stay clear. Nowadays, I stay clear of them, too. It's the furthest thing from my mind to hit one of their homes, even when I am desperate, like before the hit on Kenyon.

This neighborhood is gentrifying, and it's all good. The young and ignorant and upwardly mobile can take over most of this city as far as I care. I don't have a problem with that. My property value has gone up a bit.

Before I exit the car I scan the area to make sure there are no prying eyes. When I feel good, I grab my pack and the garbage bag filled with money and step out. I tap the lock button on my key fob and unlatch the gate that leads to a tiny courtyard area at the back of my house. What plant life exists there now mostly consists of overgrown weeds. The autumn ferns and snapdragons managed to survive, growing along the fence line on either side.

I key in the security code on the side of my door, then unlock the door and step into a small mudroom that leads into the kitchen. I drop my backpack and the money and then move quickly back outside to the car, coding and locking the back door again. I take the car around the block, take another left onto 12th, and find a parking spot across from my house. I lock the car door when I exit and then double-tap the key fob so I can hear the horn signaling that it's secure.

I have to enter the code again at the front door before I enter. Once inside, I make my way to the kitchen, where I retrieve the backpack and money and then return to the living room, opening the blackout curtains just enough so I can easily peer out at my vehicle. It isn't the first time I've had to leave a body, stuffed in a suitcase, in the back of my car.

It won't be there for long.

I don't bother to empty the bag of money. I pull out a roll of twenties, pull off the rubber band, and count it.

Seven twenties and a ten.

I pull out another roll with tens and count.

Fifteen of them.

Looks like they wrapped everything in hundred-and-fifty-dollar increments. Probably something that makes it easier for them to distribute later. They'll owe someone, maybe even Cordell, a lot of money. Who the fuck knows. Just estimating the amount of rolled-up bills in there, I figure it's gotta be in the neighborhood of fifty grand. I fold the bills I unrolled together and pocket them.

I don't bother to go through everything I have stuffed in the backpack. I pull out the cocaine. Then I grab a small plastic vial used to test cocaine and crack out of another pocket and uncap it. I flip open my tactical knife and take a tiny sample with the tip of the knife. I tap the powder into the vial and close the vial back up with the cap.

I squeeze the vial between two fingers until a little capsule contained within it breaks open to release the mixture. I shake it up and watch it turn a wonderful fluorescent blue. Exactly what I like to see. In fact, I haven't seen it turn that bright for some time. I wipe what little is left from the tip of the knife with my index finger and rub it on my gums.

I put about three grams of the powder from the bag into another pill container I carry and then slip that, along with my knife, back into my pocket. I grab the pack and the bag of money and head to the laundry room.

In the hallway before the entrance to the kitchen, there's a small room with a washer and dryer and my HVAC system for the house. The washer and dryer sit against the back wall between two walls. The wall on the left and the wall on the back are a part of the foundation. The one on the right is drywall. Everything is trimmed with wood molding. The molding that trims the drywall on the right side has a phantom hinge. I slide it open.

Pulling open the molding, I take hold of the edge of drywall and slide it out just like a sliding door to another room. The bottom edge of the drywall has aluminum edge trim, so it doesn't wear down. When I pull it out, it opens up to a wall from the floor to the ceiling, five feet wide and ten inches deep, with built-in hidden shelves.

It's where I keep my shit.

I empty the contents of the backpack and place them on the shelves according to category. The shelf where I would normally keep most of my drugs is vacant, so that's where I set the coke and the prescription meds. The bag of money is a bit tougher. I have a couple thousand banded together on a top shelf, but it's certainly not deep enough to hold a bag of money like this, so I toss the bag in the washer and cover it with dirty clothes, just until I can unroll the bills and stack them properly. I put the 9mm on a shelf with a few other weapons and then close the wall back up and head to the living room.

I peer through the curtains. The car's still there. I take out my container of coke and dump a nice pile onto the blue glass top of the end table near the curtains. I chop it up with a razor blade and make three long lines, snort one of them with a rolled-up twenty, then light a cigarette. One more look out the window, and then I lean back to finish the cigarette.

I'll have to get with Davidson today, but first I gotta finish this smoke, a couple more lines, and then dump the body.

ELEVEN

I used to make time for fishing. Nowadays, it's not even a passing thought—until now, but that's because I'm driving along 295 and the Potomac River's with me. South along 295, it'll cut a path through Virginia to the west and Maryland to the east. North, which is the direction I'm going, the highway will take a turn to follow the Anacostia, a river that empties into the Potomac at a place known as Buzzard Point. I'll drive a little farther, toward the Navy Yard and a secluded spot I know near there.

I used to have a jon boat. It had two swivel seats for sitting while fishing. I kept it stored on a trailer at the rear of my house before I had a fence. I'd take it out two, sometimes three times a month back when I was still on the department and before I got myself caught up with all this shit. Good bass fishing along parts of the Potomac. Not where I'm driving, though. The Anacostia is a filthy river.

I take an exit for a road that swerves around and back under 295, then across the Anacostia. A couple more turns and I'm on a gravel road that leads to a wooded area along the river's banks.

No traffic along here. No thugs either, no crackheads or even homeless people, just a trash-ridden landscape that spills into the river.

When I get to the spot, I park and light a cigarette. I scan the area around me and lean back to finish my smoke.

I step out of the car, scrunch the rest of the cigarette into the ground, open the rear hatch, and pull the suitcase out of the back.

I hold the handle with two hands, swing it out, and let go. It tumbles down an incline, bounces a few times, and splashes into the water a couple of feet off the bank.

It floats and gurgles as it begins to fill with water. The current will carry it out. This part of the river is deep. The suitcase will eventually sink. But I won't lose sleep if it takes its time. It's just another foul thing that found its way into the river to get swallowed up by the muck.

When I get back onto 295, I give Davidson a call.

After two rings he answers. "'Bout time you called, Frank," he says, obviously having recognized my number or saved my name to it.

"A demanding client," is what I come up with.

"Well, my boss is pretty demanding, too. Needless to say, they're all over this. Your boys at Narcotics Branch are giving us a hand, too."

"They're good people," I say, referring to McGuire and Luna.

"They got a surveillance vehicle sitting on the block now. No sign of these boys, but the car's there."

"That means they're around."

"According to one of the surveillance officers, it looks like someone broke into the house. You know anything about that?"

"You know I do, Davidson. How do you think I got the girl outta there?"

"Frank, you're turning my write-up into a damn novel."

"Exigent circumstances, brother." Before he can reply I ask, "Where you at now?"

"Sitting in my cruiser at a staging area a couple blocks away. Probably going to have to call it soon and go in."

"When do you want to meet?"

"I can't say right now. For all I know I'll be working through the night. I will need to get a statement from you at the latest by tomorrow. But keep your phone on for me, okay? Things might change. And by the way, is there anything else you might want to fill me in on, like maybe about your client?"

"You'll get everything I have when I see you. I'm not gonna leave you in the dark."

"You do that, Frank. Otherwise I'll have to go through the hassle of a grand jury, subpoenas, and all that crap."

"Well, we don't want that happening."

I hear radio chatter from his end.

"Copy," he says off to the side, then, "I gotta go. Keep your phone on." He disconnects.

I set the phone in a cup holder in the center console.

"Damn, I'm gonna need a good story," I say to myself, and then light a cigarette.

TWELVE

All I want to do right now is go home, tuck myself away for the rest of the day and through the night, but I gotta smooth things over with Leslie. I know how angry she must be. It's not the first time, but even with all the baggage I carry, which I know can affect any friendship or business relationship, I've never done something this stupid. I don't really know what I can do to fix it except to say I'm sorry and it won't happen again. I certainly can't tell her the truth. Hell, I'm so good at keeping that part of my life a secret even I believe what I say half the time.

Maybe I'll give her a part truth and tell her I'm an alcoholic. But no, we both enjoy drinking too much, and I don't want to give up that part of our relationship.

I shoot Leah a smile when I enter.

"Is she in?" I ask.

"Yes," Leah answers.

When I walk into her office, the first thing she says is, "You look like a bum in a suit," and I feel forgiven already 'cause that's how she normally talks to me.

She's sitting behind her desk. She returns to a case file she's reviewing; she's writing notes on a yellow memo pad that already has several pages turned over and tucked under it.

"I just want to say——" I begin.

Without looking up at me, she says, "I don't want to hear anything, Frankie. I especially don't want to know anything about whatever it is you're working." She sets her pen down and looks up at me. "But please tell me you're cooperating with Detective Davidson and Fairfax County."

"Davidson's the only one I've spoken to, and yes, I am cooperating."

"Well, that's a relief. And seriously, you need to get that suit pressed, definitely shower and shave. I can smell the cigarettes and sweat from here."

"I'll be fresh by tomorrow. And I'm sorry about this shit. This case has got me all worked up."

"I told you I don't want to know about the case. Last thing I need right now is getting summoned to a grand jury, which, by the way, still might happen."

"No it won't."

I sit on the chair in front of her desk.

"I'm assuming that's the Claypole file you're working on?" I ask.

"Yes. He won't take a plea, so we'll be going to trial."

"What did the government offer?"

"Aggravated assault."

"It sounds better than assault with intent to kill, but still not much of a plea offer. It could still get him the max, with a record like his."

"No judge will give him ten years for agg assault, especially the way this one went down. He should have taken the offer. He'd be out in three, less with time served."

"Shouldn't be that hard for someone like you to find mitigating circumstances."

"Quit kissing my ass. And you know I already tried to establish that. We go to trial on this, I'm going to lose. And I hate to lose."

"But this time you'll be presenting it to a DC jury."

"Trust me when I say that won't matter with this one."

"When's the trial?"

"We have a status hearing on Monday. Since he won't accept the plea, the judge will probably set a date for jury selection."

"You need me to do anything?"

"No. You've already done everything you can do."

"I can have a sit-down with Claypole if you want, maybe convince him you know best."

She looks at me like she's considering it.

"No. I did my best on that one; he's the client and the client wants to go to trial."

"It's been a while since I talked to him. Maybe I could get the story again, see if there's anything else to work with—for the trial, I mean. The time's on me. Least I can do for all the shit I just put you through."

She nods like she agrees and says, "You've already worked this one to the ground, but then it can't hurt, right?"

I agree with a nod and a bit of a smile.

"But I want you on the clock. I don't take freebies, even from you."

She's forgiven me.

"It's your dime," I tell her.

"I'll set it up with DC jail so you can meet him tomorrow."

"Make it in the afternoon. I'll probably have to get with Davidson sometime in the morning."

"All right," she agrees.

I push myself out of the chair.

"Can you clean yourself up, please?" she asks sincerely.

"I suppose so," I say, but then realize how difficult that would really be.

Thirteen

I wake up to a sweaty pillow. I turn it over and lie still for a while. I try to make sense of the dreams that fired up all that sweat, but by the time I'm focused enough, they slip away. When I go out, I go out hard.

The first thing I do after I get my brain straightened out is check my cell, but not for the time. I want to make sure I didn't sleep through Davidson trying to call me. It's a few minutes after 7 a.m. I slept maybe three hours. Wouldn't have slept at all if I hadn't downed a couple of Klonopins with a glass of Jameson. Most of the night was spent trying to figure out a good story for Davidson. One of the benefits of blow, especially good blow, is it gives you the fortitude to do shit like that.

I think I got a good story out of it.

I remember I have to shower and shave. It takes me a few minutes, but I manage to push myself up to a sitting position on the edge of the bed.

Daylight's trying to make an entrance through the curtains. It's still semidark in the bedroom, so the curtains are doing their job.

I turn the end table light on 'cause I'm not ready for the light of day. I can't remember the last time I pulled the curtains open, actually.

I down four ibuprofen with the remaining glass of water I keep on the nightstand. When I'm able to, I stand up, pull my T-shirt off, drop my boxers, and stumble my way to the bathroom.

The bathroom light is brutal. I sit on the toilet and try to take a shit, use some of the toilet paper to blow my nose.

There's a glob of mucus mixed with blood on the toilet paper; then blood trickles out of my left nostril. I wad up a bit of toilet paper and stuff it up my bleeding nostril, replacing it with a bit more until the bleeding stops.

No luck with taking a shit so I move to the sink, find the saline solution, and squirt it up my nostrils a couple of times until it drips out of my nose and into the sink.

I shave, then take a long, hot shower. When I return to my bedroom I check my cell again and notice a call that just came in from Davidson. I pull out some clean boxers from the top dresser drawer, sit on the edge of the bed, and give him a call.

"Was afraid you weren't going to return my call," he answers.

"I was in the shower. What's up?"

"I'm at the Nickel. Can you get over here at about noon?"

"That won't be a problem. You already got an Assistant U.S. Attorney assigned to this?"

"Yes. It's going to district court, so I'm here waiting to paper it."

"I'm assuming you got some arrests, then?"

"You assume correctly, my friend. We'll talk when you get here. I've got a desk on the third floor now."

I let myself chuckle. "How'd you wrangle that?"

"Me and a couple other guys from Youth Division got detailed to an FBI task force for crimes against children. The AUSA that's assigned to work with us wanted us close so she secured some space for us in an empty office."

"Sounds like a good gig for you. At least it gets you out of Youth Division."

"We'll see how long it lasts. It's good work, though. So listen, I'll see you when you get here. Hit me on the cell when you're downstairs."

"Will do. And start figuring out how you're gonna keep me out of everything. I'm too busy to deal with witness conferences and grand juries and shit like that."

He's silent.

"All right?"

"Just get down here by noon, bro." And before I can respond he says, "Later," and disconnects.

Damn, that son of a bitch didn't give me an answer.

FOURTEEN

Cops sometimes refer to the U.S. Attorney's Office as the Nickel or Triple Nickel, 'cause the address is 555. It's located on 4th Street, between E and F, about three blocks from Costello's office, and I have to deal with the parking situation again.

I circle the blocks in the area until a spot opens up, maybe twenty minutes. It's frustrating as shit because my time belongs to me now, not the department. Back when I was on the job, I wasted so much of my life in this car circling blocks. Most of the time, I'd simply give up and park somewhere illegal, put an "Official Police Business" placard on the dash, and hope for the best. It's the damn DPW you have to worry about getting a ticket from, not cops. Having a placard rarely helped. It was always a roll of the dice.

I give up and park illegally, just like old times. I throw the placard on the dash, step out of the car, and put on my suit jacket. I'm wearing my navy blue Britches suit that I bought in Georgetown back in the day, when they were still open. It's still a good suit, but I'm thinking with all the money I recovered I should buy myself some newer suits. I grab my overcoat from the front seat 'cause it looks like rain.

Davidson meets me in the lobby.

We shake hands and he says, "You've lost some weight."

"Been eating right," I tell him.

I show my retirement badge and ID to security and I'm given a visitor's sticker. After I stick it on my suit jacket I place everything from my pockets, including my keys, on a metal stand and then walk through the metal detector. I'm not carrying, so it stays quiet.

We take the elevator to the third floor and then walk to a secured door off the glassed-in reception area.

We walk along a short hallway to an open area with six old wooden desks that look like they've recently been moved out of storage. Every desk is cluttered with files and has a desktop computer with a large screen. Only one of the desks is occupied, by a young guy, heavyset, dressed in an expensive suit. He looks up at me.

"This is my partner, Detective Curtis Hicks."

We shake hands, then he nods and sits back in his chair.

"That's my desk," Davidson says, pointing to a corner spot.

He takes off his suit jacket and slides it over the back of his chair, sits, and then scoots his chair on wheels back against the wall.

"Have a seat," he says, directing me to a chair against the wall near the corner of his desk.

He grabs a fresh memo pad off a stack of pads on his desk, pulls a nice silver pen out of his shirt pocket, and writes the date and time on the top line.

"So you're looking..." he begins, and then pauses, with a thoughtful expression. "You're looking a bit tired and overworked."

"You got some nice bags under your eyes too, bub."

"Yeah, but I'm not retired. Your days should be spent fishing, drinking good scotch, and loafing around. Instead you're off chasing bad guys."

"You're forgetting—I went out at seventeen years and I was lucky to get forty percent. I gotta work."

"I always wondered why you left so early. Your boy Luna said you got burned out."

"Yeah, you could say that."

"I was telling my partner here that you're sort of a legend."

"Sort of? Is that like the minor league of legends?" I smile.

"No, I didn't mean it that way." He looks at his partner. "But he is, Hicks. Dude made more district court drug cases than his whole unit put together. In fact, all the overtime he was making put him into six figures."

"I did all right," I add.

He turns back to me and says, "No surprise you burned out, Frank. You worked too damn hard. Your seventeen years was like thirty. So are you and Costello like 'together' or something?"

"Fuck no," I say, as if I'd never consider it, which is a lie because we do have something going, I just don't know what the hell it is.

"I always liked her, even if she did turn and go to the other side."

"She's good people. Work she gives me keeps me going, so I'm thankful." He's grinning.

"Yeah, fuck that. You work to get the dopes we lock up out. What's with that?" his partner interjects.

"Give it a break, Hicks," Davidson tells him.

"It's all right. I get that a lot, but mostly from rookies."

Hicks puffs out a grunt.

"I get the occasional mope," I continue, like I don't take offense. "Mostly it's white-collar shit, though, and nothing having to do with hurting children, so you don't have to worry about me getting one of your fucking peds out. Wouldn't work that kinda crap even if I was offered." I turn back to Davidson. "Certainly don't know how you can work it either."

"It can be tough," Davidson says. "We pick up a variety of cases, but mostly those that deal with pedophiles on the Internet. Our commander at Youth Division called the supervising agent at the FBI who's in charge of this unit; because of the interstate aspect and since it involved abducting a minor for prostitution, he took it. So now it's on my desk."

"They got you partnered with the FBI?"

"They're good people to work with. I'm hoping I get a take-home vehicle out of the deal."

"Feds do have the best cars. What about Fairfax County PD? The little girl told me she lives there. They in on this?"

"FBI all the way. They took it over, but we'll keep them in the loop."

"Well, I know you'll follow it through at least."

"You want a soda or something?" Davidson asks.

"I'm good."

"I know you have to roll, so let's get started."

"Tell me first how it went the other day. You get those pieces of shit?"

"Yes. In fact, I want to show you some pictures. Tell me if you recognize any of them."

He opens a thin case file beside the computer keyboard on his desk, pulls out two Police Department Identification Number photos, and hands me one of them.

"What about this guy?"

I take the photo and immediately recognize it as Shiny.

"Yeah, he's one of them. I think that's the one they call Angelo. I just call him Shiny 'cause of his hair."

I hand the photo back. Davidson examines it again.

"Does look like he goes for the hair product."

"Yeah, Brylcreem or some shit like that, and he probably nets it every night," Hicks says.

Davidson chuckles, slips the photo back into a manila envelope, and hands me another photo.

"I recognize him, too."

"No nickname for this guy?" Davidson asks.

"No. He stays at the house, though."

"And how do you know all this shit?" Hicks asks.

His tone is a little hard, but I still don't let it get to me. I am surprised Davidson doesn't put him in his place.

"'Cause I sat on the place for a bit," is all I tell him.

I hand the photo back to Davidson, and it goes in the manila with the other one.

"That's all you got?" I ask.

"Those were the only two that showed up."

"Well, there's two more," I say, knowing there's three, but I keep Jordan Super Fly stuffed in the suitcase to myself, for obvious reasons. "They were probably still working Sixteenth and Park while these two went back to the house to re-up."

"Yeah, probably. That's why we had a lot of the boys in that area stopped and identified. Most of them didn't have any identification, and the ones that did were probably fake."

He takes out three more photos and hands them to me.

"These guys had records, though. Didn't lock them up, but I pulled these to show you."

I look them over one by one. One of them I recognize as a crackhead that frequents the area of 16th and Park. The other two, young Latino boys, I don't know.

"No, not these boys."

I hand them back.

"Would you recognize the other subjects if you saw them again?" Davidson asks.

"Hell yeah. The two you got, they talking?"

"No. They lawyered up right away."

"You got some goods on them, though? I mean once you hit the place."

"Oh yeah. Couple of guns . . . lot of drugs."

"I knew you would. I'm assuming the girl's a good witness."

"She's still at the hospital. She's pretty messed up, mentally and physically, but we managed to get a positive ID on the two I showed you pictures of as her captors. They're held without bond."

"She brought up another guy who is more than likely involved. I only got his first name—Edgar. She mention him?" I ask.

"She told us about him. We're looking into it."

"But she should be okay?"

"She'll be all right. Physically, I mean. She asked about you a couple of times. Apparently you're her hero."

"She knows I'm not a cop anymore, then?"

"I didn't tell her. Even if I did, she wouldn't have cared."

"Well, happy she's safe now."

"Amen, brother," Davidson says. He repositions the memo pad on his lap and twirls the pen between two fingers. "Okay, so when I last spoke to you on the cell, you said something about exigent circumstances that led you to kick in the door of the house."

"Yeah, I did," I say with a slight nod.

"Tell me about it."

"First, where's the bathroom? I gotta take a mean piss."

"Back out the door and directly to the left. Hit the buzzer and I'll let you back in."

"Be right back."

I walk back out.

I open the door to the men's room. It has two sinks, three stalls, and two urinals. I scan the room as if I think it'll have surveillance cameras, but I realize I'm being paranoid so I enter one of the stalls and lock the latch.

I look around the ceiling area again just to make sure, then remove the pill container from my front pants pocket. I close the toilet seat, straddle it backward, and pull out two capsules. I twist one of them open and squeeze the powder onto the inner part of the pill container's cap so it's a little pile. I do the same with the second because I want a big hit. I carefully set the cap on the toilet's water container.

I twist the pill capsules back together and drop them into the pill container for later use, and flush the toilet for the noise. I pick up the lid and snort the pile of blow up my right nostril and then sniff a couple more times to bring it all in. I wipe the inner lid with my finger to gather the rest of the powder and rub it on my gums.

At the sink I check my nose, run a bit of water, sniff a couple more times, clean my nasal passages with a little water, and then wash my hands and exit.

I buzz to get in.

Davidson opens the door.

"I think I'll take you up on that soda," I say, and then walk in.

Fifteen

The cold soda feels good going down my throat; even the burning burp afterward feels good.

Davidson reclines in his chair with the memo pad on his lap and pen at the ready. He's waiting for my answer to his question on how I came to discover the girl in the house.

Having been a cop gives me a certain advantage. I know the types of questions cops ask. I was up all night thinking about every possible question that Davidson might ask and how to answer it. How I came to find the girl is an obvious first question.

So I say, "First of all, my client does not know any of the boys you arrested and is not involved with anything illegal."

"All right."

"He's just a hardworking man who lives in Virginia with his family and does a lot of handyman work here in the city. He was doing some work on a home in the Adams Morgan area and got all his tools stolen. I'm talkin' air compressor, ceramic tile cutter, circular saw, drills, reciprocating saw, and on and on. Everything he owns to make a living. Shit's expensive, and he certainly didn't have the money to replace any of it. Well, an associate of mine who works this kind of stuff gave me a call and asked if I'd be willing to take it on 'cause he didn't have the time. He advised me that the client didn't have a lot of money, but would be willing to trade in labor. And you know my house on Twelfth, right?"

"Yeah."

"I still got a lot of work I'd like to get done, so I told him that I'd meet with the guy, but couldn't promise anything. So I meet with him and come to like him and feel sorry for him. Actually, I don't know why I took it on, except that I felt sorry for him having his livelihood taken like that. I don't work cases like this and don't know the first thing about recovering stolen property. But I do know drugs and that most of those types of crimes are committed by crackheads. And I still have my contacts on the street. One of them led me to a burglar in the area who is known to target construction sites and homes under renovation. This source of mine told me that they'd commonly trade the stolen property for crack at Sixteenth and Park. So I set up a bit of surveillance there."

"So you have photographs?"

"No. I didn't get a chance to do that. So it doesn't take me long to figure out those boys you showed me the photos of are running things pretty hard. I also manage to see some deals being made in exchange for possible stolen property. I watch them put the shit in the trunk of their vehicle, and at the end of their workday I follow them and that's what leads me to the house on Kenyon."

"So that's why you busted into the house, to get his tools back?" Hicks asks, like I'm an idiot.

"You outta your head? Of course not. I'm not crazy. For a drug house like that, I would've used one of my sources," I say with a smile.

"Sheeit," Hicks grunts.

"Seriously, though, I decide that the next day I'll sit on them at Sixteenth and Park some more and start taking pictures of the deals, maybe get some good photos of them transporting the property from the trunk of their vehicle into their house. And then when I think I have enough, I was gonna take everything to McGuire and Luna, who I knew would jump on it. They'd maybe send in one of their confidential informants to trade bait property, like power tools, for narcotics. We used to do that kinda shit all the time, and it's good for a quick hit. I figured once they hit the place, my client could ID his property and get it released back to him. It woulda been nothing more than a few hours of work and then maybe I'd finally get my kitchen remodeled. Would've saved hundreds in labor."

I sip my Coke. I can tell by the look on Davidson's face that he's a believer. Damn, I even believe it.

"I go back the next day, early in the morning, but this time to sit on their house. I wait for them to leave, which is at about ten hundred hours, and I decide to sit there for a bit to see if they got anything working at the house, too, because that'd be easier work for a CI. Nothing is happening, so after about a couple hours I exit my car to scope out the area, get the layout of the house, see if I can see anything through a window. When I'm at the side of the house, I notice one of the boys has returned and is walking up to the patio. I'm figuring he's there to re-up. I scoot myself tight against the side wall, and that's when I hear his cell phone ring. You know I speak Spanish, right?"

"No, I didn't, but go on," Davidson says.

"Well, I speak good enough to understand. He answers the call and greets some dude he calls Angelo. Had to be the one you locked up, right?"

"More than likely, yes," Davidson says.

"He's talking to him on the patio, and I hear him ask this Angelo about a girl and if he should 'let her out to eat.' Obviously I couldn't hear what this Angelo was saying, but the way this boy was talking, it sure as hell sounded like they had a girl being held against her will and locked up in a bathroom. I mean things like, 'I won't fuck her,' 'She has to eat or she's going to die on us.' Man, I knew they had someone in there. My mind started working, and I remembered on the news about some of these young teenage girls that had gone missing in Fairfax County recently, and how the police there had made a stop on these young Latino boys after it was reported they were following a young girl that just got off the school bus, but she ran away and got home."

"I remember hearing that," Hicks says.

"This boy finishes the call and enters the house. After about half an hour he leaves. I watch him get in the car and head out. I wait about twenty minutes, try to look through some windows, and don't see shit. Actually, I do see power tools on the floor in the kitchen, but that didn't mean anything to me anymore. I walk to the front door, ring the bell a few times. Nothin'. I knock hard and still nothin'. That's when I decide, based on everything I heard and what little experience and intuition I have left, that I'm going in. So I did.

"I find her in the upstairs bathroom. She was handcuffed to a chain that was secured to the floor with a heavy eyebolt. She was handcuffed in the front, and that made me think they knew she wouldn't try to escape because she was brainwashed or some shit like that. All she was wearing was her underwear. She was terrified. I didn't know what she was thinking about me being there, so I told her I was a cop and showed her my badge but covered the part that said 'retired.' All I wanted to do was make her feel comfortable. Would you believe, she didn't want to go with me at first?"

Davidson shakes his head. "Why?"

"She was convinced they'd kill her family if she left, said that they knew where she lived."

"She told us that, too."

"So then you have someone sitting on her house?"

"We have it handled. But why did you just drop her off at Leslie Costello's?"

"I've been retired for close to two years now. I don't know what I was thinking 'cept to get her someplace safe and where I knew she'd get help. I knew Costello would do everything right, so that's where I took her."

"But still, man, you should know better than that. You take a victim like her to a hospital, right? You remember that much, don't you?" Davidson says.

"I'm not a cop anymore, and I wasn't thinking straight. Now, I sure as hell know the boys you locked up ain't gonna put any charges on me and neither are you, so why are you beating me down like this?"

"I'm not trying to beat you down, Frank. I just have to ask. You should know that. Hell, you're a hero. The chief might even give you an award."

I seriously doubt the chief would consider that, but I say, "Don't even think about writing me up for an award. I'm serious, Scott."

"You're something else, Frank."

Ain't that the truth, but I don't say it.

Sixteen

I usually go out of my way to find good grapefruit. They gotta be fresh, though. They're tougher to find when they're not in season, but you can still find them at some of the better grocery stores, like the Whole Foods on P Street. I always keep a couple in the car. They're good for days like this, when my immune system needs a boost. I cut into one with my knife, suck the juice out, and chew the pulp. It's like my body knows when it's in need, because most of the time I have to force myself to eat, but not when it comes to grapefruit. I devour everything but the skin, which I drop out the car window. I feel like my body's been washed afterward.

The temperature is dropping every day. Winter's closing in. I push the button to raise the car window and recline in the seat. I watch the pedestrians passing by on the sidewalk. Most of them are law enforcement, uniform and plainclothes; attorneys; and other folks who work in this area. There are a few homeless people, though, moving like zombies. Crackheads, junkies. They're letting out from the shelter on 2nd and D, just a couple blocks away. I watch them and I gotta think the only thing that separates me from their kind is a meager pension, an occasional paycheck, my drug of choice—and, of course, grapefruit.

I light a cigarette. I inhale. I come back to reality.

The meeting with Davidson didn't go so badly. I'm thinking it was a damn good story. He even said he was sorry that I couldn't get the tools back for my bogus client and that if he had known about it beforehand, he might've recovered the power tools he saw on the kitchen floor when they were executing the search warrant. I thanked him anyway and told him my client would be all right, that I might just buy him the tools myself in exchange for his labor.

I start the car, don't even know where I'm going, but I got a couple hours to kill before I have to meet with Claypole at DC jail.

My hand on the shifter, my phone rings.

Screen shows that it's Luna.

I put the car back in park and answer, "What's up, Al?"

"Just that good hit you passed our way. How the hell'd you stumble onto that?"

"Man, don't make me go into all that again. Davidson's got all the details. Let's just say right place, right time, and leave it at that."

"I'll be getting a copy of his write-up, then."

"What'd you get there?"

"Couple of guns and enough crack and heroin to get us to district court. We're going to wrap these boys up for a while."

"Do me a big one and get them to plead out; save me from having to be a witness, all right?"

"Well, they're sure as hell not talking to us right now, but we're not done with them, so I'll let you know. We got so much on them they'll probably plead out. What do you got going for tonight? McGuire and I are going to hit Shelly's for drinks when we're done here."

"What time you looking at?"

"Around seventeen thirty."

"Yeah, I'm good for that. Haven't been there in a while."

"Evening's on me."

"Sounds good, bro."

"Okay, man, see you then."

"Yeah, okay. Be safe."

"Always," he says, and then disconnects.

It's been a while since I've done anything social. But then, I don't know many folks I can socialize with. I have to think hard about it and all I come up with is Leslie, Albino Luna, and sometimes Stan McGuire. Luna and McGuire are the only two real friends I have left on the department. We all made detective together at 7D Vice, then got transferred to Narcotics Branch. We'd been in the shit, but even they don't know the real story behind my early retirement. All they know is that I retired early, after seventeen years, and that I had had enough. The only ones who know the real story are the chief and a couple of his cronies.

I put the car back in drive and ease my way out of the parking space. Since I got some time, I make my way to Georgetown, see if I can spend some of this hard-earned money, maybe buy a new suit.

SEVENTEEN

I hate DC jail. I hate everything about it, especially having to walk in, secure my belongings, and submit myself to being searched.

When I was a cop, I'd drive my cruiser into a secured area just under the guard tower. I'd lock up my weapon, clips, and hand-cuffs in a lockbox that looked more like a P.O. box. The COs looked in the car, sometimes even opened the dashboard, then popped open the trunk to make sure I wasn't trying to sneak in any contraband. I'd get a quick pat-down after that, and drive the car into another gated parking lot. I'd buzz to gain entry into a prisoner-holding area. The entry door was made of heavy steel and the sound it made when it slammed shut was deafen-ing: steel against steel in an empty concrete vault. The only way back out was when the guards sitting on the other side of scuffed-up shatterproof Plexiglas, in an office area with several monitors, buzzed you out again. I hated that trapped-in feeling, especially when I had to rely on some underpaid, overfed officer on the other side to push the button.

Walking through the front, like I have to now, is a little less claustrophobic, but still, I leave all control behind after those doors shut, even if the sound of them closing is quieter. If I ever get caught because of the shit I do, hopefully not for anything that's gonna get me held, I might be making a trip to Canada, though more likely Mexico 'cause someone like me can get away with a lot more in Mexico.

The corrections officer escorts me to the interview room, unlocks the door to let me in. Claypole's sitting on an old wooden chair, leaning back to rest his large bald head against the dirty white cinder block wall. His goatee has grown. He keeps it well groomed, combed to split into two ponytails with rubber bands wrapped tight at the ends. He's a big man, taller than me by a couple of inches, and I'm six one. He's also got me by about a hundred pounds—a prison build. Granted, I'm not in the kinda shape I used to be, but I still have some good weight and can hold my own if I have to.

He's wearing prison-issue orange pants and a matching short-sleeve V-neck pullover with a white T-shirt underneath. Old biker tattoos cover his neck and most of the space on his arms.

He drops the chair back down on all four legs, gives me an upward nod.

"You looking beat up, Marr," he says, and then leans forward to fold his arms on the small table.

I sit on a chair at the other end so I can face him.

"I'll catch up on my sleep over the weekend."

"You got some news for me?"

"No, but I'm supposed to go over all the details of your case again, maybe see if there's something useful for trial, something we mighta missed. But we both know that'd be a waste of time, right?"

He tightens his lips, straightens himself in the chair like he's gonna say something, but doesn't. I realize that wasn't a good start to the conversation, so I adjust my tone.

"Ms. Costello thinks that's what we're gonna do, and I'd like her to think that's what we did do next time you two meet."

"What's this about, Investigator Marr?"

"I'm hoping to convince you that you're about to really fuck things up with your life."

He clenches his jaw, and the muscles going down his neck tighten, but it's not a nervous reaction. Then, impressively, he adjusts and relaxes himself. He puts his forearms back on the table and tries to act like he cares about what I've got to say.

"You nearly beat that bouncer to death. We've been over all that plenty of times before, but I think it needs to be brought up again. There are witnesses who'll say it was because he was doing his job, not letting you in the club 'cause you already had too much to drink."

"In his opinion I had too much to drink, which wasn't the case, and as far as those witnesses go, they all work at the club."

"Yeah, we've been over all that."

"And what about my witnesses? Dude gave me a hard time just 'cause I was white."

"Let me finish, here."

He nods, but just barely, as if I've been given approval to continue.

"The government's gonna have all their witnesses and I'm sure plenty of others that'll testify that you were disruptive and wouldn't take no for an answer. They'll say you threw the first punch. We know that part is true, 'cause you even admit to that."

"Hell yeah, he put his fucking hands on me. I had to defend myself."

"Some will say that he was just trying to escort an unruly man out. But let's step back and say, like you mentioned, that you threw the first punch 'cause you were defending yourself. A fight ensued and you even took a couple of nice punches yourself. The problem is you kept throwing punches even after the man was down. It ain't anything like self-defense if you stopped the threat after, what, the second punch?"

He tilts his head, with what I would take as an inappropriate half smile, as if it's something he's proud of.

I continue. "The prosecutor's not gonna have a hard time convincing a jury that he wasn't a threat after you knocked him down like that. They'll say all you had to do at that point was walk away. And trust me on this, Claypole—you sure as hell won't have a chance of beating the charge if you try to make this into a black-white thing. We both know that ain't true and all that'll do is backfire on you, make you look like the racist. So, barring some kinda miracle, you'll more than likely be found guilty. Come sentencing time, you'll be looking at five to fifteen. With your history, you'll get somewhere in between."

"Man, this is some bullshit."

"You gotta lose that pride, my man. Pick your battles, forfeit this one."

"Sheeit."

"What I'm getting at is you might want to consider the offer you've been given. You take the plea and you'll more than likely get out in less than three, with good behavior, of course."

"And what does Ms. Costello say about this?"

"I told you, she doesn't know we're having this conversation. As far as she knows, I'm here in an effort to find something new, something that might help her during trial. In fact, she's back at her office preparing to go to trial. I'm just saying, based on all my experience, that this is not a case you want to take to trial."

"Fucking three years?"

"Including the time you've been held, probably less. Shit,

that's nothin' for someone like you. Eat regular, work those free weights, clean out your body and mind."

"Yeah, a fucking vacation, right?"

I don't reply to that.

"Man, I just got back on track with my lady and now this shit," he says.

"She's still got her job, right?"

"Yeah, but she's gonna definitely have to sell my truck now. She had the good credit for the financing."

"I seem to remember you bought that used."

"Yeah, but it's still more money than she can handle every month. She already blown through all the money I made on that construction job I had before I got locked up."

"What do you owe on it?"

He has to think hard about it, probably because he's never been the one to take care of the bills.

"Somewhere around eight grand."

Something comes to me just like that, but I mull it over in my head for a second. Then I say, "What if I tell you I'll take care of that bill personally, pay it all off on a no-interest loan?"

"What the fuck you wanna do somethin' like that for?"

"You save us all a lot of time and effort and take the plea offer."

"That's crazy, man. You're talkin' through your ass."

"I'm fucking real."

"Why the hell you want to do something like that for me?"

"I wouldn't be doing it for you. I'm doing it for Ms. Costello, who doesn't want a reputation for losing, and I also know she doesn't want to have to see her client get slammed by the court. Believe it or not, she actually loses sleep over shit like this."

"I don't know, man. This is crazy shit. You're basically offering me a few thousand bucks to take an offer that puts me in prison for a few years."

"Damn, Claypole, either way you're not gonna get outta having to do prison time. I'm sitting here trying to save your ass from having to do more, is all."

"You don't know that for sure. It goes to trial, I can maybe win this."

"You can. You can try. But it's a bad gamble. You know that."

"I feel like this is blackmail or somethin'."

"You really are nothin' but a bullheaded son of a bitch."

I shove the chair back and stand. "We're done, then," I say.

"Fucking sit down, Marr! Give me a second, here."

I don't sit, but I let him have his time. He looks down at the table, slowly moving his head from side to side.

"And it's not like I'd just be giving you eight grand. You'll have to start paying me back when you get out, after you find work again."

It takes him a minute. He looks up at me.

"I wanna start fresh. I don't want this bullshit in my life anymore. You really don't think I got a case on sclf-defense?"

I sit back down.

"I wasn't there. I only know things based on the facts given to me. Based on what's been given to me and what I've been able to find myself, it doesn't look good for you."

"For real, right?" he asks. "I mean the eight grand. I don't want my girl getting stuck with anything."

"I said I would. I will. But it's between us, because if Costello ever finds out, I'll lose my job with her and more. Then you'd be messing up my life. And you don't want to do that."

"I trust you when you say that, Marr. I can see you got that way about you. Fuck, three years'll pass by like nothin' anyway."

"You said it already, but you gotta make it a fresh start when you get out. Lose that hot head of yours, especially inside. You don't wanna fuck up inside."

"I hear ya. Tell me one thing, though. Where the hell does an ex-cop turned PI get eight grand to offer up like this?"

"I know how to make good investments, and you shouldn't be asking questions like that anyway."

I pull out my notepad from my rear pants pocket and a pen from the inner sleeve pocket of my suit jacket. I slide them across the table over to him.

"Give me the dealership info on the car. I'll get in touch with your lady and take care of it first thing tomorrow."

He writes everything down and hands it back to me.

"And you tell my old lady I'm really sorry for all this shit, all right? And make sure she gets the sentencing date when it comes. I need her to be there."

"I will."

He folds his upper lip over his bottom lip so I'm not sure if it's a smile or a frown. He nods, so I take it as an awkward smile.

"All right, then," I say, and stand up.

I offer him my hand and we shake.

"Do one more thing for me, Marr?"

"Go on."

"Make sure my truck gets parked in the garage. It's gonna have to sit for a bit."

"I'll make sure," I say.

Eighteen

I've never had this amount of blow staring back at me before. Well, I did when I was a narcotics detective. There's so much here that I need to find a little self-control, or I might be picking imaginary bugs outta my hair, or worse. It's sitting there on the shelf of my fake wall, sealed up nice and tight, but not so tight that I can't get into it when I need to, like now.

Despite what I see in front of me, I still find myself thinking about planning the next hit.

Hell, you can never have too much of a good thing.

My cell rings, startling me. I quickly close up the wall and clip the edge molding in place.

I pull the cell outta my pocket.

Costello.

Damn.

I am overtaken by a sudden apprehensiveness and I'm thinking Claypole probably gave up the true nature of our conversation earlier today. I almost don't answer, but the feeling passes quickly because I just took in a bit of powdery courage. I lean against the washer, remember all the money I have stuffed in there along with my dirty laundry. I'll have to count eight grand outta that bag tonight for Claypole, that is, if he didn't just fuck me.

"What's up, Leslie?"

"I just got off the phone with Lenny Claypole. What exactly did you say to him?"

I start to wonder if she's playing me 'cause she already knows the answer, and now all she wants to do is trip me up.

"We went over the details of the case again, like you wanted. Wasn't anything new there, so I was honest and said it didn't look good for him." She doesn't reply right away, so I ask, "You still on?"

"You must have said it with conviction, because he agreed to the plea offer. He's not going to fight it."

"That's what you wanted, right?"

"Of course! I told you it would be a losing battle and I don't like to lose."

"After my conversation with him, I got the feeling he believed that, too."

"You know I like a good fight, though," she adds, like she's already trying to justify why she's letting him take the plea. "But this is exactly why I hate having to take on some of these court-appointed clients."

"It's the right thing. And it's a good thing when a hardheaded man like him comes to his senses and accepts responsibility for his actions."

"Hardheaded, listen to you. Still, thanks for going back and trying, and for being honest with him."

If only she knew. Hell, it's gonna be worth every penny 'cause of all the shit I put her through with that little girl. It's like penance.

"I feel like having drinks after work. Join me?" she asks.

"Yeah, I'm meeting up with Luna and McGuire at Shelly's. Actually, was going to call you, too, but you beat me to it. It'll be a celebration all around. They just made a great case outta that kidnapped girl I left you with."

"And here I was about to offer the same thing. Shelly's with the old crew sounds good."

"I'll drop by around five thirty?"

"See you then," she says.

I slip the phone back in my pocket and smile 'cause I now have a good excuse to wear the new suit I bought.

I open the washer and pull out the bag of money.

I take it to the living room, where I dump it out on the hardwood floor. Some of the bills try to roll away, under the sofa and under the entertainment center I have against the wall on the other side of the room from me. I scoop everything up into a nice pile and start pulling rubber bands off the rolled-up bills and separating them into stacks according to their denomination.

Two hours later, all I've managed to do is cover most of the living room floor with several stacks of ones, fives, tens, and twenties. It'll take me more time than I have right now to count up all this, so I grab a stack of twenties and then another and another and another, until I have four hundred twenties.

I count them out into eight stacks of fifty and then secure them with a rubber band. After that, I count out about another five hundred in twenties for walking-around money. I use the rest of the rubber bands for all the uncounted stacks and then put those, along with the eight grand, back in the bag. I fold up the five hundred in twenties, slip it in my front pants pocket, and take the bag back to the washer.

I head to the shower to freshen up, hopefully wash away some of that dirty money. Otherwise I'm sure I'll feel great.

Nineteen

I've been doing this for so long I know most of the tricks, even picked up a few pointers from some prisoners I debriefed back in the day. Beat all but two of the random piss tests back then, too. I was caught off guard for the one that got me when I was called in twice in one week.

It's not so hard to hide this lifestyle of mine if you stick to a defined procedure. Without certain rules, you're either gonna die or get yourself caught. Wish I knew then all that I know now, because I did love the job. And yes, there was more than a bit of self-loathing because of what that job meant and what I had become. I don't blame any of it on the work. Fuck that. It's my own damn weakness. It was and is something that has always been there, a malady I actually freed myself from when I decided I was going to be a cop.

I was a strong man through the academy, my years walking a beat, then as a vice officer, and even a couple years into my work at Narcotics Branch. I don't have an excuse for that day when I pocketed a little something for myself during the course of a search warrant. I don't even know what I was thinking when I did it, except that I could.

I'm actually okay with my life now, but the worst thing, I think, would be getting caught or found out. Especially by someone close, like Costello, or one of my good buddies, like Luna. That's why I have rules. As hard as it is, I gotta maintain self-control. And as hard as it is most of the time, I gotta force myself to be social. It'd be easy to be a recluse. I do venture out, but usually to spots in my neighborhood around U Street or downtown at places like Shelly's. It's a good spot, a comfortable hangout, and one of the few places in DC where you're still allowed to smoke cigars.

Back in the day, I used to go with McGuire and Luna, sometimes Costello. A refuge for the boys and girls at the branch. Nowadays it's the same thing, but with close people like Costello, after a long, challenging day at work or at the end of a trial, and with old buds like McGuire and Luna for a couple of drinks and a cigar, a time to catch up.

The pill container I carry with me is for a prescription I get for chronic fatigue. A few years back, when I was on the job, I convinced a doctor that's what I had. I was fatigued, but it was nothing I couldn't fix myself. All I had to do was stop snorting all that blow after work and get some sleep. I never used at work.

The meds worked for a while, but then the side effects got so bad I had to wean myself off of them. The doctor kept filling the prescriptions, though, 'cause I needed the capsules and the label showing they were prescribed to me. It's a perfect hiding spot when you're carrying. The capsules twist open easily and hold the equivalent of a nice line. I can sniff it directly out of each half of the capsules or, like I did in the bathroom at the U.S. Attorney's Office, make a nice pile on the inside of the pill container's cap. I keep about fifty capsules in the container.

The new suit fits nicely. It feels good—clean. I choose to wear my light purple dress shirt without a tie, unbuttoned at the collar, and my black leather penny loafers.

Costello lives in Capitol Hill, off Pennsylvania Avenue, near 3rd and C. It's a nice two-story connected row house, but in an area a bit like mine, which a lot of cops refer to as burglary central. She's been lucky so far. Even if her home was broken into, she'd probably volunteer to represent the burglar that did it.

It's almost seven thirty when I pull on to her block. When I pull up to the front of the house, she's sitting on a step leading up to the porch, just like a kid.

I have to double-park, but she stands up and walks down when she sees me.

Such a different woman away from work. Why? I don't know.

She's wearing a light green long-sleeve V-neck T-shirt under a faded black lightweight leather jacket and well-fitted black jeans. She opens the passenger's side door, steps in, and sits. Drops her small purse on the floor between her feet.

"Traffic bad?"

"It's DC. What do you think? I'm not that late, am I?"

"Not at all. I enjoy sitting on the steps when it's cool outside. It's refreshing. That's a new suit."

"No, just dry-cleaned," I lie, without knowing why.

"Give me the name of your dry cleaner, then."

"It's a little out of your way."

I tune the car radio to 101.1 'cause I know she likes that station. A Foo Fighters song I don't know the name of is playing again. She turns the volume up. I sort of grin and bear it.

I head back toward Pennsylvania Avenue. Traffic is not so much a battle heading toward downtown.

When the song ends, she turns the volume down.

"I know it's the weekend, but I was hoping you could come to the office tomorrow, early afternoon."

"I've never had a problem working a weekend. You know that," I tell her.

"Yes, I know, but this isn't concerning anything I have lined up. There's a couple that wants to meet you."

"A couple of what?" I joke. "You pick up a new client?"

"No. I got a call the other day, after we spoke. The parents of the child you dropped off with me gave the family of another missing child my number. Apparently they spoke very highly of you."

I turn to her briefly, then back to the road ahead.

"C'mon, Leslie, you know I don't work missing persons, certainly not a case like the one that involved that little girl."

"I'm just asking you to come and talk to them. You put me in this situation, remember?"

"Why do you have to go there? Am I gonna owe you the rest of my life because of one stupid incident?"

"Incident? Don't belittle what you've done. Frankie, they have nowhere else to go. The police have nothing."

"And what makes you think it'll be any different with me? I don't work that kind of shit. In fact, I hate working that kind of shit."

"I felt bad for them. I told them I'd set it up. Just come and talk to them. For me, please."

"Shit."

"Yes, I know. It's all 'shit' with you."

That sounded funny coming out of her mouth 'cause she rarely cusses, except when she's mad, and that's rare, too.

"Just hear their story. If it's something you can't do, then you tell them."

"So you make me the bad guy?"

"Just do this for me, Frankie."

And here I thought the eight grand I'm about to dish out was gonna give me good karma. I should've known better; I know there's no such thing as karma.

"Do the two girls know each other or something?"

"The same school is all, I think."

"What about Detective Davidson? He's the one you should be talking to, not me."

"I gave them his number, but they insisted on hiring someone like you."

"What time?"

"I set it for one p.m."

"That's good. I gotta run an errand in Maryland in the morning," I say, referring to taking care of the truck for Claypole. "And I'll talk to them for you, but that's it. I'll give Davidson a call beforehand, though."

"Thank you. And I don't even know why I have to say thank you."

"Well, you already fucked up the thank you by having to add that."

She smiles and turns the radio back up. Fucking Pearl Jam this time.

I can't find parking anywhere near Shelly's. I circle the block, then decide on an illegal space at the corner of 13th and F.

I grab my police patch outta the center console box and toss it on the dashboard.

"You're not a cop anymore. You can't use that," she says.

I shoot her a brief but hard glare. "Really," is all I say, and then I step out of the car.

Twenty

L ittle whirlwinds of smoke are carried up to the ceiling and through the ventilation system. What's left of the smoke diffuses the light to a warm glow. If you haven't been here in a while, like Costello, your lungs might have a hard time with all this lingering smoke. She doesn't complain.

Groups of people are scrunched together on large couches, in overstuffed seats, and around tables.

I spot McGuire first and then Luna sitting across from him, at a good table near the bar, under the mural. The mural depicts what I've always imagined a restful, cigar-loving Cuban village would have looked like way back when, before I was born.

Luna sees me, waves us over.

"What's up, Frankie?" he calls as we approach, then reaches across the table to knock knuckles, in the time-honored tradition. He turns to Costello. "Leslie Costello. This is a surprise. Have you finally come to your senses and decided to come back to our side?"

"Social visits only," she says.

McGuire's smoking a fat one. He nods at me, then turns to Costello.

"Good to see you, Leslie," he says.

"Good to see you, too, Stan."

We pull out the stools and sit.

Luna's drinking something "neat," a light golden color, like vitamin-enriched urine. More than likely bourbon. I enjoy good bourbon on occasion, but for social occasions I prefer a pick-me-up drink, such as rum or vodka.

They both look like they came here straight from work. McGuire's wearing a long-sleeve mock turtleneck pullover with a zipper at the neck. Looks like he hasn't shaved in a few days, but that's the look most of the narcotics guys have. Looks like he needs a haircut, too—probably sooner than later or the back will start looking more and more like a mullet. I can see a few gray hairs starting to come in along his sideburns. Luna's the opposite—squared away, clean shaven, wearing a casual button-down shirt under a tan sport coat.

"I saved one for you," Luna says as he hands me a Churchill-style cigar. I examine the label.

"Cuban."

"I still have a nice little stash in my humidor," he adds maybe too proudly.

I roll it between my thumb and index finger and smell it. I set it on the large cigar ashtray in the center of the table.

"Appreciate that, Albino. I'll fire it up with my drink."

"If I had known you were coming too, Les—"

"No worries, Albino," she stops him. "I prefer something smaller."

"So you're admitting that smaller is better," McGuire jumps in.

"Don't go there, old boy," I say, as if I need to defend her.

"Sounds like you just admitted to something, McGuire," she says.

Luna barks and coughs his bourbon.

"No worries there, counselor. I can prove it if you want."

"Okay, stand and show us," she says.

McGuire puffs out a laugh.

"What the fuck, McGuire, you should be proud of it," I say.

"Just give me a warning so I can look the other way," Luna says.

"You afraid to see your wife naked, Luna?" I ask.

"Fuck you," McGuire says. "He's the bitch in this marriage, not me."

"See what I have to put up with," Luna says.

The waitress works her way to our table.

"What'll it be?" She smiles.

I worry about what McGuire might say to that. Luckily, his lips are wrapped around his cigar; no doubt he's thinking about his dick.

"Belvedere martini, two olives, please."

"Zacapa 23, neat, and a Corona on the side," I say.

"Be right back," she advises, with another smile.

"So you got a good hit outta that house on Kenyon?" I ask them.

Luna glances at Costello, like we shouldn't be talking shop in front of her. Might not be a good thing with any other defense attorney, or even with Costello if there were a chance she'd be picking up one of the defendants as a client. But there ain't no chance in hell of that happening. She'd have to recuse herself because she took in the little girl. Besides, I'd like to think she wouldn't defend animals like them. Costello senses Luna and McGuire's reluctance, but it doesn't piss her off.

"I'm going to the ladies' room," she says with a mild grin.

She scoots the chair back, stands, and walks back along the length of the bar.

I notice both McGuire and Luna watching her backside.

"That is some fine-looking ass. You tapping that?" McGuire asks.

"Shut the fuck up," I say.

"No, seriously, because if you're not—"

"I said shut the fuck up."

Costello's my weak spot, always has been. Boys like these, once they find that weak spot, love nothin' more than to push your buttons, hoping you'll break. It's a game that started in the academy. I sure as hell won't break, but that doesn't mean they won't piss me off.

"You're getting pretty defensive there, Frankie. What's up with that?" McGuire asks.

"Just overworked, brother, and looking forward to a few drinks here with you guys, or at the end of the bar with Costello if you keep up with this shit."

"But seriously, you two an item?" McGuire asks.

"Move on with that, or I will. Shit," I say. "So how'd the search warrant go?"

"It was a good hit," Luna says, just as the waitress returns.

She sets down our drinks.

Luna downs his bourbon, hands her the glass. "I'll have another. Thanks, hon," he tells her.

"I'm good for now," McGuire says.

The waitress returns to the bar.

"Yeah, it was a damn good hit," Luna continues.

"Just found out there's another missing teenager," I say.

"You get that from Davidson?" Luna asks.

"No. Costello got a call from another family whose daughter went missing. Anything you can tell me about those boys you arrested?"

"Davidson and his Fed partners took them right away. We

didn't have a chance to talk to them. Heard they lawyered up right away, too," Luna says.

"I'll get you the info on this other girl next week. You get them to debrief in the future, maybe you can work this girl into the deal."

"Of course, brother. Keep us informed. And why are you working something like this?"

"I'm not working it. Just trying to help out, that's all."

"I could never work that kind of shit," Luna says.

"Me either," McGuire adds. "Makes me both mad as hell and sick as hell at the same time. Can't even think about it. Something like that ever happened to my daughter, you'd have to take my gun from me or I'd be wearing an orange jumpsuit."

Costello returns. She has a little cigarillo. Must have bought it at the other end of the bar. After she sits, she grabs a box of wooden matches near the ashtray and lights it. She's a social smoker, something I've never been able to understand. I fire up the cigar.

"So you guys need me to find a seat at the bar, or can I join you now? God forbid having to sit with the enemy."

The waitress returns with Luna's drink, sets it before him.

"Thanks, babe," he says. After she walks away he adds, "It's not personal. You know that."

"No, just ignorance," I say, and take another sip of rum. "You two think about it—I do most of my work for her. Maybe you shouldn't trust me 'cause I'm on the dark side, too."

"Hell no," Luna returns. "You'll always be one of us."

If only that were so, I think to myself. That honor's long gone.

Twenty-one

I've had to go to the men's room only two times since I've been here. For some reason self-control has always been easier in a social environment. It's when I'm home alone that I need more practice. That's a whole different monster. It's like chain-smoking when you're sitting alone with too much on your mind.

They ordered food for the table. I return to several plates of appetizers spread out along the round tabletop, leaving barely enough room for our drinks.

Costello's nursing her second martini. She's a lightweight. She does one more and I'll probably have to hold her up while we walk to the car. Which might not be such a bad thing. I miss her scent, especially the area at the nape of her neck where her hair falls.

I'm on my third rum and fourth beer. Don't even know how much McGuire and Luna have had, but I'm sure the food they're stuffing down their pieholes will absorb most of the alcohol. The hardest part of what I do is when I have to force myself to eat, like now. The stuffed poppers are tasty enough, but the food fucks up the high. I've gotta eat, though, or I'll be a mess in the morning. There is a certain benefit to potentially heart-attack-inducing comfort foods like poppers and fries. Consuming them, and downing four ibuprofen and a full glass of water at bedtime, will seriously reduce the risk of waking up to a bad hangover.

I can't remember the last time I had a hangover. A bit of a headache, maybe, but that's about it. I ain't so stupid that I think it's something that's gonna last. I think about that sometimes, mostly in bed when I'm having a hard time falling asleep, or when I'm depressed because I'm running low on my supply. My body will start falling apart at some point, no matter how much grapefruit I consume. The worrying has a way of disappearing soon after I wake up, and the body starts craving what has become part of its essence.

After I take my seat, I light a cigarette.

"You still have that bladder problem?" McGuire asks.

"Beer does that to me," I say with a straight face.

His head is dropping down closer to the table. He's holding himself up with his elbows. He sips the drink that's already been made into water by too much melting ice.

"Why'd you retire so early, Marr?" he asks, barely able to turn to me.

I can't count the number of times I've been asked that question, even by Luna and Costello, but that was during a time shortly after I left, when it would've been a reasonable question. McGuire himself has asked me the question before, but he's silly drunk and probably starting to feel nostalgic. We did have some fun. I had a tighter relationship with Luna, though.

I give him the standard answer. "Simple, really. I wanted my life back."

But the honest answer would be, "I was given the opportunity to own my life by taking a onetime offer. I didn't have a choice."

"I'm a lifer, bro," McGuire says.

"Hate to admit it, but so am I," Luna says.

"Brother, you came in so young, you're going to have to do thirty," I tell him.

"Thanks for reminding me."

"Quit being such pussies," McGuire says, then turns with a downward look toward Costello and says, "Nothing personal."

"Why would I take that personally, unless you think I'm a pussy?"

"I didn't mean it like that, just that you're female," he says seriously. "The bad condensation with the word, is all. Know what I mean?"

"Connotation," I correct him.

"Whatever, dude. You know what I mean, right, Leslie?"

"Yes, Stan, and I appreciate your delicacy."

"And you know I've always liked you, even if you did turn and go to the other side?" He smiles.

"That makes me feel better, Stan," she says.

"Never could understand why, though. I can understand becoming a prosecutor, maybe working for the U.S. Attorney's Office, but not from cop to defense attorney."

I stay out of this one. I know how McGuire can get, especially with too much alcohol. Costello can take care of herself. Hell, McGuire puts me through the same shit almost every time we get together. I'm sure I'd be his target if Leslie weren't here.

"Is it about the money? Because that, I can understand."

"No, most of you guys with all your OT make more than me. There are certain clients I won't take. I'd like to think that most of them deserve a chance."

"The old 'revolving door.' If you succeed, the only thing you're doing is giving them a second chance to commit more crimes," Luna says.

Luna's a good man, but a better cop. He can't handle his liquor. It'll either turn him angry or just sloppy and sentimental. I get the feeling it's gonna start moving toward the latter.

The evening is getting close to an end for me, and I sense Costello feels the same way. It takes a few minutes to get the check and then a couple more to extricate ourselves from the table, but we manage to make a break for it.

It feels cooler outside. I don't have to hold Costello up for the walk back to the car.

I double-park in front of her house.

"I can find a parking spot if you want?"

"Not tonight, Frankie. I don't like it when I've had too much to drink."

She leans over and kisses me on the corner of my mouth. She pulls away before I can turn all the way toward her.

"I'll see you tomorrow," I say.

"Good night, Frankie." And before she closes the door she says, "And thanks. For tomorrow, I mean."

"Don't thank me yet."

She smiles and shuts the door.

I watch her as she walks up the steps to her porch, opens the security gate, unlocks the front door, enters, and closes the door behind her. I wait a few seconds, notice the living room light turn on. I wait a couple more minutes and then I drive home.

When I get home, I strip down to my boxers, down four ibuprofen, a couple of Klonopins, and a full glass of water, then pour myself a bit of Jameson to finish the night off. I will have to go to bed soon or I'll have a hard time waking up. I love sleep when I can find it.

I sit on the sofa to sip my Jameson.

Costello sneaks into my head. I usually like when that happens, but I was hoping for a little more than a slight peck on the lips from her tonight, so I'm feeling a bit discouraged. I just need to give it a few minutes to let the Klonopins do their thing. It always begins with a feeling like little waves moving through the frontal lobe. A good feeling, and one that should help ease the pain in my loins.

I don't know what's in store for us. If we have a future together, I mean. Probably nothing more than the occasional fucking around like we do, and only when she makes the move. Thus far, all my moves have failed. What does that tell you? I'm not in control.

It isn't long before I hit the sack and sink my head into the pillow. I watch the clock for about two hours and the last thing I remember is 3:30 a.m.

Part Two

TWENTY-TWO

Lenny Claypole and his wife, Theresa, rent a small, two-story older brick home in Suitland, Maryland. It has an unattached garage and a tiny square patch of a front yard that's nothin' but weeds and dirt. His Ford F-250 truck—already dusty from his weeks away—is parked in front. I pull behind it. I notice an older-model light blue Ford Fiesta parked in the driveway.

I met Lenny Claypole's wife a couple of times a few months back, when I was working his case for Costello. She answers the door when I ring the bell. She looks about the same—simple, attractive, even without makeup. Her hair is dark. She wears it just below her ears in a bob cut. There's some darkness under her eyes, as if she's got too much stress or puts in long hours at work. Probably both. I can understand why Claypole doesn't want to fuck it up. She's a sweet, unpretentious woman. The two of them are an odd couple, though.

She greets me with a smile and says, "Come in, Mr. Marr."

"Thank you, I don't want to take up too much of your time."

The small home can't be more than eight hundred square feet.

I walk through a little foyer that leads into a living room area and a smaller connected dining room with a round table and four wooden chairs. She keeps it tidy. The living room is sparsely furnished—a love seat with two mismatched armchairs at each end, and a glass-top coffee table.

"Have a seat. I'll get the paperwork."

I sit on the armchair with faded floral patterns. She walks through the dining room and into the kitchen, returns shortly thereafter with a few papers and hands them to me.

Loan documents.

"So, you said I won't be responsible for having to make any more loan payments?"

"Yes. It's a service provided for families in need. It'll all be taken care of, and once Lenny gets out, he'll resume the payments with no added interest. Really, nothing for you to worry about."

"That's such a blessing."

"Please keep this between you and Lenny. It's not something that is offered to everyone, and I'd rather the word not get out. If you ever have any additional questions, you just call me. Don't bother Ms. Costello."

I grab a business card out of the inner sleeve pocket of my jacket and hand it to her. She looks at it briefly, then sets it on the glass-top table.

"This is all legal, right?"

"Of course it is. What would make you think otherwise, Mrs. Claypole?"

"I'm sorry. I'm just used to—"

"I'll take care of everything, so you don't have to worry. After today, it shouldn't even be a discussion."

"Okay."

"I will need to park the truck in the garage, though."

"That's usually where he kept it parked, anyway, because he didn't want the toolbox broken into. I always park in the driveway."

"We'll take care of that on the way out."

I glance over the loan documents.

"Desta Used Cars."

It's from one of those questionable corner-lot used-car dealerships that probably has a small lot with about thirty cars, and a trailer for an office. Spots like this one are all over DC and Maryland, and are usually the only place a person like Lenny could go to get a vehicle with no credit and a few hundred dollars down. The interest is outrageous, but I don't see anywhere in the document that there's a penalty for paying off the loan early. He already owes a couple hundred more than the eight grand, though. I got some walking-around money on me, so that won't be a problem.

After I manage to squeeze the truck into the tiny garage, Theresa Claypole gets in my car and directs me to the dealership. I was pretty much spot-on about the dealership. It takes up a corner lot, surrounded by a chain-link fence that's over six feet in height. A small mobile office trailer is across from where the used cars are parked.

The sign bearing their name, Desta Used Cars, is a large canvas banner stretching across the chain-link fence to the left of the open gate. A smaller banner is on the right side of the gate and it reads: "We Buy Used Cars for Cash $$$."

I back into a curb parking spot between two cars, near the entrance. I grab my briefcase and exit. We walk to the trailer and enter.

A thin, dark-skinned, and well-groomed man is sitting behind a small wooden desk cluttered with papers and an older-model desktop computer. He stands to greet us. The suit he's wearing isn't cut right for his small frame and looks like one of those suits you'd buy at a designer knockoff spot on M Street.

"How can I help you?" he says with a heavy accent—more than likely Ethiopian. "You need a car today?"

"Not today," I advise him. "I'm here to pay off a car for an associate of mine."

"Please, sit down."

He directs us with an open hand to two chairs in front of his desk, and then he seats himself. I pull out a chair for Theresa and then for myself. I unshoulder my briefcase and set it on my lap. I open it, pull out the paperwork, and set it on his desk for him to look at.

"Yes, Mr. Clapoh," he says.

"Claypole," I correct him.

"Yes, I remember him well. A very nice Ford 250. You are his associate in construction, I'm assuming?"

"This is his wife here. According to the paperwork, he owes a balance of eight thousand two hundred thirty-one dollars. I'm assuming cash won't be a problem?"

He examines the paperwork more closely, as if he wants to double-check the amount.

"Yes, that is correct, but there is also a penalty charge to pay off the vehicle early."

"It doesn't state that anywhere in the paperwork."

"It's a part of the agreement, as spoken to Mr. Clapoh. You can call him to verify if you wish."

"No, I don't need to call him. If it's not written down, then it doesn't mean shit."

"There's no need to be foul, sir."

"I haven't begun."

"Sir, the balance to pay in order for me to release the title will be . . ." He taps some numbers on a calculator beside the computer keyboard. "That will come to an additional three thousand two hundred ninety-two dollars, making it eleven thousand five hundred twenty-three dollars and forty cents."

"What?" Theresa bursts out.

I smile calmly and turn to her.

"Why don't you take a look at some of the cars out there, Mrs. Claypole?"

She looks at me briefly, then shoots the Ethiopian a hard glare and walks out.

I stand up and pull the wad of money out of my briefcase and drop it on his desk. I take my wallet from my back pants pocket, open it in a way that reveals a portion of my badge. I make sure he can see it. I take out some more money and count an additional two hundred forty dollars and place that next to the eight grand.

"That's eight thousand two hundred forty dollars. Don't worry about the change. Look at it, then look at me. Do I look like someone you're gonna fuck with?"

"This is a business, sir."

"You the owner?"

"Yes. You also never gave me your name, sir."

"What you are trying to pull is illegal in this fucking country. You'd be wise to take the true amount owed, 'cause if the next thing outta your mouth isn't 'Let me get the title,' then I'm gonna make one call to a good friend of mine who'll show up with a police team to check every fucking VIN, hidden VIN, and even engine-part number of every fucking car on this lot. After that, they'll come in here and go through all your paperwork and you'd better pray everything's in order, which I seriously doubt, 'cause when they get done, it won't be a matter of paying off a few fines. You will be looking at jail time."

"I am too much an American citizen! I have rights."

"You got rights, but the police don't need a search warrant to

109

do a spot check on a dealership, especially after I get done telling my friend the kinda loan scam you're trying to pull on me, and more than likely have gotten away with on other occasions."

"You cannot threaten me like this, sir. I'm going to call the police."

"What are you, a fucking dope? What do you think I'm about to do? You go on, call them. I can use the uniforms that arrive to secure the premises before the detective I'm gonna call gets here. Save me a lot of time, you shady little motherfucker. You think I'm playing? I'm about to fuck your life up."

I pull out my phone to make a call.

He stands straight out of his chair, as if he's ready to salute me.

"Sir, please, I think we can arrange something."

Twenty-three

I got lucky with the Ethiopian. He's dirty, but if he had only worked shady loan deals he'd have called me on it. I wasn't bluffing, though. I do have a friend who works with an auto-theft task force and deals with these fly-by-night dealerships. These places get into everything from re-VINing stolen cars to selling thirty-day-temp tags to drug boys. The tags alone are big business. So, yeah, he was into something, but I still took a chance, 'cause the last thing I would've wanted was my guy coming down there on a favor and then me having to explain why I'm paying off an eight-thousand-dollar loan for a felon, and all of it in cash. That would've been a good story.

When I drop Theresa off at her home, I tell her that I'll be holding on to the title until Lenny gets out of jail. That it's a procedural thing. Truth is, I want to make sure the truck is still around when he gets out of jail. She seems nice enough and supportive. Maybe she'll wait for him, but then maybe she won't. The truck's an easy couple thousand if she decides not to.

On the way back to DC, I give Davidson a call.

He picks up after the fourth ring. "What's up, Frankie?"

"Wanted to give you a heads-up about a meeting I'm heading to at Costello's office."

"Don't tell me another teenage girl's there?"

"Nothing like that. Just meeting with the family of another one that's missing."

"What does Costello have to do with that? And you, for that matter?"

"Mother and father of another missing teenager, I think from the same school, reached out to the family of the little girl I got outta the house on Kenyon. They gave them Costello's number and called her for help, specifically my help. Costello said when they called she gave them your number. You ever get a call?"

"As a matter of fact, yes. I took all their information, including the name of the detectives they were working with in Fairfax County. Best we can do is put her on our radar, but I didn't tell them that. I feel bad for them."

"Costello felt bad for them, too."

"What about you?" I hear Davidson say. For once I don't know what to say.

"Listen. I wish I could do more, but we don't work missing children either, just crimes against children, and she's missing out of Virginia, not DC."

"So was that little girl I got."

"Whole different scenario."

"Sounds to me like it might turn into the same scenario."

"I know what you're saying, Frankie, but right now she's a missing teenager from another jurisdiction. We don't pick up cases like that. Even if it was reported in DC, that still goes to Youth Division and Missing Persons, not us. We're a specialized unit, mostly dealing with pedophiles and Internet crimes against children."

"I haven't been off the department so long that I don't know that, Scott. I also know your task force picks up cases all over the country. I was just thinking there's more than likely a connection between the two girls and that's sweet media shit for your Fed supervisor. That's why he wanted the other case in the first place, right?"

"It's always something like that, but mostly it was easy because you did all the work."

"I didn't do anything on that except get lucky."

"It was all set up for us, though. Easy pickings after that. But keep me in the loop with this one. If there's anything I can do, you know I will."

"Yeah, I know."

"I'll talk to you later, bro."

"All right."

When I get to Costello's building, I use the hallway bathroom outside her office to snort the contents of a capsule; then I slap a bit of cold water on my face, dry off with paper towels, and walk out with something like a smile.

I open the door to the small reception area. Leah isn't at her desk, and I remember that it's Saturday.

I walk into Costello's office. She's typing on the laptop's keyboard while looking at the screen. She stops when I enter, slides the wireless mouse along the pad, and double-clicks.

"Don't expect me to thank you for showing up, because all this is your doing."

"Jeez, and I thought all that was behind us."

"This is a law firm, Frankie. A very small, but very busy law firm. Not a PI agency. I have two devastated parents sitting in the conference room, thinking I can help them find their missing daughter. And I can't act as their liaison between the DC police and you. Yes, I'm pissed off, because there's nothing I can do other than introduce them to you and then stay the hell out of it."

"Well, you've done your part, then."

"Now you're being snide."

I wanna say, "No, but I'm beginning to think I should've fucked you last night." But I have a feeling that would make matters worse. So instead I say, "Don't mean to sound that way. Let me go in and talk to them, see what I can do."

"I'll be here." Before I exit she adds, "I can't imagine what they must be going through. I wish I could do more."

"You've done more than enough. I'll get with you in a few."

I walk out, feeling a little less smiley.

TWENTY-FOUR

They're sitting at the other end of the conference table. I close the door behind me. The husband stands. He looks like he's around my age—early to mid-forties. He's wearing a nice gray wool suit with expensive-looking brown leather oxford wingtips. There's a briefcase on the floor beside his chair. I walk toward him and he extends his arm to shake. It's a firm handshake.

"Ian Gregory," he says.

"Frank Marr," I return.

His wife barely sits up to offer her hand. Stress is evident in her face.

I take her hand.

"I'm Elizabeth." She barely smiles.

"Why don't we sit down," I say.

He takes his seat. She seems to just float back into hers.

I unshoulder my briefcase and set it beside the chair I sit in.

"Do you work in the city, Mr. Gregory?"

"Just Ian, please. I work at the Pentagon. Private contractor."

"And Mrs. Gregory?"

"I'm a stay-at-home mother."

He reaches over, takes her hand, and they clasp their hands together to rest on her lap.

"So you got in touch with Ms. Costello through Amanda's family?"

He has to think for a moment.

"Amanda, the little girl that was found," I remind him.

"Yes, yes, of course. The detective we've been working with in Fairfax County came to our home. He asked if our daughter knew her because they went to the same school."

"What is your daughter's name?"

"Miriam," he says.

I pull out a fresh legal pad notebook from my briefcase, take my pen out of my shirt pocket, and write down her full name.

"How old is she?"

"Sixteen," he says.

"How long has she been missing?"

"Since July ninth. She said she was going to the community pool with friends. We later found out she never did."

Mrs. Gregory's head drops and she begins to cry. I notice him squeeze her hand again.

"What was she wearing when she went to the pool?"

"Shorts and a T-shirt," he says. "She has a pink pool bag and would always change into her suit in the locker room."

"Her purple sparkly flip-flops. She was wearing those, too," Mrs. Gregory adds.

"Did she go there with anybody?"

"No. She walked alone, but she said she was meeting friends there. She didn't say who," Ian says, and then as if an afterthought adds, "I don't know why I didn't ask."

"Does she have a cell phone?"

"Yes, she has an iPhone," he says, then seems to struggle with a thought. "The battery must have, you know—or maybe it somehow broke. We still keep the account active just in case."

"iPhones have an app to locate the phone if it's lost. Was your daughter's set up for that?"

"No, it wasn't," he says as if embarrassed.

"How long ago did it stop working?"

"It rang for a week or so after she had disappeared—even went into voicemail, and then a few days later it went out completely."

"Does she have any brothers, sisters . . . ?"

"Little brother. Lucas. He's ten."

"Does Miriam know Amanda?"

"We've never heard her name mentioned before. The detective showed us a picture, but we didn't recognize her. Miriam might have known her from school or through other friends, but she wasn't a good friend or we would have known."

"Did the detective share any other information with you?"

"No. He said he'd be in touch if anything new developed. We have a pretty tight community. I was able to locate her family. They only lived a few blocks away. That's how we found out about you and Ms. Costello and this other detective with a task force here, but he wasn't very helpful, either."

"You still have the family's contact information?"

"Yes, but I assumed you would?"

"No, it didn't work out like that. I'll need their contact information."

"I should have it here," he says, reaching for his briefcase.

He pulls out a small notepad, flips through pages.

"Here it is," he says, handing the pad to me.

I write the names Arthur and Louise Meyer in my notes, along with their address and landline, and Arthur Meyer's cell number.

I look at my notebook and see "Miriam Gregory" written in

the top left corner. I realize the mistake I made. It's like I've made it official that I'll be investigating this. Not only was it my line of questioning, but I pulled out my notebook to take notes. In fact, writing the name first is worst of all. The only thing that minimizes that fact is that I didn't put a date above the name. I fucked up.

"I should've asked—you want something to drink: soda, water . . . ? They have a nice coffee machine if you'd like coffee."

"No, thank you," Ian says.

His wife shakes her head, looks like she wants to leave.

"I really need a soda. Do you mind?"

"Of course not," Ian says.

I stand and begin to walk, but remember my briefcase. I grab it.

"Be right back," I say, and exit quickly.

The bathroom is empty. There are two stalls. I take the end stall, against a wall. I close the lid on the toilet seat, examine it briefly to make sure it's clean, and then sit on it.

"Fuck," I say to myself. Close my eyes.

Eyes still closed, I pull out my pill container.

I usually have more self-control during the daytime, especially when I'm doing something for Costello. I just need a boost so I can clear my head.

So that's what I do, but this time I snort three capsules.

After I flush the toilet a second time, I push my nostrils shut one at a time and sniff hard.

It's like a wide stream rushing in my head converging to a point and then swirling like ripples. Immediate clarity. I believe this is how I'm supposed to feel naturally, how all of us are meant to feel all the time, but that feeling was taken from us.

I walk out of the stall, check my nose in the mirror to make sure it's clean. A couple more sniffs and I exit.

I walk back into the office and a few steps past the doors to the conference room to a counter that has a coffee machine and a sink and a small built-in refrigerator underneath. I grab a can of soda from the fridge and walk back to the conference room. I take a swig and then enter.

"Didn't mean to take so long," I say, and then sit back down.

I look at the notebook again and the lone name at the top of the page. I pick up my pen and write the date above the name.

October 16.

Twenty-five

Ian grabs two five-by-seven photographs of his daughter from his briefcase and stretches his arm over the table to hand them to me.

The first one is a head shot.

"That's her school photograph," Mrs. Gregory says.

She's smiling. Her shoulder-length brown hair is nicely combed and folds over her ears, covering the sides of her neck. Her eyes are light blue in color, like her mother's.

I look at the other photograph. She's standing on a brick patio, screened-in porch behind her, and wearing that same smile.

She's a pretty girl, and the smiles seem genuine, like smiles kids are supposed to have. But I'm not a good judge of things like that. For all I know, there's something hidden there.

I set the photos on the table beside my notebook and then finish off my soda. I hold in a burp and it becomes a hiccup instead.

"Excuse me," I say.

I look at the notes I've taken thus far, most of them basic investigatory stuff—names and contact information of friends, known hangouts, and hobbies. Surprisingly, they seem to know a lot about their daughter. They even had a prepared list of contact information for her friends. Most of the parents I dealt with when I was a cop had given up on their kids shortly after the kids learned how to walk.

When I was a uniformed officer, we were always called to take missing persons reports. It was nearly an everyday occurrence. Most of us used to dread the calls, especially if the case involved a child. A detective was called to the scene after a brief interview with the parents. First thing we did was a walkthrough of the house and surrounding area. Most of the time, after spending a couple hours on the scene, the kid was located, usually somewhere else they weren't supposed to be. There were also those dreaded times, after exhausting all efforts, when we had to make the call for the watch commander to respond. After that, the Missing Persons Unit was notified and a command center was set up. Those usually turned into cases like this. Damn, I felt bad for those detectives who caught cases like that, 'cause you knew it wasn't going to turn out well. Most of them end up like this one, where the parents never know. Sometimes a body is found. As awful as that must be, at least those parents were given closure.

There's nothing I can tell the Gregorys that they haven't heard before. One thing I know they haven't heard yet is how bad it really looks—the chances that they'll ever see their daughter again. That's one of the reasons I decided, when I made the decision I was gonna go for my PI license, that I would not work missing persons. By the time a PI gets hired for something like this, it's usually too late. The case is cold as hell, even damn near freezing. I can't tell these folks all that. Shit, what kinda person would that make me? Hell, I feel even worse having to take their money.

"My fee is forty dollars an hour, plus gas and incidentals. I have to be honest with you. Something like this is probably gonna take a lot of hours, and incidentals can include anything from paying for information to travel expenses."

They look at each other, but don't have to talk. That bond over time where the slightest expression or something in the eyes can replace words.

"Whatever it takes," Ian says.

"All right, but I'm going to be straight with you. I'll work it through next week. If I don't come up with anything by then, more than likely I never will. I want you to be ready for that."

She looks at him like before, but he doesn't turn to her this time. He doesn't want to read her face. He simply nods.

"Just a couple more things, then."

I hand each of them my business card.

"All my contact information is on there. Leslie Costello simply did a favor by introducing us. She's an attorney and has nothing to do with what I do. I only work for her on occasion. So there's no need for you to contact her, all right?"

"We understand, and tell her it's appreciated," he says.

"I'll need to visit your home and go through her room, her belongings, if that's okay."

"The detectives in Fairfax County already did that, but yes, that would be fine."

"Did the detectives take anything?"

"No, they didn't."

"A girl's appearance can be changed—"

"Are you suggesting she ran away?" Mrs. Gregory interrupts.

"I'm not suggesting anything, Mrs. Gregory. Please let me finish. Does she have any birthmarks, scars, moles, anything that can help me identify her other than these pictures?

"She has a birthmark on her right outer thigh. It is light brown and small, but it looks like Australia."

"And you're sure she wasn't dating anyone?"

"Yes, we are," Ian says firmly. "She wasn't allowed to date until seventeen."

"Did she go to the movies with friends, the mall, anything like that?"

"Of course. We weren't that strict," he tells me. "And the friends she went with are on the list we gave you."

"Now, please, just bear with me, because I have to ask these questions. I'm sure you've already been asked them. But I don't see any boys' names on this list. She didn't have any friends that were boys? Doesn't mean she had to be dating them, but she is a teenager, after all."

"To be honest, Detective Marr, there could have been. Maybe she didn't tell us, but not because she was hiding something. Probably just because it wasn't a big deal. I really don't know."

That appears to affect him 'cause he seems like the type of man who needs to know, maybe even control, everything.

"She's a good girl," Mrs. Gregory says, as if she's trying to convince me.

How do I respond to that?

"Is Monday a good day for me to come by your home?"

"I'll be at work, but Elizabeth will be home."

"Around one p.m., then?" I ask Mrs. Gregory.

"That'll be fine," he says for her.

She nods accordingly.

Leslie's in her office plugging away at the computer. I remember all those days of nothin' but writing. I don't miss that shit.

"Are they still here?" she asks.

"No, we're done."

"And . . . ?"

"And I guess I'll see what I can do."

"That's good. Good. I don't have any cases that need an investigator right now, so I'm glad you're taking this on."

"Get me out of your hair for a while, huh?"

"You know better."

I wish I did.

"Then how about dinner tonight? On me."

She considers it, but I can't read her so well right now.

"It's been a while, and I'm really craving oysters. We can hit the Old Ebbitt."

"Why not," she says. "It's going to be packed on a Saturday night, though."

"No need to worry about that. I've got my connections."

"Oh, I know you do."

"All right. Pick you up from your porch at around seven?"

Her mouth turns up. She says, "My stoop."

First thing I need to do when I get home is tuck this shit I have stashed in my pocket out of reach, take a couple of Valiums, and try to nap.

Home alone I have a tendency to binge, and the last thing I want is to get all wired up before the dinner. Once I start something like that, the next line is the only thing on my mind.

I can do without for a bit of time as long as I know I have something to come back to. Doesn't hurt sneaking a couple little lines here and there throughout the evening, 'cause that'll balance me out. But I got to find a bit of sleep first and then a nice long, hot shower.

When I get home I call a buddy of mine who works the bar at the Old Ebbitt. There was a time when I was a regular at the bar at the Old Ebbitt. Haven't been there in a bit, but I always keep important numbers handy. He said he won't be working tonight, but he'll make sure they hold a booth for us in the main room.

I strip down to my boxers and lie on the bed, on top of the covers.

I close my eyes and try not to think about anything, especially the missing girl.

TWENTY-SIX

Leslie's wearing her faded leather jacket again. Also those black jeans I like so much. They hug her with meaning. So does the long-sleeve designer T-shirt with a scoop neck.

The cool air is comfortable. Gotta love this time of year. Winter's closing in, and hopefully bringing a bit of snow with it, but not so much that I can't get around. Depending on the situation, though, that might not be so bad.

I park a couple of blocks from the Old Ebbitt. The White House is in view across 15th Street, nicely lit up. We walk a block and then cross G Street and it's a few steps more to the restaurant's beautiful old revolving-door entrance. I see the small area inside jammed with people waiting to be seated.

We nudge our way to the front booth, and when the hostess finds a second I give her my name. My boy came through, and after a couple of minutes, we're escorted to a nice booth toward the back of the room. Leslie hangs her jacket on a hook attached to a post on the edge of the booth and we sit across from each other.

When the waitress shows, we order a round of martinis and a dozen of the mix-and-match oysters. That'll determine what we like best, and we'll probably order another dozen after that. We're both oyster junkies. Me most of all 'cause it's a great source of protein with minimal effort. I could live on them.

"It's nice getting out like this. We haven't done that in a while," I say.

"It is nice."

Our drinks arrive before the oysters.

She lifts her martini glass, carefully holds it across the table toward me.

"Cheers to a good idea, Frankie."

I lift mine and we clink glasses, but only spill a little. I want to tell her to take it easy on the drinks tonight 'cause she's such a lightweight, and well, you know . . . I might have bad intentions.

Halfway through the martinis, the plate of oysters shows. I don't hesitate, and neither does she. I dab a bit of horseradish on a small plump one and stab it with a little fork, lift it out of the half shell. A single bite and then I let it slide down. Leslie tilts her half shell back and slurps it in. Without a doubt, it looks a hell of a lot better the way she does it.

There's a fine, demure look on her after, a kind of smile but not one meant for me. Something like being brought back to a pleasant memory.

She sips her martini, peeks at me over the glass.

"You miss the job, don't you?" she asks as if she knows it's something I've been thinking about.

"Yeah, sometimes, but it wasn't the same a couple years after you left. The new mayor messed everything up."

"A change in regime can do that."

"Tell me about it. The focus changed with it. It was all about making the quick hits, build up the stats. Started not being so fun anymore. What about you? You miss it?"

"I miss certain aspects of the job. I liked working patrol."

"You were a good officer, but you had another mission in life."

"I did, but I didn't realize it until I became an officer and went back to school."

"And everyone that knew you just thought you were using the department to work your way through college."

"And they were right. But I didn't know where it was going to lead. You know that."

I nod because I do know. That's why I respect her.

"I always thought I would just make rank. Slowly climb the ladder," she continues.

"Yeah, I remember. You would've made a good commander eventually."

"No, that position is too political. I would have settled down at lieutenant."

"Smart girl."

She takes down another oyster, her lips moist with brine after, and her eyes seem to grow larger.

It doesn't take long to get through a dozen oysters. I manage to get the attention of our busy waitress, and we order another dozen. I down my martini and order another one of those. Leslie's still nursing what she has left.

"I'll have another, too," she says.

"Take it easy, champ. You know how that goes to your head," I tease.

"I'm not the lightweight you think I am."

"You were tougher when you were a cop and hit these spots on a regular basis with us."

"You saying I'm not tough anymore?"

"Just when it comes to liquor, maybe not so much."

"It's called a healthy lifestyle, Frankie. Makes me tougher than you think."

"You'll outlive me, then."

"Don't say things like that. I need you around."

If only I knew what she really meant by that.

We drive with the windows down on the way back to her home. The temperature has dropped, but only slightly.

I turn onto her block. Before I pull to the front of her house, she asks, "Do you want to find a parking space?"

TWENTY-SEVEN

It takes a moment before I realize where I am.

Leslie's under the covers beside me, sleeping on her side with her back toward me. Her arm is tucked over the top cover, nuzzling it close to her face. The side of her breast is only partly exposed and a paler shade of ivory than the skin on her forearms.

The curtains are open. It's barely light outside. A large holly tree with its waxy green leaves and red fall/winter berries obstructs the view to her neighbor's house and vice versa. But I still want to close the curtain.

Once I'm up, I'm up.

I didn't sleep all that long, but I slept hard. Haven't done that in a while. Costello's better than having to down a couple of Klonopins with some Jameson.

I don't want to wake her and I don't want to go home, so I lie on my back and roll to my side so I can look at her some more.

How her delicate neck curves into her shoulder.

Twenty-eight

Sunday rolled by like nothin', and I'm already looking forward to the next time. But who the hell knows when that'll come. Just her.

It rained most of the day, too, which made matters worse, 'cause after I left Costello's house at about 11 a.m., I spent the afternoon and most of the night on a monstrous binge.

Hard Monday morning.

Fall wind's howling outside my window.

I sit on the sofa to have my coffee and go over the notes from my interview with the Gregorys. I have a couple of hours before I have to be at their house. I figure I'd better get some phone calls done, try to set up interviews with Miriam's friends from the list, and call Amanda's family, see if I can get in to talk with her.

I've broken just about every rule there is to break in the so-called PI code, but I need to be careful about stepping on toes with respect to Amanda's investigation. I had dealings with PIs when I was a cop, and I have to say, they pissed me off more than once. Normally I couldn't give a shit, but I like Davidson, and Luna's a real friend.

I curl over the pages of my notes to a fresh page and mark the date and time.

My first call's to Davidson to let him know I got hired by the family of the missing girl. We talk for a bit. He's not concerned, actually figured I would get hired, but it's a different matter when I tell him I'll be contacting Amanda's family to set up an interview.

"You want to be careful about talking to her," he tells me. "She's a victim in an ongoing federal investigation."

"Yeah, and the last thing I'll be talking about is your investigation, so no need to worry. All I want to do is show her a photo of Miriam Gregory and see if she knows her."

"I'm not going to say don't do it. Just know the edge, Frankie."

Yeah, he can say "don't do it," but that won't stop me. I wouldn't be breaking any rules, either, just making enemies. I've been hired to investigate a case, and she's my only lead right now. He can make things tough on me if he wants, but it doesn't sound like he's trying to do that. It's always been helpful that I'm a retired cop. Now, if boys like Davidson knew I was forced into retirement, that would be entirely a different matter. I'd be through, an addict, another waste.

So for the sake of courtesy and cooperation, I tell him, "Understood, buddy. No worries there."

"And if you get any information I can use, you'll call me, right?"

"Of course."

The next call I make is to Amanda's father, Arthur Meyer. It's his cell phone. I light up a cigarette before making that call.

I'm thinking it's going to go straight to voicemail, but he answers after the fourth ring. "Hello."

"Mr. Meyer?" I ask.

"Yes," he answers.

"My name is Frank Marr. I'm a retired DC police detective."

"I know who you are," he says kindly. "I wanted to meet you and thank you personally, but Ms. Costello said she'd thank you for me. How are you, Detective?"

"She did, and thank you, I'm fine. I appreciate that, but I'm calling for another reason. Unfortunately, I'm looking into another case similar to your daughter's. I was hired by a family whose daughter is still missing."

"Yes, I know the family. They were recently in touch with us. I gave them Ms. Costello's number and the number of the detective in DC in charge of our case. I hope you don't mind, but I also gave them your name."

"I know. I spoke to the husband and wife the other day. Because the two cases are so similar, I really have to interview your daughter."

It takes him a moment, and then he says, "She's been through . . . a lot. I don't know. Can't you just get the information you need from Detective Davidson? Or the FBI?"

"I've already spoken with Detective Davidson several times. I knew him when I was on the department, so he's been very helpful. What I really need to do is show Amanda a photograph of the missing girl. That's all. See if she knows her. Maybe ask one or two other questions. It's something I have to do in person."

"I certainly don't want to stand in the way of you possibly finding this other poor girl. It's just that—"

"I can appreciate your concern for your child, Mr. Meyer. I can't imagine what she went through. The last thing I'd want to do is make it more difficult for her, but I should tell you, in the short time I spent with her, I found her to be a very strong young girl."

"She is very . . ." he begins with difficulty. "Yes, she is." It takes another brief moment. "I can come home early from work tomorrow, say, around four? I'd like to be there, too."

"That'll be fine. Thank you, Mr. Meyer."

"No, thank you, sir. We can't thank you enough."

Damn, if I don't feel taken aback by that. Didn't think I could get so affected.

Shit.

I snuff out the remains of my cigarette and light another one.

TWENTY-NINE

I was able to get in touch with all three of Miriam's girlfriends. The parents were okay with my meeting with them. Well, except for one.

I'll meet the first girl, Carrie Deighton, shortly after she gets home from school. She doesn't live far from the Gregorys' house, so I told her mother that I'd come over when I'm finished there. The second girlfriend on the list is Tamara Moore. Her parents agreed only to a phone interview, and I set it up for Wednesday at three thirty, when she gets home from school. And then there is Justine Durrell, also on Wednesday, but at four thirty.

We'll see. I'm not expecting much, but there are times when some of these younger kids will more willingly offer up information to someone like me over their parents. But that experience of mine is based on my work with kids in DC who are little thugs, soon-to-be thugs, or wannabe thugs. There's a big difference between them and these teenage girls. At least I'm thinking there is.

Strong wind gusts outside. What leaves are left on the few trees in my neighborhood are shaken free.

It's still a few hours before rush hour, so I decide to take I-95 to the Lorton Road exit. It's just a few minutes out of the way, but I know that area.

Lorton Prison used to be there. The department had a facility behind the prison where we'd go through civil defense and firearms training. There used to be cows roaming around behind the barbed wire that stretched along a dirt road leading to the facility. Back then it was farmland that surrounded the prison.

It's been some years since that time. Now there's a retirement community, and a high school on one side, and some sort of community arts center and a golf course on the other. The redbrick watchtowers and most of the housing units surrounded by tall brick walls still remain on a portion of land that the county hasn't decided on what to do with yet. Maybe a future mall? I certainly wouldn't shop there. Too much torment in that land.

Miriam Gregory's home is located in a quiet community off Lee Chapel Road, in Burke, Virginia. It's almost an hour outside of DC, but then I did take a longer route, so it could be less than an hour. A lot of pockets of small communities in this area, and it looks like a lot of land yet to be developed. That'd be a shame. I'd like to think nice wooded areas have a purpose, and I don't mean for hiding bodies.

I can't imagine how Amanda got herself involved with those Salvadoran boys in DC, but then this dude Edgar would be the one to talk to about that. Suburban life. It's never been something I've desired. But maybe if I grew up in an environment like this, my life wouldn't have turned out the way it did. Then again, probably would have. I might have gotten so bored I'd have turned to drugs sooner, maybe even have gotten myself locked up. You didn't want to fuck with Fairfax County back then. They'd slam you for a joint. Not the case nowadays. It's not even a slap on the wrist. Not even that.

I pull to the curb in front of their house, step out, and shoulder my briefcase.

Nice landscaped yard. A lot of fall colors. I walk up the driveway along the edge of their grass to a redbrick walkway lined with mums.

Elizabeth Gregory opens the front door before I even step up to the porch, as if she's been waiting for me.

"Detective Marr, please come in."

I still like being called detective even though I'm not one anymore, but I think she knows that and it's meant as something respectful.

"Good afternoon, Mrs. Gregory."

I follow her along a short hallway to the living room, where she invites me to sit on one of two matching armchairs across from a sofa and separated by a large wood coffee table. It is a well-ordered living room. I sit down, thinking she might want to talk before taking me to her daughter's room.

"Would you like a cup of coffee?"

"No thank you."

It is obvious she is taking some kind of sedative. She is too calm, but her face still gives away all the sleepless nights she's been having.

She sits on the sofa, picks up a cup, and sips from it.

"Tea," she informs me. "Chamomile. Would you like tea?"

"No, I'm good, Mrs. Gregory. Is there anything you'd like to talk about?"

"No, no, there isn't, really. I think we covered everything. There is something, but I know it's something you can't answer. You seem like someone who would not have a problem speaking his mind."

"Yes, that's true, but then it would also depend on the question."

"The police here always seem to have such rehearsed lines. I imagine there are only certain things they are allowed to say. I just really want—need—to know what you think, what the possibility is, based on your experience or whatever, that she is still . . ." She wipes away a tear. "I'm sorry."

"I'll be honest with you, Elizabeth. I don't normally take on missing persons cases."

She seems surprised.

"Now, it's something most cops have experience investigating, so I know what to do, but it is not something I take on as a private investigator."

"Then why my daughter?"

"Because you need me."

More tears now. She grabs a tissue from the end table and wipes her eyes.

"And the reason cops don't answer questions like the one you were about to ask is simply because they can't. Not because they're not allowed to; it's just an answer they don't have. Any answer I might come up with would just be bullshit."

She smiles kindly.

"Would you mind if I asked you something very personal?"

"You can ask."

"How is your marriage?"

It takes her a moment. "Are you married, Detective?"

"No, ma'am. I never got around to it."

"Well, after time, marriage becomes something comfortable. Ours was always comfortable, but then it got shaken up by a terrible storm."

"So your daughter saw that it was comfortable?"

"Yes, yes, she did," she says, like she understands why I asked. "We fought like most families fight. Never talk of divorce. My husband has to travel a lot because of the work he does. He can also be emotionally distant at times, and has a hard time showing affection, but he loves Miriam and I know Miriam knows he loves her. So she didn't run away, if that's what you're getting at. I know the police detective here thought that is what happened, but she didn't. I hope you don't think that, especially after you were the one to rescue that other girl and the situation is so similar."

"The similarities between the two are another reason I took on this case, but I still had to ask."

"I understand."

"Would you like to show me Miriam's room?"

THIRTY

I'm checking out the room, and it's what I would imagine a typical teenage girl's room to be like. Maybe a bit too tidy, like the rest of this house, but I'm sure Mrs. Gregory straightened it up.

There's a twin bed with several stuffed animals on it. There's a little nightstand with a single drawer and a bedside lamp. There's a study desk with three drawers and a laptop, and beside it a dresser with four drawers and a vanity mirror. There's a sliding door that opens to the closet and to the right of that a small bookcase.

"Would you like me to stay?"

"Only if you want to. It's not necessary, though. But tell me first, did the police find anything they thought might be useful, like a diary or maybe something on her laptop?"

"She hasn't had a diary since she was eleven years old and she only uses the laptop for schoolwork. Everything the police have, you have. It's on the list we gave you. I know it's not much, but she only had a few close friends."

"Will I need a password for the laptop?"

"No."

"Thank you. I shouldn't be long."

"I'll be right downstairs, then."

"Okay."

I'm used to looking for drug stashes, sometimes secreted where you'd least expect to find them, so how hard can it be to find a teenage girl's secret hiding place?

I look everywhere I would normally look, including areas of the carpet that look like they may have been pulled up. After squeezing all her stuffed animals, I go through the drawers, including, admittedly, the drawer containing her underwear, which is something I'm not comfortable with but had to be done. I dig through the closet, her clothing, boxes, and even shoes. I move to the bookcase and go through all the books, hoping to find photographs or pieces of papers with notes or phone numbers.

Nothing.

I find a high school yearbook for last year. She would have been a freshman. I search the pages and find her picture. She looks a lot younger. I guess these are the years they grow quickly. I search through the *M*'s and see Amanda's photo.

I tear off a piece of paper from my notepad and mark the page with it, then I set the yearbook on my notepad.

I go to the desk, search through the few papers she has, and then the drawers.

Nothing.

The last thing I do is go through the laptop.

I check the icons for anything that might indicate an account for email or social media, but don't find anything.

I click the icon for Google hoping I will find something useful on the bookmarks bar or in the browsing history.

It's another dead end.

I'm not surprised, though. If I wanted to hide something from my parents, the laptop they gave me would be the last thing I'd use.

So much for that secret hiding spot and that smoking gun of a diary I was hoping to find.

I walk downstairs with the yearbook, find Mrs. Gregory sitting on the sofa. She sees me and stands.

"It took a little longer than I thought," I tell her.

"Please, have a seat."

"That's all right. I'm meeting with one of your daughter's friends from the list you gave me. I don't want to be late."

"The police already did that. I know my husband gave you the list for your investigation, but can't you just compare notes with the detectives here, speed things up?"

"It doesn't really work that way, and even if it did, I'd still want to talk to her friends. By the way, I couldn't find anything having to do with social media on her laptop. Was she on Facebook, Twitter, Snapchat or anything like that?"

"Certainly not Snapchat. And she wasn't allowed to use social media on the laptop because that was for schoolwork. We did allow her to have Facebook on the iPhone, but she never used it. I guess it's become more of a grown-up thing."

"I wouldn't know. I'm not the social media type." I smile.

She forces a smile in return.

"You said you have a son."

"Yes. He's in school. The school bus will be dropping him off at the corner soon."

"Oh, school. I was wondering why he wasn't here."

I pull the yearbook from under my notepad. "Can I borrow this for a day or two?"

"Of course."

"I'll be going, then."

"Thank you, Detective."

She walks me to the door, but before she opens it to let me out she says, "I know I keep saying thank you, but I really do mean it."

"And I appreciate hearing it."

The first thing I do when I get to my car is take a pill container out of my briefcase, but not the container with the blow. I need a couple of Valiums.

I chase them down with a swig of Jameson, out of a flask I carry in an inner pocket of my suit. The Valiums will take a bit of the edge off my desire for coke. Klonopin is good for that too, but doesn't last as long. Since that big score, I've been using more than I normally do.

I'll have to find some good grapefruit on the way home.

THIRTY-ONE

Carrie Deighton lives in the same community, just a few blocks away. The home is of similar design, but there's not much attention paid to the landscaping. Carrie's mother opens the door. I introduce myself. At her request, I show my identification, and then she invites me in.

Carrie is in the kitchen, sitting on a barstool at a tall breakfast table. She closes a book she's been reading.

Her mother offers me a barstool across from Carrie, and then sits next to her. I'd like to tell the mother I'd rather talk to her daughter alone, but I have a good feeling she'd say no, and that would diminish my credibility with her daughter. It is going to limit my line of questioning to something less personal, but I gotta go with what I got. I'm sure she hangs with certain boys. I'm equally sure she won't share that kind of information when her mother is sitting next to her. It is definitely a handicap having a parent around when you need to conduct an interview.

Shit, I wasn't even offered coffee, so what does that tell you?

"I appreciate you meeting with me, Carrie."

"No problem," she says.

I take out my notepad, flip to a new page.

"How long have you and Miriam been friends?"

"Since middle school."

"Fifth grade," the mother steps in.

"That's a long time. In kid years, anyway."

They don't even crack a smile.

"When was the last time you saw her?"

She looks at her mother. "I told the other officers this. Why do I have to answer the same questions?"

Before the mother can answer I say, "Because I'm new to the case, and it's better to hear it directly from you than read something on paper."

The mother nods.

"What was the question again?" Carrie asks.

"When was the last time you talked to Miriam?"

"I don't know exactly. It was summer vacation, though."

"She was reported missing on July ninth," I say. "That would've been a Friday."

"It doesn't seem like it was that long ago," Carrie says.

"She told her parents she was going to the community pool here. Did you go there with her sometimes?"

"Yes. It was summer, so we went to the pool a lot."

"Would you mind writing down the names of friends you guys went to the pool with or met there?"

She looks at her mother again.

"The police have all that information," the mother says.

"Yes, ma'am, but I don't. I don't know why there should be a conflict here, Mrs. Deighton. It's my job to try to find Miriam

Gregory. I need your daughter's help to do that; there are a lot of pieces to put together and a lot of time has passed. So will you help me try to put those pieces together?"

The mother places her hand on Carrie's shoulder and nods.

"Thank you." I tear off a sheet of paper and hand it to her, along with a pen. "Phone numbers, too, if you have them."

She writes several names, looks up their phone numbers, and writes them down. All girls and all of them on the list I already have.

"Thank you very much, Carrie."

"You're welcome."

"Do you know a girl by the name of Amanda?"

"I've heard the name before, but I don't know her. It's a big school."

"What about Edgar?"

"I've heard his name, too, but don't know him either."

"Who have you heard mention his name before?"

"I don't know, people at school. Not even friends." She hesitates, but this time she doesn't look at her mom for reassurance. Her mother doesn't seem to pick up on it, though.

"What, he hung with a different crowd?"

"Yes." This time she looks at her mother with an expression like she's had enough.

"What, honey?" her mother asks.

"I don't know those people, Mommy."

"If she says she doesn't know them, then she doesn't know them," the mother tells me. "Who is this Edgar, anyway?"

"He's just a kid that goes to her school and is on another list I have. That's all. I believe she doesn't know him, but maybe your daughter can tell me if she knows about him?"

After another reassuring tap on the shoulder from the mother, Carrie says, "He just hangs with the loser crowd is all."

"Kids that don't study, kids that skip out on school, drink; what do you mean by losers?"

"All of the above."

"Drugs?"

"I don't hang out with any of them."

"We've already established that, Carrie."

"I've heard they're into pot, stuff like that."

"You've seen them smoking at your school?" the mother demands.

"No, Mother. They're just losers."

"Did Miriam hang with any of them ever?" I ask.

"I saw her with one of the older boys before."

"But not Edgar?"

"No. I told you I don't even know what this Edgar looks like."

"What about the one you saw her hang out with? What does he look like?"

"I don't know. He's just a boy."

"White kid, African-American? About how old?"

"He's white and I think he's a junior."

"Describe him for me—hair, how tall he is."

"Brown hair. I don't know how tall. Average, I guess."

"Does he drive?"

"I don't know."

"And you're telling the truth, Carrie? You don't know these boys?" the mother asks with concern.

"No! I don't hang out with losers, Mom."

"Did you mention these losers to the police when they interviewed you?"

"I don't remember."

"No, she didn't," the mother says angrily.

"It's okay, Carrie," I try to comfort her. "Sometimes things come back to you later, things you may not have thought were important way back then. And that's why I like to ask the same questions. So you did good."

She manages a meager smile, the kind of smile you might give a loser.

THIRTY-TWO

I stop at the Chinese takeout on 11th Street and grab steamed chicken with vegetables and steamed white rice.

I eat it when I get home. I cut up a nice grapefruit for dessert.

I pour myself some Jameson, set up a nice pile of powder with a few lines beside it, and light a cigarette. I sit back on the sofa with Miriam's yearbook. I go through it page by page, checking out every photograph and reading every inscription made by her friends. I find two boys with the first name Edgar.

The first one's a freshman. Edgar Rawlin. He doesn't fit the profile. Too clean-cut, and when I first talked to Amanda she said Edgar took her to the Salvadorans' house in DC. This guy's too young to drive, but that doesn't mean he won't drive. Still, he doesn't fit the bill.

The second one is Edgar Soto, a junior. He's a good-looking kid, the kinda face that might charm some of the younger girls. He's got something he's trying to grow on his chin to make him look tougher.

I bookmark both Edgar pages with torn paper.

I look at the photos of Miriam, the ones given to me by the parents.

Such a pretty girl. Seems like she could do a lot better than a little punk like Edgar, if one of these is the Edgar I want.

Damn, makes me glad I'm not a father. If I had a daughter, she'd be in a boarding school for girls. One of those schools with tall gates all around at least thirty miles from the closest town.

Thirty-three

I'll be meeting with Amanda at four o'clock. I have some time so I decide to head up to 16th and Park, sit on it for a bit and see who's out playing.

I find a nice parking spot on the west side of 16th, about a quarter of a block up. I don't see any of the regulars. Maybe it's just the wrong time of day, or Davidson and his boys, and maybe Luna, have been hitting them hard. Might even be because Shiny and his crew were taken out of the picture and they were the only ones running the corner. If any of these are the case, then it'll stay clear for a while, but not for long. Once things ease up, someone else will take control and be out there slingin'. Might just be the opportunity Cordell Holm was waiting for, unless he was already in control. Time will tell. I'll stick around for a couple hours, see if anything transpires.

I could walk around the neighborhood, show Miriam's photo. There's a few Latino-owned markets and restaurants all along Mount Pleasant Street; a short walk west of here there's a community of people who've lived in this neighborhood for a long time. Showing her photo around would be an appropriate next step. But I don't want to do that until I've exhausted everything else, especially until after I talk to Amanda and Edgar, if I can find him.

It's doubtful, but still possible, that if Miriam was abducted by the same crew that abducted Amanda, showing her photo around might get back to the wrong people, especially with all the crackheads, drunks, and thugs roaming this area. I honestly don't believe those boys on Kenyon were acting alone. That house was more of a holding cell, the first stage in the process.

If at one time Miriam was being held at that house, then she's either been taken outta state to someplace like New York, forced into prostitution somewhere around here, or, Lord forbid, she's dead. If it ever comes down to me having to hit the street, I have some sources I'd want to get with first.

After a couple of hours of sitting, I'm satisfied that it's a dead end for now.

I drive south toward the 14th Street Bridge, where I'll catch I-95 and make my way to Amanda's home.

THIRTY-FOUR

Amanda Meyer's home is in one of the newer communities of Burke. The homes are larger, with more siding, less brick, and even less land. Long stretches of wooded areas with creeks and aqueducts separate most of the communities around here; the Meyers' neighborhood is on one side of such a wooded area, and the Gregory family is on the other. They're close enough to be part of a larger community, but still far enough that school might be the only place they'd run into each other.

Mrs. Meyer answers the door.

She's an attractive lady, with a welcoming smile.

After I introduce myself, she greets me with an even more welcoming, but brief, hug. When I enter into the foyer, I am greeted again, but this time by Mr. Meyer and an unexpected, very long and uncomfortable hug.

"Okay, okay, now," I say after a couple seconds, and I try to tactfully break free after giving him a couple of pats on the back.

He releases me. "So good to finally meet you." He beams.

I certainly didn't expect this; with the exception of maybe

Costello, but only on certain and very special occasions, I'm not the huggy-bear type.

I'm invited into the den and offered a large leather recliner to sit in, as if Mr. Meyer would be honored if I took his spot. I thank him, but sit on a firmer armchair with green leaf patterns. I set my briefcase on the floor beside me.

"Amanda is in her room," says Mrs. Meyer. "I'll go get her."

Mr. Meyer sits in the leather chair.

"Would you like coffee or anything?" he asks.

"I'm good, thank you."

"I can't thank you enough."

"You have already," I say. "How is your daughter doing?"

"She's seeing a psychiatrist. It's terribly hard on her, but she'll pull through."

"What little time I spent with her, I sensed she's pretty tough."

"Yes, she is," he says, and I see his eyes begin to tear. "Sorry." He wipes the tears away with the back of his large hand.

"So I imagine the FBI has been here a few times to interview her?"

"Yes, three times already. The first time with an agent who specializes in forensic interviewing of children."

I don't have time to ask further questions, as Mrs. Meyer enters with Amanda.

She's wearing a long-sleeve pajama-type shirt so I can't see the track marks, but there is still visible bruising on the bit of area I can see around her wrists. I stand and expect another hug, but instead she stretches out her hand. I offer mine for a gentle, polite handshake.

She looks different, but without question, better. Still, something in her eyes shows me she's been through hell. Drug abuse is something I know all too well. But it's not something I'm fighting. I'm uniquely comfortable with my position in life. Unfortunately for Amanda, all the drugs they forced on her in a short period of time will be the least of her battles.

"Good to see you, Amanda."

"You, too." She smiles and then sits on a love seat, at the side closest to the chair I was sitting on.

I sit back down.

"I know you've heard this a few times already, but you're going to get through this."

A slight smile.

"So I imagine you've also had a ton of questions thrown at ya already, huh?"

"Yeah, pretty much."

"Well, I just have a few more. I'm sure you've been asked some of them before."

"Okay."

I turn to the parents. "Would you mind if I talked to Amanda alone? It's not anything she can't share with you later. It's just easier to talk when the parents—"

"We understand," he interrupts.

"Thank you," I say.

He throws a loving smile Amanda's way, then stands.

"We'll be in the living room, sweetie," the mother says, and they exit.

Mr. Meyer closes the sliding doors, but not all the way. I can see them as they walk into the living room.

"You're not really a policeman," she says directly.

"No, but I used to be, and you know what they say: 'Once a cop, always a cop.'"

"But you don't work for the police."

"Sometimes I do, but I wasn't then. I'm a private investigator now. I'm sorry I lied to you, but I needed you to trust me then."

"I know. It's okay."

"The important thing is you're safe now, right?"

She nods her head a couple of times.

I'm not gonna question her about what she told the FBI. In connection to me, I mean. I gave Davidson a good story, and I'll stick to that.

"Did your parents tell you why I wanted to talk to you?"

"Yes, about a missing girl."

"Yes. She's from a neighboring community and went to the same school as you. I'm working for her family, trying to find her."

I unzip my briefcase, pull out my notebook and a case jacket I put together for Miriam Gregory. I open the file and take out the two photographs of her. I hand the head shot photo to Amanda and she takes it.

"Do you know her?"

"A policeman showed me another picture of her already."

"Yes, but I'm working for the family. What did you tell the policeman who showed you the picture?"

"That I don't know her, but I've seen her around."

"When was the last time you saw her?"

"Last year at school. I don't remember when exactly, just that it was around school. I never talked to her or anything like that."

"Do you know any of her friends?"

"No. I don't think so, anyway."

"Okay." I take back the photo and slip it into the file.

I reach into the briefcase and pull out the yearbook. I open it to the marked spot for the older Edgar. Edgar Soto.

I hold it up with one hand and point to the photo. "What about him?"

Several nods and then, "That's Edgar."

THIRTY-FIVE

This is the kid that introduced you to those boys in DC?"

"Yes."

"Did the FBI show you a picture of him, too?"

"Yes, it was a larger photograph, but looked like the same yearbook picture."

That means he wasn't arrested; they couldn't get a juvie arrest photo. But it also means they're onto him and for all I know already picked him up and charged him with some shit like conspiracy. Once the police have him, it'll be next to impossible to talk to him, unless he gets out on bond, which I seriously doubt. Judges usually don't fuck around with these types of cases. And if he's a smart boy, he'll know better than to talk and more than likely will lawyer up right away. They usually set up debriefings, but those take time. My case will quickly turn from freezing cold to dry ice.

"I'm sure they asked you all this before, but I have to ask some of the same questions. Do you know where Edgar lives?"

"No. He never took me to his house."

Slick kid.

"Did you ever communicate with him through social media or texting?"

"No, I'd just see him at school."

"He drove you to DC, though. What kinda car does he drive?"

"They asked me that, too. It's light blue. I think like a new Camry or something. I always thought his parents were rich if they let him drive a car like that."

"You see him driving that car a lot?"

My cell phone rings.

"Hold on," I say, and pull it out to look at it.

Costello. I let it ring and go to voicemail. She'll leave a message if it's important.

"About his car, did he drive it a lot?"

"Yes. Sometimes he'd pick me up at the school bus stop and take me himself."

"Was anyone else with him when he picked you up?"

"No."

"Any of his buddies here ever go to DC with the two of you?"

"No. It was always just us."

"Did you ever hang out with him around here, someplace he liked to take you?"

She hesitates.

"It's all right. That's why I wanted to talk to you alone."

"He'd take me to this place off a path near South Run Park."

"You'd go smoke weed there and stuff?"

"Yes."

"Does he hang out there a lot, maybe with some of his buddies?"

"Yes. That's where they would go to get high and sell their weed."

"What days and around what time do they go out there?"

"It used to be every day right after school."

"You said it was a path. Where'd he park the car?"

"At South Run Park, usually at the very far end of the parking lot."

"Why were you nervous to tell me that? Did you used to sell too?"

"No, it's not that."

"Then what?"

"Because we did other things together."

"You and Edgar?"

"Yes."

"You mean something more than just kissing?"

"You swear you won't tell my parents?"

"That's something I think you should tell them when you're ready. I won't. Did you tell the FBI or other detectives any of this?"

"No. I'm sorry. Is that bad?"

"No, because I'll take care of it. Don't worry. Where is this South Run Park?"

"It's off the parkway, right past Lee Chapel."

I turn my notepad to a blank sheet and hand it to her, along with a pen. "Can you draw a map, show me how to get to South Run and then the path?"

Thirty-six

I follow Amanda's hand-drawn map, which does a good job of guiding me to the Fairfax County Parkway. I don't like to use Google maps for certain things, especially shit like this, 'cause the information is definitely logged. You never know.

It's about five o'clock and the beginning of the rush-hour traffic, but traffic is going the opposite direction. I make the right turn and find South Run Park a short distance ahead on the right. I turn in and follow the road to the parking lot. The rec center is ahead on the left, but I keep right and drive to the other end of the lot, where it borders the wooded area. Several cars are parked in the lot, but none that fit the description of Edgar's car. I park anyway. Before I can exit, my cell rings again.

Costello.

I answer with "What's up?"

"Did you get my message?" she asks coarsely, like she's upset.

"No, haven't had time. I'm just finishing up in Virginia. Why?"

"Fuck you, Frankie."

That throws me off.

"What the hell's the matter with you?" I ask.

"I called Lenny Claypole's wife earlier today——"

Oh shit . . .

"——to tell her about the sentencing date and a bit more about the plea offer. She thanked me for some kind of service I supposedly provided that paid off their car loan."

"Let me explain."

"Yes, you will explain, but let me finish. I talked to Lenny Claypole, and from what I could gather, it sounded a lot like the two of you came to some sort of arrangement that if you paid off his car debt he'd accept the plea. What the fuck are you thinking? Are you trying to get me disbarred?"

"Of course not. You know better than——"

"I don't know what I'm going to do here."

"You're going to do nothing."

"Do nothing? Are you on drugs?"

That's almost funny, 'cause I know it was just one of those statements only made in anger.

She continues. "Do you realize what you've done? I don't care what type of deal you think you have with my client. I'm his advocate. Do you know what that means? Damn."

"It won't fuck anything up. Just let me explain."

"Do your best, Frankie."

"I told him you wanted me to look into everything again, see if we could possibly find something helpful for trial. When we were done and I knew we had nothing, that everything had been exhausted, I simply advised him, based on my experience, that it didn't look good. I broke it down for him and he came to his senses and said he'd take the plea."

"And that wonderful offer you made to pay off his car loan had nothing to do with it?"

"That was just something I offered because his wife can't afford the car payments."

"Then they lose the damn car. You lie to the wife about some 'special service' I offer and you manipulate Lenny into taking a plea deal. That's sure as hell what it sounds like. In some warped way you think you're helping me out because I didn't want to go to trial and lose? The fuck, Frankie!"

"I was helping him, and I guess you, too."

"That was foolish and incredibly inappropriate. And where the hell would you come up with eight thousand dollars? In cash, no less."

"You think I don't have savings? 'Sides, he's going to pay me back."

"So you made some sort of contract with my client?"

"No, he's good for it. Leslie. It was just a favor. Granted I didn't think it through. But I thought I was doing a good thing. You're the one that put it in my head with all this 'second chance' shit."

"Please don't put this back on me. You really fucked up."

"Okay, I fucked up. I'm sorry."

"That's just not good enough. You've done some funky shit in the past, but nothing that compares to this. Oh, wait, I forgot about the little girl. Silly fucking me. I don't know, Frankie. I just don't know. I need some time to digest this. Don't call me and don't come to the office."

"What are you talking about? You're seriously overreacting here."

"I'm not overreacting. I told Lenny if he wants to go to trial then that's what we should do and not to worry about whatever deal the two of you made, but he said no, to take the plea."

"So what does that tell you?" I ask, before she can continue.

"You just don't get it, Frankie. Back the fuck off. I'm done with this." She disconnects.

I slip my cell back into the left inner pocket of my jacket.

It takes me a couple of seconds, but then: "Fuck! Fuck! Fuck!"

THIRTY-SEVEN

I find the narrow bike path that winds its way through a wooded area, just about where Amanda's hand-drawn map said it would be. The drawing shows where there's a split in the path near a large boulder. Follow the path straight and it leads to Burke Lake. Take it to the left and it leads to another community development.

She has a little *x* that marks the spot when you go left. It should be on the right side of the path near a creek. Find two large fallen trees, one on top of the other, at the bank of the creek and that's where they'd hang, sitting on one of the fallen tree trunks like it's a bench and smoking up their weed.

I follow the directions, and sure enough, there it is. A small dirt path, probably made by thousands of footsteps, leads to the creek and the two fallen trees.

No one's around.

I walk the short distance to check out the area. The ground surrounding the crisscrossed fallen trees is littered with empty beer cans, a couple of forties, a pint bottle of whiskey, and cigarette butts. The walking path I took to get here is nicely kept, but it seems this little area is a neglected spot. Probably because the park authority wouldn't normally walk off the beaten path to find all this litter at my feet. This mess made by thoughtless teenagers is not so obvious unless you're standing over it. Too many shrubs and trees to conceal it. That's more than likely what attracted them here in the first place.

I head back to the car.

When I get there, I open the door. I sit for a second or two, and then I smash my head against the top of the steering wheel two times, very hard.

"Damn," I mumble, and then feel the blood trickle down my forehead.

THIRTY-EIGHT

I smoke a couple of cigarettes laced with cocaine for the ride home. It amps me up, but not for long, 'cause it's just a quick fix. I don't even know why I do it. It's a waste of good coke.

I call Leslie on her cell, but she doesn't answer. I leave a message for her to give me a call back so we can talk. I try the private line at her office, but again no answer. Last, I call the main number, and Leah picks up.

"Hi, Leah. Can you put me through to Leslie?"

"I'm sorry, Frankie. She's not available," she says in a way that I know Leslie told her she doesn't want to take my calls.

"Just tell her I called, all right? That it's important I talk to her."

"I will."

I disconnect the cell and drop it in the center console.

"Idiot. Such a fucking idiot," I tell myself.

The guilt sets in when I decide I can't do any more work today.

I wouldn't have the guilt if it were any other case.

When I get home I grab a beer from the fridge, settle myself on the sofa, and get ready for what I know will be the beginning of a serious binge.

Thirty-nine

I've been up all night.

I'll need some help to make it through the rest of the day, so I replenish the supply I carry around, and then I put two grapefruit and some toast in my stomach.

I'm no rookie. I've gone off on binges before. My record's three days, and I haven't even hit twenty-four hours with this one. I've got some time before I start to shut down. My head feels muddled in a cloudy haze, though. This thing with Leslie's driving me nuts. I want to call her again, but I know she won't pick up. I need to fix it, but I also know I can't. I convince myself that she'll come around with time. Time has a way of doing that.

To start the workday off, I give Luna a call at his office to see what kind of information I can get from him.

"I need to know if Davidson picked up this kid yet," I say after we exchange pleasantries.

"Why don't you ask him yourself?"

"Because I'd have to fill him in on everything I'm doing and

I'm not ready to go there yet. I just need to know so I don't waste any more time trying to find this kid. He's the only lead I got."

"What's his name again?"

"Edgar Soto."

"Do you have a date of birth?"

"No, just that he's seventeen, maybe eighteen, and lives in Virginia."

"Hold on."

I hear him typing on a keyboard and breathing into the phone.

After a minute, he says, "Nothing in the system, not even NCIC. If he just got locked up, it might not be in yet."

"What about Live Scan for an arrest photo? That goes in right away."

"Now you're making me get out of my chair."

"I'll buy the rounds at Shelly's next time we go."

"You know I can get in a lot of trouble doing this shit for you, right?"

"Yeah, and that's why I'm bribing you."

"Hold on a second," he says, and I hear the phone receiver hit the desk.

Almost five minutes later he returns with, "You still on?"

"Yeah, go ahead," I say.

"There's nothing for Edgar Soto in the system, but you know that doesn't mean anything. If he was processed as a juvenile I wouldn't see it here."

"I know. Appreciate it anyway, bro."

"No problem. Talk later."

It looks like I'll have to give Davidson a call.

I tell him I don't have shit and I need some help if I'm ever going to find out what happened to Miriam Gregory. I ask what he's got on Edgar.

"Amanda popped him on a photo array and that, along with her statements, was enough for a judge to sign off."

"A good defense attorney will tear that shit apart."

"Based on what the victim said, this Edgar took her to DC a couple of times and on several occasions the defendants gave her drugs and solicited her for prostitution. They even told her how much money she could make. Edgar was there when they talked and even tried to convince her himself. She didn't want to do it, so one day they got her high as a kite and he just left her there. He's good to go."

"Sounds like it. It'd have been tougher if she wasn't a minor."

"I won't argue with that."

"When are you gonna snatch him up?"

"We're working on that."

"When you do, you won't forget about Miriam Gregory, right?"

"Don't worry, I won't."

Damn, he's being evasive, like this is some top secret shit.

I know Davidson's good at what he does, especially when it comes to interviewing. I still got this feeling that our boy Edgar will clam up, especially if they pick him up at his house. That'll put his parents with him, and you can bet the first call they make is to a lawyer. By the time they get him in the box, they'll be lucky if he admits to holding her hand.

FORTY

I have a phone interview with Tamara Moore later this afternoon, and then in person with the other girlfriend on the list, Justine Durrell. After the conversation I had with Davidson, I make the decision to call the parents of the two girls and reschedule the interviews for tomorrow. I want to set up at the South Run parking lot for the day, just in case Edgar decides to play hooky. I don't know what the chances of him showing are or whether he hangs there anymore. It's the only solid lead I got, so I have to play it out, especially if I might lose him tomorrow. I have a feeling that's why Davidson was being so secretive. They're probably working on a search warrant for his house. We always liked to hit them early in the morning, catch them before they could wipe the sleep outta their eyes. Let's hope that's what Davidson is thinking.

After a hot shower and a nasal cleanse, I put on one of my older suits, one I used to wear for court when I was a cop. Makes me feel like one again.

I grab the notepad and the Miriam Gregory case jacket from

my briefcase and slip them into the backpack. I check the pack and make sure I got what I need.

I slip on my overcoat and step out into a light rain.

It's a cool rain and I look up so it can hit my face, but only for a second. More than that'd be silly.

The traffic lightens at the 14th Street Bridge, and it doesn't take long to get to the parking lot at South Run. There're only a few cars parked here, but not at the end where the lot meets the woods. It's a fairly large parking lot. Occasionally I'll see a woman walking out of the rec center to her car or someone pulling in and parking to go inside. Most of them look like mothers, taking advantage of their kids being at school.

The light rain eases to a mist and I'm nearly through a pack of cigarettes.

I turn the radio on and it's still tuned to 101.1. This time, "Hurt," by Nine Inch Nails, an oldie I like and used to listen to back when I was in the academy with Leslie. But it makes me sad 'cause I think about her even more. I switch it off.

I notice a car pulling in to the parking lot. It's a light blue four-door.

When it gets closer, I see that it's a Honda Accord, not a Camry. It parks a few spaces over from me, the passenger's side facing me. I lean down beneath my window.

The passenger steps out first. He's a white kid with wavy brown hair and can't be more then seventeen. The driver steps out, but I can only make out the back of his head 'cause the car obstructs my view. He moves toward the rear of the vehicle.

Damn if I didn't get lucky. He sure as hell looks like Edgar Soto to me.

They walk across the lot to a gravel road and the opening to the path. They disappear into the wooded area.

I slip on my leather tactical gloves and move my car to a better position a couple of rows behind his—a spot that gives me a better vantage point to see the entrance to the path.

About an hour and a half later I notice Edgar come walking from the path and heading back to his car. The distance from the path to his car is far enough that whoever he was with would've appeared by the time Edgar hit the gravel road.

I shoulder my pack, exit my car, and act like I'm fiddling with my car door while he makes his way to his vehicle.

He doesn't notice me.

I begin to move toward him while he's unlocking the driver's side door.

He bends in like he's trying to find something. That gives me the time I need to get behind him.

I set my pack on the pavement.

"Edgar," I say.

It startles him, and he hits his head on the metal portion of the doorframe. He grunts something and quickly turns to face me.

He takes me for a cop right away and tries to push out and run, but I'm bigger than him by at least six inches and a hundred pounds. I grab him tight by his right hand and squeeze his fingers until he cries out. I twist his arm up and around so he can do nothin' but turn with it. That's when I shove him face-first against the glass of the rear passenger door.

"What the fuck . . ." he huffs.

I push my weight against him, look around me to see if anyone is watching.

Not a mom or a friend in sight.

I pull out my cuffs secured between my belt and the small of my back and click them tight onto the wrist of the arm I'm twisting behind his back.

"What are you—"

173

"Shut the fuck up," I tell him, and then I cuff his other wrist so his hands are secured behind his back.

I grab him by the hoodie of his zipped-up jacket to hold him up against the car while I lean over to the driver's side so I can unlock all the doors. I do a quick pat-down, starting with his ankles and working up.

"What's this?" I ask, after squeezing his left front pants pocket.

"Just my cell phone. What the fuck are you doing this for?"

I check to make sure it's a cell phone and put it back in his pocket. I squeeze his other pocket and feel what appear to be small zips with weed. After doing pat-downs for so many years, you learn what is what. I'm rarely wrong. When I'm done I force him around the car to the front passenger door.

"What are you doing? What do you think you're doing? Let me the fuck go!"

"I said shut up." And I gut-punch him so he curls down and has to gulp for air.

I quickly open the passenger door of his car and muscle him into the seat.

"Wait, wait . . ."

I grab him by the chin with my left hand, push his head back against the headrest, and say, "One more word, Edgar. I swear, just give me another fucking word."

I take the seat belt and buckle him in. There's nothing he can do with his hands cuffed behind him, so I step back and shut the door. I hurry around to the driver's side, grab my backpack, and notice the keys to his car on the pavement under the open door. I pick them up and get in the driver's side, set my pack on the floor behind the front seat.

I start the car and back the fuck out.

I scan the parking lot as I drive out, but don't see anyone around.

"Please, sir, please tell me what you want."

I know I warned him, but I allow it just one more time. I start to think maybe I shoulda thought this through a bit more, but I'm impulsive like that. Now I gotta deal with it.

He's moaning something I can't understand, and I just wanna knock him into some white light so I can have time to mull everything over in my head.

"What's your last name, Edgar?"

I look over, see tears streaming down his face. He knows I'm not a cop now. It's gotta be terrifying, especially if you know what I know about me.

"Here's the deal. I ask only one time from now on, and if you don't answer, I'm gonna hurt you. I'll hurt you bad. What's your last name?"

"Soto," he struggles out.

"You just sit there and shut the fuck up, and I mean no crying, too, and maybe you'll come outta this okay. You say one more word without me asking and you'll get hurt. Clear?"

"Yes, sir."

I turn the radio on.

He's got it tuned to some shit I can't stand. I find the classics station.

"Everything I Own," by Bread. Haven't heard them in a bit. My mother used to play this band. It makes me smile, but not for that reason, mostly 'cause having to listen to this song would drive Leslie nuts. I'm pretty sure she wasn't even born when this song came out. I remember hearing it as a little kid, through my mom's closed bedroom door. I sort of figured it was her alone-time music.

I turn to look at Edgar. He's too scared to look back.

By the time the song ends I got this worked out in my head.

I turn the radio off and head to I-95 to make my way back to DC.

FORTY-ONE

I know Edgar's gonna say something. Kids like him are stupid that way. I don't wanna have to smack him down or do something else to hurt him while I'm driving, so I lay out the story for him.

First I ask, "How old are you?"

"Seventeen. I'm only seventeen."

"Then you're old enough to make big decisions."

His lips purse and his jaw muscles tighten. He's struggling hard to hold back those big-boy tears.

"You're gonna have approximately forty-five minutes to consider what I'm about to tell you. I might already know the answers to some of the questions I'm gonna ask, so I want you to be real careful about what you say. You're no use to me if you lie."

He sniffles and says something unintelligible.

"I need to know you understand me, Edgar."

"I understand. Please tell me what this is about."

I smack him hard on the side of his face with the back of my hand. Not enough to make him bleed, but hard enough that it stings like shit and he'll have a bruise to show for it.

The The Second Girl

"You don't ask me questions. Only give answers."

"Yes," he says through clenched teeth.

"What's your friend's name, the dude you walked into the park with?"

"Sir, he's just a friend of mine. He smokes sometimes and hangs with me there, but that's all."

"Fuck, are you a moron?" And I raise the back of my hand again.

"Greg," he blurts, before I can smack him. "His name is Greg."

"Greg what? Give me a last name."

"Greg Thomas."

"Okay, then."

It doesn't take me more than twenty minutes to get to the Wilson Bridge. I take the exit for I-295 to DC. After a couple of miles, I pass the police academy on the right. Haven't seen that building in a bit. There are some good memories there for sure.

I follow the same route as I did the first time I went to the Anacostia River.

Aside from the occasional whimper, Edgar is surprisingly quiet. But when I make that turn to enter the deserted park area, I can hear his labored breathing.

I stop at the spot where I kicked Jordan Super Fly into the river.

I put the car in park and turn off the ignition.

"If this has to do with what I'm doing, I'll stop. I swear I'll stop," he snivels.

I raise my hand to smack him again. He tucks his chin into his chest, expecting it, but I don't follow through.

"Tell me why you think you're here."

He has an expression like he has to consider what I asked, like he just realized I might be fishing for information I don't have.

"You tell me," he says bravely.

This time I do smack him, but harder, and he didn't have time to prepare. Blood trickles from his left nostril.

I grab him by the back of his neck and have to lean over the console to push him against the passenger door.

"You think you're a fucking tough boy?" I ask, not expecting an answer. "I ask. You answer. It's that simple. And that's the last time I'll say that. Tell me why do you think you're here?"

"The weed, sir, because of the weed."

"No, little man, that's not it. I don't give a shit about you and your cute boyfriend dealing weed in the woods. If that were the case, he'd be here with you."

I let go of him, grab the key out of the ignition, then my backpack, and step out of the car. I walk around, open his door, and drag his crying ass out.

He pleads with me.

"Get on your knees," I order him.

"Please, please. Whatever you want, just please."

"Get on your fucking knees," I say, helping him to his knees so he's at the edge of the steep bank and facing the river.

I stay behind him so he can't fully see me.

I unzip the pack, find a photograph of Miriam, and reach over his shoulder so it's in front of his face.

"Remember, I'll only ask once, so be very careful about lying."

I put the photo back in the pack, pull my Glock outta the holster, and put the barrel to his head with enough pressure so he knows what it is.

"Oh God . . ."

"Tell me her name," I say, pushing the barrel hard enough so his head tips with it.

"Miriam! Miriam!"

I take the gun away from his head.

"I'm her uncle," I say, in a way that even convinces me, and since I'm on a roll, I go with the story in my head. "Now I'll tell you something. I know all about the shit you do. I've followed you to the house in DC where your buddies live. Because of what I do, things like this come easy to me. You know what I mean?"

He cries again. I don't expect an answer.

"Where is Miriam?"

"I don't know. I swear to you I don't know."

"Then you're no use to me."

I press the barrel against his head again.

"No! No! Wait a minute. Wait. I took her there a couple of times. She wanted to go with me. I swear I just took her there."

"You took her there and then what?"

"Nothing. We—"

"What do you mean nothing, you little fuck? There ain't no 'nothing' about this."

"I mean I bought my weed from them. She came with me a couple of times. Don't get mad, sir, please. You told me to tell you the truth. She liked to get high, and she went there with me because they had other stuff."

"What other stuff, drugs?"

"She liked crack."

"Crack? You telling me she went and did that on her own, you lying fuck? You forced it on her."

"No, no, really, I swear I'm not lying to you. She was into drugs before we met. She bought her weed from me. She wanted other stuff, like blow, but I told her I didn't deal that shit. We hung out together, so I started taking her with me when I had to buy my weed. They had an interest in her, so they turned her on to that other shit, not me. I'm sorry, but that's the truth."

"What do you mean they had an interest in her?"

"She's pretty. They liked her."

"You were her boyfriend and that was okay with you?"

"No, no, it wasn't like that."

"You're nothin' but a piece of shit."

"I'm sorry. I'm really fucking sorry."

"You're sorry for what, specifically?"

"For taking her there."

"Tell me where she is now."

"I left her at their house. She wanted to stay. It wasn't anything she didn't want to do. I shouldn't have let her."

This kid's nothing but a little sociopath. I almost wanna believe him, but he's lying through his bloody teeth. I know he had a bigger role, because he brought Amanda there, too. I wanna keep him talking, so I let him go with it.

"She's only sixteen years old."

"I don't want to die. I'm telling you the truth."

"Is she alive?"

"She was when I saw her."

"When did you last see her?"

"It was in the summer. It was a long time ago. I don't know exactly. I really don't. I think it was July."

"Where did you see her?"

"I told you. At the house in DC."

I slap him on the right ear with the butt of the gun. I know that's gotta hurt.

He cries out, tries to tuck his ear to his shoulder, and then he starts crying again.

"She's not there anymore, so where would they take her?"

"You're gonna kill me. You're gonna kill me, aren't you?"

"Where?"

"I don't want to die, but really, sir, I don't know."

"Do they work prostitution? Is that what it was?"

"I don't know. Maybe."

"You lyin' shit. Answer up."

"They've had girls in the house before, but then they go. They never stay. I don't know where."

I want to ask him how many girls he recruited for them, but I don't wanna give up Amanda. It's best to stick with the lone crazy uncle story, the uncle whose sole interest is his niece.

"Who was their supplier?"

"You mean the drugs?"

"Yes, dopey, the drugs."

"I wasn't in like that. I just bought a couple ounces of weed from them."

"How long would you hang out there?"

"Sometimes it was quick, but sometimes we'd hang out and play cards."

"An hour, two hours, three?"

"I've hung out there for almost half a day before."

"So you got to know them pretty good?"

He's afraid to answer.

"You wanna live, right?"

He nods several times.

"This is how you live: Give me the names of everyone you know from that house or from the street. I want all of them."

"Okay, okay," he says quickly, then bows his head like he's gotta think. "I don't know last names, though."

I know that's probably true. Most of the players, this punk not included, don't offer that kinda information. Asking one of them something like that might get you into trouble.

"Give me what you got."

"There's Angelo. He was in charge of the house. Then there's his brother José, and Andrés and Viktor, who I believe are their cousins. There's also Salvador and this little kid, maybe thirteen years old, that ran errands for them. His name was Manuel, but we called him Little Manny. And then, umm . . ."

"You hung out playing cards, probably drinking and smoking. People had to come and visit. Tell me about that," I offer, trying to jog his memory.

"Sometimes a lot of people came by, but I didn't get names. It's not like I was there every day."

"I'm gonna hit you hard, boy."

"Don't, just don't. Gimme a sec. I can't think straight."

I allow him a couple of seconds, and he says, "There was this older guy who came by to play cards once. He wasn't Latino. I don't know his name, but they called him Pequeño Diablo when they talked about him in Spanish and Little Monster when they talked to him."

"What'd you call him?"

"Sir, I didn't call him fucking shit. I didn't mess around talking to him."

"But you think his nickname was Little Monster."

"That's what they called him to his face."

"Describe him."

"He was short, much shorter than me, but built. I mean, he looked seriously dangerous. He was African-American and had cornrows."

Sounds like someone I knew when I was working narcotics. He was one of Cordell Holm's boys. Called him Little Monster 'cause that's exactly what he was when he had to act as an enforcer for Cordell. If he's still working for him, then that's likely one of the main reasons Cordell has been able to hold on to his position longer than most.

Looks like something good mighta come out of beating this kid down.

FORTY-TWO

I can't spend any more time here with this kid. At this point, I'm confident he'd let me cut off his dick in order to survive. That's a thought. I don't like it messy, though. So what the hell do I do with him?

"You see that river, well, if you wanna call it a river. River makes it sound like it should be something tranquil. It's nothin' but filth. For me, far from tranquil, 'cause I like to fish, but I'd never fish this river. You look at it, boy, 'cause I put one in the back of your head you'll be a part of that river. Part of what makes it filthy. I'm not finished with what I have to do, because I have to find my girl. So you better believe me when I say if you fuck that up and do something stupid like call the police, or, even dumber, any of the boys out there who you're working with"— I wait a moment, think, watch the muddy surface of that river barely move. Then: "I'll kill you, Edgar."

I snatch him by the hoodie and push him face-first on the ground. I press my knee with good weight on the small of his back until he grunts. I search his coat pockets again, pull out a nice little wad of cash. I search his pants pockets and take his iPhone and eight small zips, each containing a dime's worth of weed.

I sit him up and then help him stand. I shove him against the car and squeeze his balls until he squeals like a little girl.

"Naw, nothin' there," I say, but still hold on. "You need to understand that this is real."

"Please. Please, I understand. I won't say—" He starts to cry.

"Shut up. I don't wanna hear all this crying, just a simple yes."

"Yes."

I pull him back up and open the door. I help him to sit and then buckle him in. I toss the cash and his little knife on the floor at his feet, but keep the weed and his wallet.

I walk around and get in the driver's side and start the car, but before I drive, I search the contents of his wallet and find his driver's license. I grab my notebook and write down all his information.

"I'm not going to even ask you if this is a good address. It doesn't matter. I got your date of birth, your Social, everything I need to find you. And I can find you."

I search the wallet again, but this time for some folded papers I saw, along with a couple of cards. One of the cards is an ID for access to a community pool. The other one is his student ID. The addresses match. I find two torn pieces of paper. I unfold them.

The first one has "Justine" and a phone number written on it. I recognize the number and obviously the name.

The second paper just has a phone number with a Virginia area code.

"Who is this for?" I ask.

He looks at it briefly and says, "Just a dude that buys an ounce of weed from me once a week."

"What's his name?"

"Robbie. I don't know his last name."

"You're quite the businessman, huh?"

He doesn't answer.

I keep the pieces of paper, return the IDs to his wallet, and toss it on the floor at his feet.

I check the contacts in his iPhone, but it doesn't power up.

"What's with this?" I ask. "A businessman whose cell phone doesn't work?"

"That's why I was going to the car, to charge it."

I see the charger cable hanging out of the center console. I plug in the phone, but it still doesn't have enough juice to power on. I leave it plugged in and set it in a cup holder.

I drive.

Rush hour fires me up. I can't imagine being one of those commuters. Poor saps. This is their life, twice a day, five days a week. I'm not even halfway to South Run and I've been driving for an hour and a half. I'm about ready to jump outta my skin.

It's dark by the time I pull into the parking lot. Sign in front says it closes at dusk. There are still a few cars in the lot and lights on in the rec center. Staff is probably closing up shop, or maybe the rec center is still open and it's the park that closes. I don't know, but just in case it's all closed up I wanna make this quick; some bored cop could decide to check it out.

I pull into the space he parked in before.

I pick up his iPhone again. It powers on. I find his contacts.

"I see your boy Angelo in here."

"Please, sir, don't call him."

"You wanna go back to the fucking river?"

He shakes his head.

"Shut up, then."

I get my notebook and copy down the number, then continue scrolling and find numbers for Andrés, Edgar's smoking buddy Greg Thomas, and then José. I don't find a number for Amanda or Miriam. Maybe he had enough sense to delete them, or maybe he just keeps them on torn pieces of paper, like Justine. Was she going to be next on the list?

He's got so many names in here I'm tempted to keep the iPhone. I don't want to fuck up Davidson's case, 'cause I know he'll take it, and that's what'll connect Edgar to Angelo and company.

"You got Little Monster's number in here?"

"No, sir. I told you I won't mess with that guy."

Cell phones are gold, and as much as I don't want to stick around this parking lot with this handcuffed mutt in the front seat, I take a little time and go through it. I copy down all the numbers with a 202 area code, and a few others that look interesting.

When I'm done, I set the iPhone in the cup holder in the center console.

"Lean down," I order him.

He obeys. I release him from the handcuffs. There's blood around his wrists.

"Don't even get outta the car, just slide over when I exit. You roll out right away and go home. I have nothing better to do tonight, so I might set up at your house to make sure you're still there."

I open the door and step out. I watch him as he slides over. He doesn't look at me, just skids in reverse and heads out. I wait until I see him make a left turn on the parkway and then walk back to my car.

I wait in the car for about an hour, passing the time listening to the radio and snorting a few lines. In that time, a couple of people have walked from the rec center to their cars and left. When I'm comfortable, I leave. Once I get to the light at the parkway, I ease out to look in both directions. No vehicles are parked off the road. A few cars roll by in both directions, but nothing that appears sketchy. I know he won't be around. He's too scared and probably at home locked in his bedroom, wearing a clean pair of shorts and sneaking a peek out the window every so often to see if any strange cars are parked in front of his house.

FORTY-THREE

I need to pace myself, or I'll crash. I've crashed into that wall of hysterics before and it ain't fun.

I take it easy when I get home and snort only about a quarter. When I start to come down, I take a couple of 10mg Klonopins with a double shot of vodka, go to bed, and wait.

My mind is racing and keeps me up most of the night. Can't stop thinking about Leslie, and then of course there's the case and all that has to be done. Most of the cases I pick up are simple. You hit the street, knock on doors and try to find good witnesses, maybe take a few photos or reinterview key witnesses. It's not like what I used to do during a narcotics investigation. That's what this case is like. I don't miss having to search cell phones in an effort to locate certain players and then figuring out how to okeydoke them after. Luna was good at that shit. I was good at interview and interrogation, fieldwork, and kicking in doors. Role-playing or having to okeydoke someone plays a smaller part in what I do now. Most of the time I have to do it out of necessity or to save my ass.

When I wake up, I don't remember falling asleep.

My cell phone's ringing.

I unplug it from the charger on my nightstand, clear my throat, and answer, "Frank Marr."

"Mr. Marr, this is Detective Shawn Caine, with the Fairfax County Police Department."

I check my clock for the time.

Not even eight thirty yet.

"Am I catching you at a bad time?"

"No. What can I do for you?" I ask, even though I already know why he's calling.

"Mr. Gregory gave me your phone number. I'm the detective assigned to their daughter's case. I was also working the Amanda Meyer investigation. That was very good what you did there, getting her home safely. I wanted to reach out to you, see what it is you're up to with respect to Miriam Gregory."

"What it is I'm up to?" He's fishing, and the last thing I'm gonna do is pass on information. That is, unless doing so would somehow benefit me.

I know exactly how and why a cop does this. They got rules and a special way of doing things. I'm not saying I always followed the rules back then, but nowadays I don't have to follow them at all. Probable cause isn't something I have to worry about anymore. These detectives do, and that's what can mess things up for me.

"Well, Detective, that's confidential information, but I know you have a job to do, so Mr. Gregory would be the one to talk to about what I'm up to."

"I know all about PI confidentiality. Mr. Gregory said he hasn't heard from you so he doesn't know what's going on."

"When I have information I think he should know, he'll be the first one I call."

"Listen, it's the family's right to do what they want with their money. If they want to give it away, then that's their call, but it seems to me all you've been doing is making the same rounds I've already made. And the last thing I need is you interfering with an ongoing investigation."

"Detective Caine, I'm a retired police detective—"

"I know you are," he interrupts.

"When I was working, the last thing I'd ever want was some PI stepping on my case, possibly screwing the whole thing up for me. You got your job and I got mine. Be assured that I know what I'm doing, and if I do pick up a good lead that might result in locating Miriam Gregory, you'll be the second call."

"I've spent months trying to locate her . . . That family has been through a lot. They don't need someone giving them false hope. After Amanda Meyer was found, they got excited, thinking there might be a connection."

"And you don't think there's a connection?"

"I'm not saying that, but I've been investigating missing children for a lot of years, and she's been missing for a long time. I think you understand."

"I understand, because the last thing I want to do is give the family false hope, but I'm also not gonna sit on my ass either, waiting for her body to show up at a morgue."

"Watch yourself, Mr. Marr. We both know that since you located Amanda Meyer there are some possible new leads. I'll be following through on those. I just want to make sure we're not walking on each other here, or that you don't get yourself in trouble mucking up an ongoing investigation."

This is starting to take a bad turn, so I try to back up, 'cause the last thing I need is more enemies.

"I copy that, Detective. And by the way, have you been in touch with Detective Davidson? He's working Amanda's case."

"I have."

I decide to throw him a bone. Edgar's gonna be in police custody anyway, so he's already a done deal; I won't have access to him anymore. I know how the Feds work, and there's a strong possibility Detective Caine doesn't know the Feds are probably in Edgar's house right about now. In fact, if he did know, I think that's where he'd be instead of talking to me.

"You may already know what's going on this morning, but in case you don't, you might want to give Davidson a call on his cell."

"Okay," he says, not inquiring further, because that would give up that he doesn't know what's going on.

"We both want the same thing," I tell him.

"Maybe, but the motives are different."

"No, not so different. You see, unlike you, this case wasn't assigned to me, and certainly wasn't one that I wanted to take on. But I did, and it has nothing to do with the money."

"We'll be in touch, then."

"All right, Detective. You stay safe."

Damn, that's not how I like to wake up in the morning, so I lie back down to work the day out in my head.

FORTY-FOUR

After my over-the-phone interview with Tamara Moore, I drive to Justine Durrell's home in Burke, Virginia. The phone interview was a waste of time, but for good reason. Tamara seems like a good girl.

I have to hand it to Edgar, 'cause he opened up a few doors in this investigation for me. Who knows? It might have been easier for Detective Caine if he'd known about Edgar when Miriam first disappeared. But then, like I said, the good cops (and I think Caine falls into that category) have rules. I have a feeling that going head-to-head with a wannabe tough boy like Edgar in a regular interview setting would not have worked as well. Don't get me wrong. I know a few good cops who still go old-school like I did with Edgar, but not necessarily to my kind of extreme. I admit I do get carried away sometimes.

Justine Durrell's mother is wearing running shoes and a workout outfit. It's a bit too tight around the thighs and ass, but I get the impression she likes that kind of attention.

She walks me to the living room, but doesn't offer me a seat.

In a sharp tone, she calls out, "Justine, get down here. That investigator's here to talk to you."

The living room is spacious, a bit too open, so I ask, "Would you mind if I interview your daughter in the den, maybe in private? It's totally up to you. It's just that some of the information concerning the missing girl is something I'd like to share with your daughter alone."

"I don't care where you interview her. I'm going on a run. And see if you can scare some sense into her while you're at it. I don't know what to do anymore, and you look like a man who knows how to scare someone."

"I'll have a talk with her," I say, and then notice Justine making her way down a flight of stairs that leads from a second-floor hallway.

She's tall and slim, maybe a little too slim. She's wearing baggy gray boys' sweatpants and a black T-shirt with sleeves that fall just over her bony shoulders.

"I'll be back in forty-five minutes," her mom advises, but I'm not sure who it's directed at.

Justine plops herself on a large sofa.

"You the only one home?"

"My brother's at a friend's and my dad's at work."

"This'll be a good spot to talk, then."

I sit down, grab my notepad and the case jacket from my pack, and set the pack on the floor.

I ready my pen.

"You having problems with your mom?"

"She make that obvious to you? Because she sure does with everyone else."

"Yeah, she did, a little. How do you get along with your dad?"

"What does that have to do with Miriam Gregory?"

"Damn, you don't sound like a sixteen-year-old. You are sixteen, right?"

"Yes."

"Well, I'm not one of your peers, so I think you need to step it down a bit, okay?"

She doesn't say anything, just looks away. She probably heard her mother and that fucked up her attitude. I'll stay away from the family thing.

"I think you know I've been hired to try to find Miriam Gregory."

"Yeah."

"She's been missing for a long time, but it's like I have to start from the beginning again. That's why it's important I talk to you and all of Miriam's friends. She been a friend of yours for a while?"

"Since elementary school."

"That's a while. When was the last time you saw her or spoke to her?"

She almost answers right away, but then pauses to think about it.

"Early summer. I don't remember exactly when, though."

"Was this in person or over the phone?"

"In person."

"Where did you see her?"

"At the park."

"Okay, Justine, let's start over. It'll make it a lot easier on the both of us if you don't just feed me bits and pieces. I don't know this area. I'm a DC boy. So when you say park, for all I know you're talkin' about Lafayette Park."

"South Run Park."

"It just so happens I know a little bit about that park. I'd like to show you a couple of pictures; tell me if you know any of these kids."

I pull out a photo of Amanda and then the yearbook with Edgar's photograph. I show her Amanda's first.

"She's a bitch," she says.

I admit, but only to myself, that I am taken by surprise.

"What's her name?"

"I think Amanda, and she's not a friend of mine."

"I got that impression. Why is she a bitch?"

"She stole my fucking boyfriend."

"Did the police ever show you a picture of her?"

"No, and I don't understand why you are."

"I'll get to that."

It actually makes sense they wouldn't show her a picture. Miriam went missing months before Amanda, and they didn't know about Edgar until Amanda. I'm sure Caine is only a few steps behind me with interviewing Justine. At least I would hope he is. I open the yearbook and show her Edgar's photo.

"Is this the guy who used to be your boyfriend?"

Now she's really surprised, but she can't hide it like I can. I can almost hear her thinking, *How did he put that together?*

"Yes, that's Edgar," she tells me.

I wanna tell her how lucky she is he got taken away by Amanda, but I bite my tongue.

FORTY-FIVE

W hen did you and Edgar meet?"
        "Last year, but we didn't really hang out until sum-
mer."

"So he knew Miriam?" I ask, even though I already know.

"Of course. She was—is—my best friend. I mean, she's not
dead, right?"

"I wouldn't be trying to find her if she were. Do you know a
guy named Greg?"

She's got that look again, wondering how I know all this.

"Yes."

"Go on."

"He's just a friend of Edgar's. Do they have something to do
with Miriam?"

"Aren't you all friends?"

"Yeah, I guess."

"You have a cell phone, Justine?"

"I used to, but my mom took it away. Why are you asking me
all these questions?"

"Okay, I'll be straight with you, but that means you gotta be straight with me. Trust me, girl, I'll know if you're not."

I shoot her my best, sort of hard but not too threatening look and she blinks, so that means I win.

"I know all about Edgar and his little weed-dealing crew at South Run. I know all about the two of you and your relationship. I know Miriam was mixed up in it, too. I don't think it's something your mom, or, for that matter, the police, is gonna take lightly. Am I right?"

I'm pretty sure the little nod she gives me means I'm right, so I continue.

"I used to be a narcotics detective in DC, but I played with the big boys, not the minors. You guys are too easy. It didn't take me long to put together the connections. I still need your help, though. There's still a lot I don't know, mainly, where to find Miriam. So I don't care about the drugs you're doing or the friends you're hanging out with. The only thing I care about is finding your friend Miriam, okay?"

"Okay."

"But don't get me wrong. If you lie to me or hold anything back, I'm going to give your mom everything I have, including a number she can call to have you get a piss test."

"You can't do that."

Teenagers who haven't been in and out of the system most of their lives are too easy to read and even easier to play. Justine's obvious, like an actress in one of those low-budget films who tries too hard.

"Of course I can. We both know how that piss test will turn out, and we both know what your mom is gonna do, especially after I talk to her. I wouldn't be surprised if you find yourself in one of those out-of-state all-girls boarding schools after Christmas vacation. You answer my questions, and everything will stay between us. I'm not a cop, so I can do that. You don't answer, I go to your mom and I also go to the cops."

She unslumps herself from the sofa.

"Who do you get your drugs from now, since you and Edgar broke up?"

She's unwilling, but I sense it's fear that's holding her back.

"You don't want to test me, Justine. I don't want to have to mess your life up more than it already is."

"Greg helps me out."

"You got some sort of allowance? How're you paying for it?"

She looks down.

"Wait, don't answer that. I don't wanna know."

According to Edgar, Miriam liked crack, so I gotta assume she does, too.

I take a chance and ask, "What about the crack? Who're you getting that from?"

"I don't smoke crack!"

"I'm not playin', girl. I know when someone's using that shit. I can smell it on your skin. It's a sweet smell. I know it well. You might have your parents fooled, but not me."

"You can't talk to me like that."

"You already know you don't have any rights in this household. Just remember the piss test."

"I get it from a friend of Edgar's, from DC. He gave me his number once."

"I know you're still smokin' that shit, so how do you connect with him now, this friend of Edgar's?"

She's looking down again.

"Your home phone?"

She doesn't answer.

"Maybe you sneak out at night to meet up with him? Or after school? That'd be easy, right?"

"It's like I'm in a prison. My parents have everything locked up, even the windows. If I didn't have to use the bathroom at night, they'd probably lock me in my bedroom."

"When was the last time you saw this guy, then?"

"Last week."

"So you get in his car and he drops you off at the bus stop or something and you walk home from there?"

"Yeah, pretty much."

Sixteen years old.

Fuck.

It's obvious what she has to do for whatever amount she's getting from him, so I'm not going to embarrass her by asking again.

"It can't be for long, though, because you have a curfew."

"Just as long as the bus would take," she says.

"Has he ever picked you up at home or dropped you off at home?"

"No. I'm not stupid."

"So he doesn't know where you live?"

"No. Why?"

"Some of these boys in DC don't fuck around, Justine. It might seem like an adventure, but trust me, it ain't. They can take it all away from you, the life you think you hate and more. So this dude, was he a friend of Miriam's, too?"

"She knew him. Sometimes we all drove around together."

"Did you ever go to where he stays in DC?"

"No."

"Do you know if Miriam did?"

"I don't think so. She would've told me if she did."

"What about any other homes in DC? You ever visit anybody else there, maybe go with Edgar?"

"Once with Edgar, we visited some friends of his."

"Do you remember any of their names?"

"No; they were Latino, though."

"What did you do there?"

"We got high, mostly."

"They ever ask you to stay there?"

"Yeah, of course, but we didn't."

"They ever take you anywhere else?"

"They took us to this club once in Adams Morgan. I forget the name. It had the word 'village' in it."

"Columbia Village?"

"That's it. They had pool tables."

"Anywhere else? Maybe someone's home?"

"No."

"So those Latino boys never tried to force either you or Miriam to stay?"

"No. Why would they do that?"

"Are you getting your crack from one of those boys?"

"No, not them."

"Tell me who you're getting it from, then."

"I can't."

"So you're telling me the last time you talked to Miriam was in the summer, around July?"

"Yeah."

"You said she's your best friend. Are you worried about what happened to her?"

"Yeah, of course."

"It's just that you seem so nonchalant about everything."

"I'm not nonchalant."

"You don't seem to want to help me find her."

"I don't want to talk to you anymore."

"What's the guy's name you get your crack from?"

"I said I don't want to talk anymore."

"Then I guess I'll hang out and wait for your mom."

"You're a real asshole."

"I know I am. What's his name?"

"I just know him as Playboy."

"Playboy? You telling me you don't know his first name?"

She hesitates, and then says, "Calvin, but everyone calls him Playboy. Please don't have him arrested. I need him."

"I'm not gonna have anyone arrested. I told you. I just want to find Miriam. If I ever talk to Playboy, he'll never know I talked to you, so your relationship will be just fine. Don't worry. What does he look like?"

"He's a black guy, keeps his hair short and tight."

"How old? Is he a big guy? Describe him."

"He's in his early twenties. He's a couple of inches taller than me."

"So he's about five eight. What does he drive?"

"A really nice Lexus."

"Color?"

"It's black. Shiny black."

"Two- or four-door?"

"Two doors."

"Did you ever see his car tags, what state they're from?"

"No. Why would I look at his car tags? He's from DC, though."

"Do you have a code name you use with him for crack?"

"Code name?"

"When you called him. I know you didn't come out and say you wanted some crack."

"We didn't call; we texted. And we call them jellybeans."

"That's a good one. What about someone named Robbie? You know him?"

"How do you know all this stuff?"

"Because it's my job. So who is he?"

"A friend of Edgar. He's just a pothead, that's all."

"I'm going to need to see your cell phone, Justine."

"My mom has it. What are you going to tell her? You promised—"

"Calm down. I'll tell your mom that you have contacts of other friends on there and I just need to copy some numbers, all right? That's all she'll hear. You can listen to the whole conversation if you want. I won't burn you with your mom, and like I already told you, I won't burn your Playboy. But you're gonna have to keep your mouth shut or you'll lose everything. You understand that?"

"Yes."

"I mean it. You wanna keep your little adventure, then you'd better make sure someone like Playboy never learns about our conversation."

"Don't worry. I'm not stupid."

There is irony there.

Forty-six

Life can be hard, especially for a bored suburban teenager on drugs.

After this job, I'm done with teenagers.

Hard to believe I used to be one. I might even feel a little bad for my parents.

No, not really.

When you think about it, I'm not much different from some of these kids. The only thing that separates us is I don't have to worry about my fucked-up parents anymore.

So why didn't they take Justine like they took Amanda, and more than likely like they took Miriam? Maybe Playboy can answer that question.

But then there's Edgar. He said he brought Miriam to the Salvadorans' house, but maybe they didn't have to use the tactics they used for Amanda. Maybe Miriam was willing. Crack is some powerful shit. It rots you from the inside out.

Cocaine is a monster, but crack is the devil. You can keep the monster in a closet, but not the fucking devil. It'll possess your life and get you to a point where there's nothing left but the devil himself. I've seen it enough times on the job. I was smart enough not to take that first hit. I know how weak I am. It would've changed my life from something manageable to something out of my control. I feel like that's happening now sometimes, but I believe in the power of good grapefruit, Valium, Klonopin, and a few hours of sleep.

If Miriam was willing, then she's either dead or working in one of those row house brothels you'll find on almost every other block in certain sections of DC. And shit, this isn't a competition. I'm hoping Caine gets to Justine and gets the information I have. Unfortunately, I can't give it to him because I can't chance Justine sending up a flare to warn Playboy. I need Playboy on the street, where he's easier to get to. Also Justine might disappear for good if that happens. Then again, she still might.

Even though I don't have anything I want to share yet, I feel obligated to check in with the Gregorys. I get out of my suit first and slip on some jeans and a casual shirt. After that, I plop on the sofa and light a cigarette.

Ian Gregory answers the home phone, having just walked in the door after his commute from the Pentagon.

I fill him in on what very little I can tell him and add, "I do have a couple of leads, and I'll be following through on those first thing in the morning."

"Detective Caine called me the other day. Have you been in touch with him?"

"Yes, I have."

"So are these leads something he should also know about?"

"Let me work it through my way, Mr. Gregory. I still stand with what I said before. Give it through the end of the week. If I don't have anything solid then, I never will."

"But you said you have leads? That's good, then."

"A lead is simply something that needs to be worked. If I develop something solid from it, then I'll call you right away."

"Thank you for keeping me informed."

I'm such a bullshit artist, but Ian Gregory is either clueless or won't tell me how much trouble his daughter really got into. I don't think he's clueless.

After I get off the phone with him I snuff out my cigarette and light another one. My house has always been a comfort zone, but since this mess I made with Leslie, I find that it's less comforting. It's true what they say. You never know until someone's gone. But she's not dead, and I'm not dead, so there's hope.

Cell phone rings.

"Frank Marr," I answer.

"Hey, Frank, this is Davidson."

"What's up, Scott? You got good news for me?"

"Afraid not, and that's what we have to talk about. You have time to stop by the office here?"

Oh shit. I can tell by his tone that something's up. I'm hoping Edgar didn't get stupid brave and give me up.

"Talk to me now. What's going on?"

"Need to talk in person. It's sensitive. If you haven't had supper, I'll order a couple of sandwiches from Jack's."

"No, I'm good. I can be there in about an hour. Why don't we meet at the FOP Lodge, though? I could use a beer."

"Like I said, it's sensitive. You know how it is there. I'll owe you a dinner some other time, though. So I'll see you at about six o'clock?"

"Yeah, I'll be there."

I'm thinking supper may not come for a while.

FORTY-SEVEN

I'll admit it. I think about running, getting the fuck outta Dodge. I've got the stash. I've got the cash, and I certainly know where to get the good fake identification. But then I figure that although Edgar might be a little stupid, he's not that brave. He's gotta know that if he turns me in, I'll give up everything I know about him. And he knows I got a lot to give up. Even without that, it'd be his word against mine, and he's a piece-of-shit coconspirator in a juvenile abduction and rape case.

Yeah, I'm not gonna run.

But I still walk into the Nickel clean. No backpack and no pill container. Just in case.

Scott answers the door of the unit's third-floor office after I buzz it a couple of times.

He's wearing tan BDUs and a navy blue polo shirt with a gold embroidered MPDC badge on the left chest. He looks tired.

"Thanks for coming in." He smiles.

"No problem, brother."

"I don't think I've ever seen you not wearing a suit." Davidson smiles again.

"That's because you've never seen me at home before, and that's where you dragged me out of."

"Well, I appreciate you taking the time."

I follow him to his desk.

Davidson's partner, whose name I forget, is sitting at his desk, and a man and a woman wearing pricey tan tactical pants with several zippered pockets and open vests with even more pockets are sitting at the desks that were unoccupied the last time I was here. Everything about them is fresh. It's how I know they're Feds.

A large man with short spiky hair and a black suit is leaning against a wall. He shoots me a nod like he knows me. He has a visitor sticker like mine. I notice part of the silver badge secured to the left side of his belt. It looks like Fairfax County.

"Frank, this is Special Agent Donna Hernandez and her partner, Agent Chad Hawkins."

She offers her hand and a "Good to meet you," and we shake, and then Chad offers his, but with only a slight smile.

They seem relaxed, sitting on their chairs on wheels and leaning against the wall. Scott's partner is relaxed too, but with his feet propped up on his desk.

"And I think you know Detective Caine over there," Davidson says with a motion of his head toward the large man against the wall.

"We've spoken on the phone," I say.

He straightens up and reaches out to offer his hand. We shake. He returns to his wall.

"Have a seat, Frank," Scott says, offering me the chair in front of his desk.

He sits down, and then I do, too.

I notice three boxes that contain bagged and tagged evidence.

"Looks like you just executed a search warrant," I say.

"Yeah, Edgar Soto's home."

"So you got the punk. Good job. He talk?"

"No. That's why we appreciate you getting down here."

"I'll do what I can," I say reluctantly.

"Did you ever find Edgar Soto and talk to him?" Davidson asks.

"Whether I did or didn't is privileged information. You know that."

"C'mon, Frank, we need your help with a couple of things here."

"Talk to me, then."

"If you interviewed him, he might have given you some information we can use."

"You mean information that'll help you with the Amanda Meyer case?"

"Yes, and anything else you may have talked to him about."

I sense that he's digging for something more.

"What, you need something to use before you interrogate him? You got Edgar in the box, right?"

"Well, no, but we do have him in a bag."

FORTY-EIGHT

W hat the fuck happened?" I ask, trying not to sound too thrilled. As bad as it is, I like this scenario better than the other.

"We hit his home at a little after six hundred hours. His mother actually answered the door for the knock-and-announce. She was surprised as hell we were there and didn't have a clue. While I was trying to calm her down because of the search warrant we had, the entry team made their way in to clear the house. It's a big house, real big, but it didn't take long for them to find him."

"How was he killed?"

"Can't say yet," Scott tells me, and now I know he's fishing. He won't give up the crime scene.

"Mother didn't hear anything?" I ask.

"Slept soundly."

"What about his father?"

"They're divorced," Hernandez says.

I forgot they were there.

"Was there any sign of forced entry?"

"We have guys there still looking into everything."

That's a load of bullshit, I think. They know. They're just keeping it from me. I'm not a brother in blue anymore, so I can't expect them to share everything.

"So you think this has anything to do with Amanda? Maybe one of Angelo's boys got to him?"

"We don't know what to think."

"So I'm sure you got a detail on Amanda's house, then?"

"We have agents there," Hernandez says.

I look her way again. She's cute. Petite. The sidearm tucked into her fancy tactical thigh holster is almost the size of one of her shapely forearms.

"That's good to hear," I reply.

Damn stupid kid, Edgar. I'm sure the first thing he did after I left him was to mouth off to the wrong person about our little encounter at the river, and that's what got him killed. Because they got scared.

I think about Justine. She might be in danger, too, or already dead.

"Well shit, that's too bad; but what do you need me for?"

"Frankie, we're going to need everything you have."

"What is it you think I have?"

"Everything you got with respect to Miriam Gregory," Davidson says. "And anything else you might have, especially if you interviewed the decedent."

"Detective Caine has been working that case much longer than I have, but then I'm sure that's why he's here, right?"

"I know how you guys work," Caine advises me, with a bit of authority. "Your rules aren't our rules, so I'm thinking maybe you got better results than I did."

He's starting to piss me off, so I don't acknowledge him.

"I hear you used to work this kinda shit when you were on the job," Hernandez says. "I heard you were really good at it."

I'm starting to like her, but I know she's just working me, like Davidson is. They're holding back on something real.

"I was okay," I tell her, and then to Davidson I say, "You got McGuire and Luna on this?"

"Definitely; they're on it."

"All due respect there, Scott, whatever it is I have, which is probably less than what your new friend Caine has, is confidential. I have clients to protect. You and I go back and we're talking a murder investigation, so I'll do what I can to help, but I have to call my client first."

"Understood."

I notice Caine shaking his head. It wouldn't be too hard to knock that sly smile off his face, but I don't want to have to deal with the repercussions. I might have some more serious repercussions to deal with here later on.

"Mind if I go into the other room to make a call?"

"It's all yours, but use the open room over there."

I walk a few steps into the adjacent room. It's separated by a small archway. It's close, but still far enough that they won't hear my conversation unless the room is bugged, which I seriously doubt.

I'm not about to call the Gregorys and scare the hell outta them with this. It's Justine I'm worried about, and it's her mother I call.

She answers. "Hello?"

I speak low so they can't hear me in the other room. "This is Frank Marr, Mrs. Durrell."

"What can I do for you, Frank?" she asks like she's known me for a long time, but I think it's just that she's had one too many. I guess that's how some of those suburban wives work it off—chase down a nice healthy run with a coupla drinks.

"I have a follow-up question for Justine. You mind if I talk to her for a second?"

"Not at all, Frank. Hold on."

I hear the phone set down and then, "Justine! You have a call!"

Shortly thereafter, a click as a phone is picked up in another room. "Hello?"

"This is Frank Marr, Justine. Mrs. Durrell, are you still on the line?"

I hear a click from the other phone.

"She hung up," Justine says.

"I think I made it clear when I was there, but I want to make sure you understand that the boys you're playing with are dangerous."

"You made that clear. And I'm not playing with them."

"That boy you're rollin' with is bad news, Justine. You need to stay clear of him, especially now, or you might get yourself caught up in the police investigation. I need you to really understand that, all right?"

"You don't have to keep telling me."

"Don't get smart."

"I'm not getting smart. I couldn't text or call him even if I wanted to. His number's on my cell phone that my parents took, and I don't have it memorized, okay?"

"Good. Also, like I said, the police are probably going to get in touch with you soon. You need to tell them what you know. Everything."

"You said I could trust you, and now you call me back like two hours after you were here and tell me this."

"You *can* trust me, so you need to trust me when I say these boys are dangerous, so stay away from them."

"Okay, okay. I have to go."

"You call me if you need anything."

"I will," she says, and hangs up.

She's a smart girl made stupid by addiction. I hope she'll listen. I don't even know if Playboy is involved with all this shit, but I got a bad feeling anyway.

FORTY-NINE

I walk back to the other room but don't sit down. It appears that I'll always have to keep a few steps ahead of these guys when it comes to this case. I can't hold on to the information Justine gave me today. I may not be responsible most of the time, but sometimes I have good sense. Luckily, these boys here move at a much slower pace than I do. They set things up differently. They have to get everything cleared with their supervisors. Then they have to brief, debrief, and map everything out. That can take them anywhere from several hours to several days. All I have to do is pack my backpack with a few essentials, get in my car, and go. Despite all that, I gotta be careful. They're not giving me details related to Edgar's murder for some reason, and I'm beginning to think it's not because I'm no longer a sworn member and a part of the fraternity.

"I didn't call my client."

"I heard you talking to somebody," Davidson says.

"I was. It's a source I have."

"So why didn't you call the Gregorys?" Caine asks.

I look at Davidson and ask, "Did Detective Caine give you a call after I said he should, or was he already in on the search warrant?"

"He called, but after we discovered the decedent, we asked if he could stop by."

"I just wanted to make sure you were still in charge."

I hear a chuckle from the other side of the room, but don't know from who. It wasn't Caine, though.

"You guys got some bad blood together or something?" Whatshisname asks.

"Not me; maybe he just doesn't like retired cops who have to work to supplement their pension."

"It ain't nothin' but a thing," Caine says, as if it's a song lyric.

"Let's get back on track, guys," Davidson says.

"Well, Caine, despite what you might think of me, I'm glad Davidson called you in. That means Miriam Gregory will be on your mind while you're working this."

"Yes, she will be."

"It's not a competition. We all want the same thing," Hernandez adds, and I think I'm falling in love now.

"You know you still have a couple of Angelo's boys out there, right? Or did you pick them up?" I ask.

"They're in the wind," the silent one, Hawkins, says.

Well, they're not keeping that from me, so maybe things aren't so bad.

"I'd say they're good suspects, then, right?"

"We're on it," Hawkins replies.

"You might want to get an undercover or someone like Luna in Columbia Village in Adams Morgan. My source said they used to hang out there."

"Appreciate that. We will," Hawkins says.

"That's a start," Davidson says.

"There's another girl, Caine has her information, Justine Durrell. She was a friend of Edgar's. You'll want to talk to her. Just do me a favor and make it look like it comes from you, Caine, not me. I promised her I wouldn't tell anybody about her friendship with Edgar. And she's more afraid of her mother than she is of you guys, so use it."

"She used to hang out with Edgar Soto?" Caine asks.

"That's what I said."

"She never told me that."

"Like you said, you got rules of engagement, and I don't walk on eggshells when it comes to juvies."

"So you're saying you beat it out of her?" He smirks.

"The only bruises you'll find on that girl are inside, and she got those long before she met me."

"Is she connected to Amanda Meyer?" Davidson asks.

"No, they weren't friends."

"What about the defendants who abducted Amanda? Does she know them?" Davidson asks.

"Yeah, she does. I might have to talk to her again on behalf of my clients, so like I said, keep my name out of it. I don't want her to clam up on me."

"I got you on that," Caine says.

"Don't worry," Davidson adds.

"I have a feeling if you tell her Edgar Soto was murdered, she'll give you everything she knows."

"Is she your source?" Davidson asks.

"Give me a break, Scott," I say. "And if you have a detail on Amanda, you might want to get one on Justine, too."

"You think she's that involved that she's in danger?" Caine asks.

"I don't think it's that she's that involved, just that she hangs with the wrong people, and that might be enough to get her hurt."

"I'll get one of our marked units to sit on her house until you all get everything worked out," Caine says to Hawkins.

"Appreciate that."

"So you don't think we look at her as another suspect in the Amanda Meyer case?" Davidson asks.

"My opinion, no, she wasn't involved in all that. She's just a girl who wants to have fun."

FIFTY

I feel better since they agreed to provide Justine with a protection detail, so I hold off on giving them Playboy, at least for now. I got an idea for an okeydoke I want to play on him, and these guys'll just get in the way. I need to get with Luna first. I can trust him to keep things to himself, especially if there's something in it for him down the road, like a good bust.

"Have to admit, you know a lot more than we do about some of the players in this investigation," Hawkins says.

"Players? I told you that girl isn't a player."

"You said you have a source. Sounds like a good one, too. You gave us a possible good lead with Columbia Village. Does your source know the decedent?"

"I've got a hundred good sources. All you guys need to do is talk to Justine Durrell on this one, and take it from there."

"So tell us about your conversation with Edgar Soto," Hernandez says out of the blue, and suddenly I'm falling out of love.

"I never said I had a conversation with Edgar Soto. And like I told Davidson, even if I did have a conversation with him, and I'm not saying I did, it'd be privileged information."

"Enough with this privileged information shit," Whatshisname says. "This is a fucking murder case."

"And I'm not trying to hinder that case. If I did talk to him, the only thing we'd talk about is Miriam Gregory, and if he knew where she was."

"And what makes you think there's no connection between the two?" Hernandez asks.

"Very well could be, but unless I find Miriam Gregory, I'll never know. What the fuck's this about, Davidson?" I ask, because it's starting to feel like an interrogation.

Davidson doesn't say anything, like he's deferring to the big boys or, rather, boy and the woman beside him. They all got their position now, except for Caine. He's just a guest.

"What if we told you there's a witness who observed a man in a suit who fits your description. He was with the decedent yesterday," Hawkins says.

"I'd say there's a lot of men in a suit who fit my description."

"I don't know. You don't look like the average bear," Hernandez says.

"This is bullshit, Scott. You know I wanted to talk to him. He was the only lead I had. For that matter, he was the only lead Caine had, and now he's dead. Does wanting to interview the kid make me a suspect in his murder? This is ridiculous."

"I'll give you more of the ridiculous, then," Hawkins says. "We have a witness who saw you fight with the decedent and then force him into his own car and drive off. Does that ring a bell?"

I belt out my best laugh. It sounds genuine, because I'm genuinely taken by surprise. They won't know the difference.

"What, another witness? You said the last one saw a man who fits my description. Now you got one who puts me fighting with the kid? You guys are outta your fucking minds if you think I was involved in something like that."

I look at Davidson again, but he won't look at me directly. I'm starting to worry about whether I'm going to walk outta here. Fact is, it would look like I was having a little scuffle with the kid, and maybe a concerned mother called 911, maybe even got Soto's tag number before we drove off. If a unit did respond, then they'd find it easy enough during the course of the preliminary investigation. Someone could've provided a good description of me, even put me with my car. Another witness possibility is his weed-dealing partner, Greg. He could've seen it go down from the wooded area. Either one of these options would suck.

"Davidson, what're you thinking, pulling me down for some shit like this? You're seriously reaching. If you had me for something like that, then all this would've played out differently and you know it. I'd have had my door kicked in instead of a former old buddy politely asking me to stop by."

"We have your old police photo, and you haven't changed that much. A photo array is being shown to the witness as we speak."

Now I know these guys are amateurs. They shoulda let Davidson run with the interview. He might've had a better chance. They're full of shit, and this is all a fishing expedition. They would've shown that photo array first thing, not waited until I got here. There probably is a witness, and that witness probably did provide a good enough description that led to all this, but the witness couldn't identify me in a photo array, so now they're reaching, trying to okeydoke my ass, like I'm some fucking rookie. Whatever it is they have is circumstantial at best, but I've seen good cases made with less, so I'm still more than a little concerned.

"Next time you want to play my ass, at least do it in the

comfort of my own home. That's where I'll be if your so-called witness pops me in the array. I'm fucking out of here."

I start walking toward the door.

Davidson is the only one to follow me, but he doesn't try to stop me. That's when I know I'm safe.

"Are you sure you want to walk out like this?" he asks.

I stop when I turn to walk down the hall and we're out of the others' line of sight.

I face him and ask, "What the fuck are you thinking, Scott? How could you think I'd have anything to do with that kid's murder?"

"Listen, man, I know you can be heavy-handed at times, but I also know you had nothing to do with the murder. You wouldn't be walking out of here if I thought otherwise. But we both know you talked to Soto. You might've been the last person to talk to him. I just don't understand why you won't share whatever it is you talked about."

"You want something from me, Scott, try asking."

"Okay, then. Was it you who the witness saw with the decedent?"

"No."

I hear a door open behind us. I look over my shoulder, and out walks Deputy Chief Garrett Wightman, the last person I'd want to see right now.

"Now I'm beginning to understand," I tell Davidson.

FIFTY-ONE

Wightman has always had this walk as if he's approaching a microphone on a stage before a large audience. He's wearing a uniform. White shirt and tailored pants, cut just right. The gold badge on the left side of his chest shimmers under the bright fluorescent lights. The right side of his chest is stacked with award bars and special tour bars. And, of course, he's got the hat on his head. That's his pet peeve when it comes to patrol. He had an officer written up once for not wearing his hat after a long foot chase with a robbery suspect.

He sees me right away, and doesn't acknowledge me. It looks like he might even try to walk right through me, but he veers to the right a bit so he's closer to Davidson.

"I'll let him out, Detective. I'd like to have a chat with him first. And I'll need a write-up from you before you leave, so I can brief the chief in the morning."

"Copy that, Chief," Davidson says, looks at me briefly, as if he doesn't have a clue what's going on, then turns and walks back to the main room.

Wightman turns and looks at me with an empty stare.

"You have a special monitoring room in there, Chief?"

He steps closer, like he's ready to slap my face and challenge me to a duel.

"So you're a *private investigator*," he says, enunciating "private" and "investigator" so it sounds patronizing.

The hall is narrow; the only way to the door is through him, and I'm not about to try that. He'd have me on assault with intent to nudge or some shit like that. So I mentally prepare, because he's a man who loves to hear himself talk.

"I know you're crooked, Marr. You always were. They should have let me fire you when I had the chance. You shouldn't have been allowed to retire like a regular officer."

"You got a fucking point, Garrett?"

"I'm getting to it. I know the chief did the right thing by letting you go that way. Reality is, a lot of good cases you and your partners made would've gone south if it got out you had a . . . *drug problem*," he says, with that same extra emphasis on "drug problem," "and I'm sure you still have one. Men like you don't change. So I need to make sure you understand that if you somehow manage to muck this case up for my boys out there, I'll find a way to take away what little retirement we allowed you to have and more." He lets that hang. Not blinking. Calm.

"Don't worry, Marr. No one here knows about your sordid history. In fact, Detective Davidson thinks you're a 'hero,' having rescued that little girl. Some of us know better, though, and that's why you're here. Unlike before, I hate to let you go now and walk out that door. Those agents in there will get to the bottom of it. I only wish I could go to that poor family who you somehow suckered into hiring you and tell them to fire your ass. But we both know I can't do that. You remember the saying, what we all at one time or another told the bad guys that got away—'Time is on our side because this is all we do, twenty-four/seven.' You just make sure you never sleep, Marr. Ever."

"Don't you worry, Chief."

"I'll show you out now."

He turns and does an about-face and I expect a march, but he only walks with short steps to the door and opens it to let me out. I muster my best smile and walk out the door and toward the elevators.

I have a sneaking suspicion that if I were still wearing the suit I wore when I picked up Edgar, this might have played out differently.

The first thing I'll have to do when I get home is toss that suit and dress casually for a while, especially when I'm in Virginia. I'll miss that suit. It means a lot to me.

I push the down button on the elevator.

FIFTY-TWO

I gotta be more careful.

Davidson let me down. It doesn't matter that he doesn't think I had anything to do with the murder; he misled me.

Hell, who am I kidding? I'm guilty as sin, but not for the murder of Edgar Soto. But Davidson doesn't know that, and the least he could've done is give me a heads-up instead of leading me into the lion's den and treating me like a common suspect.

I don't know why they were playing me like that if all they were after was whether I talked to the kid on the day of his murder. I'm fairly certain a lot of it had to do with Wightman putting a bug in Agent Hawkins's ear. Whatever the motivation, it's fucked me up. I feel like I'm being watched, like Wightman had my house bugged. I know it's ridiculous, but I can't stop scanning the living room, checking the light fixtures, the walls, and then my landline. After all, I have experience with this sort of thing.

Fuck, do I hate Wightman. He mistakes order for effectiveness, certainty for smarts. Despite that, I don't hold anything against him having to do with what happened in the past. If I were in his shoes, I would've tried to screw my ass, too. Hell, I deserved much worse than I got back then. Like Wightman said, the private deal I got was about the cases we made, specifically the subjects I placed under arrest over the course of my career. I could not even count. It would be a field day at district court and superior court, though. All those defendants, with all their advocates. I shudder to think about it. Costello's so pissed off at me now that if it ever got out she'd probably jump on the bandwagon.

I also know that I shouldn't have been able to walk out of the U.S. Attorney's Office an hour ago. I'm going to have to be more careful.

Starting now.

I walk up the stairs to my bedroom and find the suit I was wearing. I crumple it up and toss it on the bed. I search my closet and find one more suit of similar color and toss that on the bed, too. I head back downstairs to the living room, where I wad them up; I place the suit jacket I was wearing yesterday in the fireplace first. It's a little chilly outside, so this is nothing unusual, unless I'm being watched. I've burned clothing before. It can take a while, and it stinks. I'm also sure it's not that good for you to inhale, but then again, I put a lot of shit up my nose, so how much worse can this be?

I squirt the jacket with lighter fluid and set it on fire. It gives off a lot of smoke. Too much. I realize I didn't open the fireplace flue, so I quickly pull it open and secure the chain. The smoke still isn't getting pulled up the chimney. I run to the front door and open it to allow ventilation. I can feel a cool breeze being drawn in. After a minute I go back to the living room. The thick smoke is being carried up through the chimney now. I drop a log in there to help it along. It's a bright flame.

After a couple of minutes I drop the pants in and push the log around with a poker.

I sit on the sofa and light a smoke to watch the first old work suit burn. I'm sorry to see it go like that, but I'm happier I didn't wear the one I just bought. I like it better. It fits me well.

When the material burns down enough, I stir what's left of it and drop in the other suit. I sit back on the sofa to watch it burn for a bit, then close and lock the front door, then go to the laundry room.

After I slide the wall open, I grab the bag of money out of the washer. I rearrange a few items on a bottom shelf and carefully stack the wads of money along the shelf. It takes me a while to finish. When I'm done it looks like a small wall of tiny paper tubes stacked one on top of the other.

I notice the pill container of Oxys I took from the house on Kenyon. I open it and take out two, then close up the wall again and head back up to the living room.

I down the Oxys with some bottled water and sit back on the sofa to enjoy the fire.

FIFTY-THREE

I haven't had a rough morning like this in a while.

I soak my head under a hot shower until the headache eases off enough that my frontal lobe doesn't feel like it's trying to force its way out of my forehead.

After my half pot of coffee and a couple of grapefruits, I replenish my supply from the secret wall and grab a couple more of the Oxys from the pill container and a few rolls of currency. I have a feeling it's gonna be a long day.

I call Luna on my cell because I'm still paranoid about the landline. We talk briefly. He doesn't have a clue about what I just went through. I'm sure both he and McGuire have been kept out of the loop because they're close to me.

I set up a meet with him for lunch and ask him if he can give me a couple of PDID photos, one of Angelo and the other one of Viktor. He agrees after I tell him I'll buy.

We meet at a hole-in-the-wall sandwich spot on Florida Avenue NE, a few blocks from Narcotics Branch. It's just Luna. McGuire's papering a case at district court. We all used to frequent this place a lot. The sandwiches are stacked. We'd get them on the go, find a nice spot with a good view, eat them in the car, and feel like taking a nap afterward.

I leave my car parked in the lot and hop in Luna's cruiser. It's a black Ford Expedition. He keeps it clean. The police radio is concealed and built into the glove compartment. He has it dialed into the citywide channel, so unless there's an emergency or some kinda detail, it's relatively quiet.

Luna's idea of a nice view is parking off New York Avenue, near one of those sleazy motels we used to hit all the time, and watching the prostitutes hanging out in the parking lot and on the balconies just outside their rooms after a hard night's work. I could never figure out if it was the view of all the working girls hanging out on the balconies smoking cigarettes and joints, hair up, dressed somewhat normally and not looking so bad from a distance that Luna was after, or if his eye was on work and who they were talking to and meeting up with.

Back in the day, he'd watch through small binos, copy down descriptions of people and vehicles, tag numbers and room numbers, so I'm thinking work, but you never know. We all got our vices. I never asked and I never will.

Sitting watching those women now, I can't help but hope that I might see Miriam. But I know how slim the chances of that happening are. Old-school pimps run most of the girls here. The ones the pimps control usually do the route from New York to New Jersey to here and back again. And most of these girls are older. Some of them try their best to sell themselves as teenagers, but once you get close enough, you realize how off they are. No amount of makeup can hide that shit.

No, Miriam got herself caught up with something else entirely, and unless she was sold off to a pimp, she won't be anywhere around here. The boys on this side of town don't play nice with the guys they refer to as "the Mexicans" or simply "'migos," because as far as they're concerned, all Latinos are Mexican.

I don't have much of an appetite, but try to eat nevertheless. I still got taste buds and the sandwich does taste good, so that helps.

Luna came through with my request and hands me two PDID photos.

"Remember, you get any information on their suppliers, you call me," Luna says.

"You know I will."

"And you're buying at the Old Ebbitt when we go."

"Now you're getting pushy."

"You haven't seen pushy yet, brother. You've been asking a lot of favors of me recently."

"I know. I know. So what do you got working with this Edgar Soto homicide?" I inquire.

"Routine shit. Lot of names on his cell phone we're looking into. Most of them come back to cells, so they're not listed in the Haines phone directory. We got a nice stash of weed out of a storage shed in his backyard. He had it stashed under the lawn mower. No father so I guess he's in charge of mowing the lawn; it seemed like a good spot."

"One of those names on his phone Calvin or Playboy?"

"Playboy is. How the hell did you get that?"

"A girlfriend of the girl I'm looking for is running with him. I interviewed her. His first name's Calvin, but everyone calls him Playboy. The girlfriend knew the decedent. I had a feeling Playboy did, too, and also might be good for information as to my missing girl's whereabouts."

"You give that to Davidson?"

"Fuck no. Well, I gave him the info I had on the girlfriend, but that's it. I don't like the Feds he's working with. They're rookies, and I'm sure they'll find a way to fuck it all up."

"That's a good unit Davidson's with, Frankie. They do good work. It's hard work."

"I'm not gonna argue with that. I know it takes a special person to do the kinda work he does, but this has to be worked like a narcotics investigation. That's my way in."

Luna takes a bite of the pickle that came with the sandwich, chews, and looks toward a group of girls gathered together on a third-floor balcony.

"Look at them there. It's like they think they're on some kind of vacation," he says.

"I'm sure what they're smoking up makes them feel like they are."

He turns away to take a bite out of his sandwich, chews a couple of times, and swallows. I'm surprised he doesn't choke.

"All right, then, you got any other names I should keep on the radar?" he asks.

"Boy named Greg Thomas. He's Edgar's running partner. I think he's worth looking into. And then some kid who I only got a first name on, Robbie. All I know is he's another friend of Edgar's, buys weed from him. Both of them probably involved in his little weed-dealing business, too. You'll roll them easy enough."

"Man, I hate dealing with juvies. Especially the suburban wannabe kind."

"I hear ya there."

"So what's your angle? You expect me to do the work for you?"

"No. I'll do all the work and you'll get all the glory. Don't worry yourself about that. You got anything on Playboy yet?" I ask evenly.

"No. He was a name just like all the other names we're working."

"This Playboy might work the area of Sixteenth and Park,

maybe even live somewhere in 3D. He has short-cut hair and drives a newer-model two-door Lexus. That ring a bell?"

"Can't say it does. I haven't worked that area since you left."

"Okay, here's what I'm thinking. Remember that crackhead we used to use for over-the-phone okeydokes 'cause she had such a sweet young voice?"

"Yeah." He chuckles. "Tamie Darling. You'd never guess such a sweet voice'd come out of something like that."

"You're right about that. You still working her as a special employee?"

"Occasionally."

"I used her once a few months ago to sweet-talk this witness into a meet so I could drop some papers on him. Then I did some spring cleaning and sorta misplaced her number."

"And now another favor. Man, they are piling up."

"This isn't a favor. I told you, you're the one that's gonna reap the rewards. Let me do it the way I do it, and if it's what I think, *you'll* be buying the rounds at Shelly's."

"Go on, then."

"I have good information that this Playboy is distributing narcotics to minors and soliciting minors for prostitution. Also, I know he personally likes his girls very young. I believe he's either the supplier or connected to whoever was supplying Angelo and company. So I'm thinking why not pull the same game we used to back in the day when we needed to lure in a drug boy for a buy?"

"If he was supplying Angelo and his boys, then he's a lot more than a little drug boy. I don't think he'd fall for something like that."

"I agree he might be a bigger player, but he's got this weakness."

"And if he bites?"

"I have a good description and know what he drives. Our girl

232

won't be there, but I will. All I do is follow him back to wherever he might go."

"You're assuming a lot."

"If it doesn't pan out, then it's my waste of time, not yours."

"So you follow him back to wherever—then what?"

"I don't know yet. Gonna have to play that part by ear."

Fifty-four

I set up the meet with Tamie Darling at a safe spot I've used with her in the past. It's a vacant lot on Sherman Avenue, near Howard University. A construction company working in the area uses it to store some of their larger trailers.

I get there early and drive in and park between two of the trailers.

Drug addicts are unpredictable, but they usually make the best confidential informants. Darling makes her living as a special employee for the police department, so she's generally more dependable than most users and takes what she does seriously. Her habit depends on it, so she's very good at what she does, especially role-playing. I was the one to originally sign her up and give her a number, so she still does the occasional job for me. Only difference is I pay more for her services than the department does.

She shows up after about twenty minutes. I notice her in my rearview mirror walking across the lot toward my car. She's still thin as a rail and moves like a drunken model walking on a narrow runway.

I hit the button to unlock the doors. She slides into the front seat with a "Hey, sweetie," and sets her overloaded fake Gucci purse on the floor between her legs.

"How're you doing, Tamie?"

"I'm doin' just fine."

She pulls a pack of cigarettes out of her purse, taps one out.

I fire it up for her with my lighter.

She takes a long drag and blows the smoke toward the partly open passenger's side window.

For a crackhead she doesn't look so bad. She's not homeless, so she wears clean clothes and takes care of herself most of the time. Her dark skin is smooth and relatively blemish free, but she still has that distinctive smell that can only be associated with smoking crack. It's slightly nauseating and sweet and finds its way into their skin, like what they're smoking up is seeping back out from the inside.

"Appreciate you getting here on such short notice."

"No problem, sweetie."

She scoots herself so that her back is leaning against the door-frame and she's facing me.

"You lost some weight since the last time I seen you. Or maybe it's just that I never seen you outta a suit before."

"I'm going casual for a bit," I tell her. "Also might be sitting in this car for a while."

"Starting to feel more retired, huh?"

"That, too."

"So what do ya need from me today, honey?"

"A simple phone call is all, and for that sweet voice of yours to sound like a cute suburban teenager. You think you can manage that?"

"You mean something like this, sweetheart?" she says, trying too hard to sound cute.

"Minus the sweetheart and maybe a little more Caucasian."

"I can do white girl."

"You're gonna be talking to a DC drug boy who goes by the nickname Playboy. He's got a thing for white Virginia high school girls. I'm thinking the more innocent you sound, the better."

"Innocent?"

"Young, sweet, virgin . . ."

"Oh fuck. Virgin?"

"Yeah, white teenage virgin."

"Shit, Frankie, that might have to cost double."

"You pull this off, I'll take care of you. Don't worry about that."

"So like what do you want me to talk about?" she asks, using the kind of voice I'm looking for.

"That's very good, darling. You're calling for a high school friend of yours, Justine. She got herself grounded."

"Justine. Okay."

"I'll write it down for you. But she got herself grounded and her mom took away her cell phone. You talked to her in school today, and she gave you Playboy's number to call him for her and see if he can hook the two of you up with some rock."

"Suburban white girls on crack. That shoulda hit the news. I mean, 'That should be on the news.'"

"These kids hide their lifestyles well. So listen up. Your friend's name is Justine. You go to Lake Braddock High in Burke. Her mom picks her up directly from school, so she doesn't take the bus anymore."

"So why wouldn't she just use my cell phone to call him herself?"

"Good question. Because you wouldn't let her. You want to meet him for yourself. You don't have a crack connection, just weed. But don't overthink it, because he's not gonna. The only thing that's gonna be doing the thinking for him is his dick, but that's only if you can pull this off."

She belts out a throaty smoker's laugh.

"You just make sure to sound sweet and tempting, and all he'll be thinking about is hooking up with that voice of yours."

"What name do I use?"

"Your real name. Tamie. Just don't give him a last name. I don't wanna have to follow him all the way from Virginia, so tell him you have a driver's license and can meet him in Georgetown because you've hung out there before with your friends. You can meet on Wisconsin Avenue where it ends just under the bridge, and you'll be standing right on the sidewalk there."

"But I won't be standing there, right?"

"No, of course not. That's the point. All I want is for him to show up, and then I'll follow him after he gets tired of waiting. Make up a description, like you're short and blond and wearing black jeans or something. But be sure to tell him that you have to get the car back before dinner so you have to meet him right after school at, say, four thirty or so. It can't be later than that or you can't go. And as innocently as possible make it clear that it'll be worth his while to show up."

"Innocent as possible? How the fuck does that sound?"

"Don't use words like 'fuck.' In fact, no cusswords at all."

"That just wouldn't sound natural. What the fuck would he want to do with a girl like that?"

"Tamie, you're a sixteen-year-old white girl from Virginia. That's all you need to be thinking. You watch TV shows, like re-runs of *Friends*?"

"I seen it on occasion."

"Well, it's like the girls on that show, but not the sassy one with black hair, more like the blonde."

"Okay, I think I got it."

"Just don't push the sixteen-year-old girl thing too much or he might get spooked. Lead him just enough to pique his interest and let him ask the questions."

"Okay."

I grab my notepad and write down what she needs to remember. I hand it to her.

"Justine, she's grounded for skipping school. Lake Braddock. You're in the eleventh grade. You're calling from school and on break before class. You want to buy a fifty. She calls crack jellybeans."

"Jellybeans." Tamie chuckles. "That's silly."

"You want to meet him on the corner of Wisconsin and Water right under the bridge, four thirty. Get a description of the car he'll be in."

She sets the paper on her lap. "I got it, but what if he asks what kind of car I'm driving?"

"Tell him it's a newer-model gold Volvo 40. Cops don't use cars like that."

"You got a thing for Volvos, sweetie."

"They're dependable. Now get into character, girl."

"Have I ever let you down, Frankie?"

"Never, darling."

FIFTY-FIVE

I have a few cell phones I use for undercover work. I have one that carries a Virginia area code. I set it to record a message greeting and then hand it to Tamie.

She reads from my notepad, "Hi, this is Tamie and I'm not here so please, please leave a message."

She hands it back to me after it beeps.

"How was that?"

"Good for me. I'll keep your message on here until I'm done with the investigation, so if it doesn't work out today and if he calls back, I might have to get right back with you."

"I'm around."

"Are you ready for the call?"

"Yeah, hold on." She takes a last drag from her cigarette and drops it out the window. "Okay."

I enter his number and tap it to call, then hand her the cell. I can barely hear it ring, and after the third ring a faint, indistinct voice at the other end.

"Is this Playboy?" Tamie asks in a voice that would have me fooled if I closed my eyes.

I lean closer to Tamie to hear as best I can.

"Hi, Playboy. I'm a friend of Justine's."

I can't hear what he says; then he asks, "Who she?"

"Justine, from Lake Braddock High School. In Burke. She said you hooked up a couple of times. She gave me your number."

"Yeah..." The rest is inaudible, so I move back to a comfortable reclining position and light a cigarette.

"She can't call you. She got—I mean, she's grounded and her mom took her cell phone away for skipping school...I don't know how long she's grounded for...No...Okay, I'll tell her to call you when she's not grounded...Yes, she really, really wanted me to call you for a big favor...Well, we were hoping to get what she got from you before—you know, some jellybeans. I can even drive to DC to save you a trip. I just got my license."

I give her a thumbs-up for the "license" part.

"I'm almost seventeen...No, I'm white, I mean Caucasian."

She turns to me and shrugs, like she doesn't understand why he said or asked what he just did. Maybe it's something he can sense, 'cause I wouldn't know the difference if I wasn't looking at her.

"Blond hair. I'm short, but not too short. Justine said you're cute...Seriously...Yes...Well, I'm in the eleventh grade... Uh-huh...I have to go to my next class soon, but I can leave here at three...What's 'five-oh'?" She shoots me a look and smiles because she knows what it really means. "Police?" she asks, and then chuckles, but it's a little more refined than her usual deep-throated cackle. "I'm only sixteen. How can I be the police...? No, seriously. You'll know when you see me...No, that's so silly...Oh, I drive a gold Volvo. My mom bought a new car, so I got this one...Uh-huh...We'd really like to get a fifty...No, just a fifty. That's all we can afford...Oh, I don't know, Playboy." She chuckles again. "For another fifty? Well, yeah, I guess we could work out some sort of trade. Like what are you talking about...? Uh-huh, I can wait till we get together, but I would like to get an extra fifty...Okay, we can talk more then...I don't know where that is. I know Georgetown and was wondering if we could meet there...You know where Wisconsin ends, just under the bridge by the water...? Yes...I go shopping there sometimes with friends, so I know that part of DC...It has to be around four thirty because I have to get home by dinner or I'll get grounded too...Yes, I promise, Playboy...Okay... Okay...I'll see you at four thirty...Oh, wait. What kind of car do you drive, so I can look out for you...? Oh, I like Lexuses, and black is my favorite color...Okay, I'll be standing on the corner right under the bridge...Okay, bye-bye."

She disconnects and hands the cell back to me. I check it to make sure it is disconnected and then put it in the center console compartment.

"He'll be driving a black Lexus?" I ask.

"Yeah, he said it's new. One of the sporty ones."

"Black's your favorite color, huh?"

"Had to make sure he knows that." She grins.

"Well, it sounded like it went well, except for that 'five-oh' part. Talk to me."

She taps out another cigarette and I light it for her.

After a deep draw on the cig, she says, "He asked that typical shit, 'How do I know you ain't five-oh?' but I'm sure he doesn't think I am. Like you said, his dick does the thinking for him."

"Does it sound like he was tight with Justine?"

"Oh yeah, he been getting himself some of that."

"He told you that?"

"He didn't have to tell me that directly. I know a man, and the way he talked about her, I know he getting it."

"What else?"

"He acted all skeptical at first, like he didn't know who I was talking about, but then he opened up."

"What was all that talk about another fifty?"

"He wants to tap a bit of that sweet young Tamie ass is what."

"Straight out said that or insinuated it?"

"Insinuated, I guess. It's not like he said he wanted me to give him head, but that's sure as hell what he meant. I can tell you that for certain."

"So he never asked for sexual favors directly, but you know that's what he wanted?"

"Hell yeah, sweetie. That's what he meant when he said I could trade a little somethin' for the extra fifty."

"You know how to read these mopes. Does it sound like he'll show?"

"Fuck yes he'll show. Like you said, he got a dick that does the thinkin' for him, but the head be too swollen to think straight."

FIFTY-SIX

These things rarely go the way they're supposed to. I'm hoping for the best, though. I get to Georgetown just before three, an hour and a half before Playboy's supposed to show.

Wisconsin Avenue ends at Water Street. Any further and you'll find yourself in the Potomac River. I make a right turn onto Water Street from Wisconsin. It's a small road under the Whitehurst Freeway, and follows the Potomac River on one side and the southern edge of Georgetown on the other. It ends after a few blocks, under the Key Bridge and at the beginning of a busy hiking and biking trail. I don't drive that far. After a couple of blocks I make a U-turn and drive a few blocks past Wisconsin in the other direction. I don't see any cars that match the description of Playboy's Lexus, or anything else that might be suspicious.

Parking is tough anywhere in Georgetown. I loop around a couple of times until I see someone pulling out of a spot on the south side of Water, about half a block from the intersection at Wisconsin. It gives me a good vantage because more than likely he'll come in off Wisconsin, like I did.

I back into the space and park between a nice BMW and a U-Haul van. I'm not concerned about getting made for a cop by the corner drug boys in this location, 'cause you won't find any corner drug boys around here.

When I was a cop fresh out of the academy I had to walk a beat, but not in a place as "up-and-coming" as this neighborhood is now. In fact, nothing was up-and-coming when I came on. It was still like it was when I was a kid. Every neighborhood, including Georgetown, was what it was. But things changed. Everything did. Communities like Georgetown eventually lost landmarks like the Biograph, and then the Key Theatre. But all that resulted afterward was that those businesses were replaced by other businesses.

This city is all about tearing down to build up. That should be DC's new catchphrase. There's nothing wrong with progress. Just know what you're going to do with all the collateral damage resulting from that progress.

I crack the window and light up a smoke while I still can. It's doubtful he'll show up early like I did. In all my experience working idiots like him, they never have; they'll either show up late or not at all. But then again, none of the drug boys back then were showing up for who they thought would be a cute underage girl on crack. Nothin' to do now but stand by and play the waiting game.

I got everything I need in my backpack just in case it turns out the way it's supposed to, and I get stuck on surveillance through the rest of the day into the night. I can go through the whole night if I have to. Shit, I've done it before. I got a strong back and my legs don't cramp that often.

When four fifteen rolls around, I snort the contents of a couple capsules, put them back together, and drop them in the pill container. I check myself out in the rearview mirror just in case a bit of that white powder is stuck around my nostrils or the whiskers of my upper lip. I'm clean. Don't know why I thought otherwise. I've been doing this long enough that I'm damn good at hiding it, but the routine checks have become habit.

It's a busy Friday, so more than a few cars roll by, but I don't see the one I'm looking for. Then, as if right on cue, I see a shiny black Lexus occupied by a black male roll up to the stop sign at Wisconsin and Water.

I recline myself a bit and look through small binos cupped between my hands. He fits the description Justine gave me. He's looking around, obviously trying to spot her. A car behind him honks. It seems to startle him, and he makes a right turn, heading in my direction. I slide down further below the window, but stay up just enough so I can clock him driving by. I sit up and look over my shoulder as he makes a quick U-turn about a half a block down. I scoot down again as he slowly passes my car and pulls to the curb near the intersection in an illegal spot five cars ahead of me. I have to look around the parked cars, so I only get a glimpse of his vehicle. But that's all I need.

He's got his hazard lights on; it looks like he's giving my fictional Tamie a little more time.

Sweet Tamie. She's worth every bill. And there were a couple hundred of 'em.

I start my car up.

It's almost four forty.

The undercover cell in the center console rings. I take it out. It's Playboy trying to call Tamie. It rings through to voicemail. I wait for it, but he doesn't leave one. It rings a second time. Again, no message. He rolls out a couple seconds after that call attempt and makes a left on to Wisconsin. I quickly maneuver my way out and follow.

By the time I turn onto Wisconsin he's almost at the canal.

Another car makes a left turn onto Wisconsin from Grace, cutting in front of me. That's a good thing. Now I'm two cars behind him and that makes for better cover. I cross over the canal and notice that he hit the red light at M Street, but it looks like he's staying on Wisconsin. The undercover phone rings a third time. Boy's sprung, he won't give up on her. I pull to the curb just before the cut that leads to Blues Alley and wait for another car to pass me before I continue to follow him. I change to his lane, but stay two cars behind.

The light turns green and he continues traveling north on Wisconsin. It's getting pretty congested, everyone making their way home early on a Friday. We get caught up in crawling traffic before we hit N Street. I'm still two cars behind.

Traffic clears after the signal. He merges into the left lane and takes a right on Q Street. No more calls on the cell. I think he's given up at this point. I take the right on Q, but slow down to let him get far enough ahead of me so he won't notice my car. If he sees it once I'd better make sure he doesn't see it twice or I'm done, especially if it's going to be a long tail and a possible surveillance afterward. Tailing someone with just one vehicle is tough. You gotta have a minimum of three cars to do it right. I've had a lot of practice, so I'm still pretty confident in my skills.

I allow another car to pull out of a parking space and get in front of me, then hope he travels at a decent speed so Playboy doesn't get too far ahead.

He makes a left on 23rd, crosses Massachusetts Avenue, bearing right onto Florida, headed toward Adams Morgan. Hits a signal at 18th Street and puts on his left-turn blinker, but once the signal turns, instead of heading north on 18th, he crosses it and bears left to stay on Florida. He hangs another and I can see the Third District station on the right. A couple of marked units are parked half a block up.

At this point I'm fairly confident where he might be headed. If it were the area of 16th and Park, where José and his boys used to hang, then he probably would have continued east on Florida to 16th and made that right. Traveling this direction, I'm guessing he'll be headed in the vicinity of 17th and Euclid.

I'm almost a block behind him when he hits Kalorama. The boy's good about obeying the traffic laws. He makes a full stop. By the time I get across Kalorama he's got his right-turn signal on for Euclid Street. I speed up a bit so I can catch up, but hang back when I notice he's moving slower, like he's checking out his 'hood. I double-park on Euclid at the intersection with Ontario and watch him make a left on 17th. I continue slowly and notice him park along the curb on the east side just a few feet from the intersection. Halfway down the block I double-park again. A couple of cars pass me on the left, having to merge into the other lane.

I notice some players hanging on the northwest and northeast corners. Very likely slingin'. A couple of them look like lookouts, so I drive slowly like I'm looking for a parking spot. I got good tint on my car, other than the front windshield, but still I'm not worried so much about being seen once I park.

Playboy steps out of the driver's side, turns to acknowledge one of the players on the northwest corner. He walks between another parked car and the front of his vehicle to the sidewalk. One of the boys, who I make for one of the lookouts, and another boy, walk toward him and they do some handshake shit and start talking.

I make my move and find a space between two cars on the south side of the street, in front of a row house connected to other row homes on the west and a newer three-story condo building where there used to be a mom-and-pop market, on the east. Most of these homes on the south side are good homes. The market used to be run by a Korean family when I last worked the area. I know this area well. It's controlled by Cordell Holm. We used to hit it on a regular basis when I worked narcotics, but despite the arrests and all the drugs and guns we managed to seize, we had little to no impact. It's cleaned up a little, but there's still deals that go down on the streets or the cuts between the school on 17th, and sometimes the lobby area or halls of an apartment complex on Euclid called the Ritz. A lot of the homes in this area are dirty, but nothing I'd want to hit nowadays. And yes, I have thought about it on more than one occasion. Problem is it'd be rare for any of them to be unoccupied for the amount of time I'd need to get in and out. It's nothing like the boys on Kenyon. They didn't do their business on their own block.

Cordell's got family members in several of these homes, cousins and probably grandparents, so it's not anything I'd take a chance on. Doesn't matter how much shit I think I might get out of hitting the right one.

I back in tight and tilt my seat back, but not so much that I don't have a good view ahead of me. I've got a good distance, here.

Playboy meets up with another male subject on the sidewalk in front of a three-story row house with an English basement near the corner. Kid looks like he's twelve years old. After a short chat, Playboy walks the few stairs to the stoop of one of the red-brick row homes and enters. I don't know that home. There used to be a lot of Latino worker-types that rolled in and out of a couple of the houses there a few years back, so I always figured it was either an illegal rooming house or gambling or both.

I grab bottled water from the floor behind the passenger seat and then my flask and palm-size binos outta my backpack. I take a swig from the flask and sit back. I might have to sit for a bit.

FIFTY-SEVEN

Crackheads walking up to the corner like clockwork. The boys taking them down to a cut behind the row home on the corner across from me to do the deal. Every hour or so a marked unit rolls through, making its rounds. It's a unit working the evening shift, occupied by two young officers who look like they're fresh outta the academy. The drug boys don't even disperse when they see them. Couple of them simply spit on the ground before the unit passes, showing the cops they ain't nothin'. I look at them and think about all the ways I can hurt them—physically. These two officers think they're hurting these boys by stepping out once or twice, writing up parking tickets on a couple of cars (including Playboy's), or squarin' up with a couple of them, probably advising them to move on, but all the kids do is walk a few feet, spit on the ground, and find a stoop to sit on. Never did like that spitting-on-the-ground shit. It's disrespectful; but then that's why they do it.

Eighteen hundred hours. I can see northbound and southbound gridlocked traffic on 16th from this distance. Steady traffic making its way up 17th too. Probably commuters thinking they can trim a few minutes off their commute. They cross Euclid, heading toward Columbia Road. Every so often a couple of cars will pull to the corner curb along the crosswalk behind Playboy's car. They make their deals and roll. Not even that obvious. It looks something like a brief conversation between two unlikely friends, followed by a handshake. These boys know a lot of people. A lot of them with Virginia and Maryland tags. I use my binos and note the tags with Virginia plates. A large majority of them are regular-looking people, like they're just getting off work. After all, it is Friday.

A lot of the same type of people, mostly men, are starting to walk up, too. Some of them are wearing suits or looking like they just got off a construction site; the majority of them are walking south on 17th from somewhere farther up the street. A lot of them are taking the stairs to the row house Playboy stepped into. They knock a couple of times and get let in. Some step back out after about fifteen minutes and others after about thirty. Looks like Cordell and crew got themselves into the brothel business.

Most of the parking spots have been taken up by residents of this area, so these folks who are walking either live within walking distance or find parking a couple blocks away, maybe at the parking lot behind the school. There's a driveway that's out of my sight, just a few steps north of the row house, and that leads to the lot behind the school. Police need to run an op here again. Light up some of these mopes. They're so close to a school that the sentence can be double the time. I scan the area, see if I can mark any sign of an op, but then I remember those two officers rolling through like clockwork, and realize maybe not. But then again, when we were running something, we'd never tell anyone. Let everything look like business as usual. Those drug boys spot that marked unit long before it rolls up to the corner.

Evening eventually settles in, and the sky darkens. The street-lamps flicker in unison, with little electric crackles, then settle into a dull, yellowish glow.

The row house has had steady traffic, like there's a previously set-up time for the clients. I don't see some of them exiting, so I'm thinking either they might have some gambling going on or these guys are leaving through a rear door. There's a cut behind those row homes that leads to the driveway and the school lot and the rear of the Ritz.

Hell yeah, Cordell's got himself a good spot to work his dirty deeds. I'm just hoping I'm right that one of those deeds is running teens. I got nice circumstantial shit with Playboy and his connection to Justine, and her friendship with Edgar and, of course, her best friend, Miriam.

Several primary and secondary sirens wailing nearby. Hearing them in the distance takes me back. Stirs up the adrenaline, but only a tiny bit. I need a snort to make me feel better, so that's what I do.

Primary unit being drowned out by all those secondary units. They whoosh close by, sounding like they're on Columbia Road, heading toward 18th. It's the center of Adams Morgan, where all the restaurants and nightclubs are. Might be just a couple of drunks getting started early, or maybe a good street robbery. The lookouts positioned on the corner look in the direction of the sirens; then it's quickly back to business.

I'm starting to feel like the binos are getting suctioned to my eyes. Every so often I break away to check my surroundings. There are a few brave (clueless) people who I make as residents walking by, but I see mostly drunks and homeless crackheads— your basic assortment of street lepers. I'm once again grateful for the windows' nice tint; no one notices shit. I got everything I need in hand's reach, so there won't be any real movement.

I notice a young boy riding a bike south on 17th. He hops off his bike in front of the row house. The corner boys don't seem to acknowledge him. The kid rolls his bike to the steps and leans it against the railing. He walks up the stairs, and before he enters, one of the corner boys yells something at him, and he turns. I can't hear well enough to know what he yells back, but I can make out the kid's face. He's Latino and sure as hell looks like the kid at 16th and Park who always held the parking spot for Angelo.

I grab my notes from my pack and find the names Edgar gave me, including those of the other boys who rolled with Angelo. I find the kid's name: Manuel, but they called him Little Manny.

FIFTY-EIGHT

The sky turns gray and the darkness darker. Night is coming earlier. Fall is a welcome season. Let it bring some of that breezy cool air through this city, so I can roll down the windows on occasion.

Tonight, it's bringing a light rain, but I can't use the wipers. Fortunately, it's not a downpour, so it doesn't obstruct my view through the front windshield. I turn the key in the ignition so I can crack the window open just enough to keep my breath from fogging up the windshield.

I don't know why, but I start thinking about Leslie and wonder what she's got going for the weekend. Usually one, sometimes two of those days would include me. I'm really hoping it will again someday. Not much can bring me down, but this situation with her definitely is. Didn't know I could feel this way. It's like my heart has turned into an aching muscle—poetically speaking. And now since that occasionally overwhelming passion for Leslie has been realized and gone unfulfilled, that pain has found its way to my brain. I think they call it heartsickness, something I have been avoiding for a long time. I'm brave, except when it comes to those "affairs of the heart." I take another swig from the flask, see if that'll help suppress this sensitive side of me.

I focus my attention back on the house. The patio light either has a low-watt bulb or the fixture is dirty as shit, but it's bright enough for me to make out some of the faces as they exit. One of them is Little Manny. He's carrying a white plastic grocery bag with what looks like "Safeway" written on it. He hops down the stairs, scoops up his bike, and rides south on 17th to Euclid. I watch him until I can't see him anymore, as he cuts left in the direction of the Ritz.

I check my watch for the time.

It's rolled by.

Almost twenty-two hundred hours.

Little late for a kid that young. Parents might forgive it if he's bringing home a little something that helps with the food and rent, though. He's carrying something good in that bag. Probably money that's going to Cordell. Narcotics Branch or 3D Vice has gotta know about this place. The chief more than likely has them working on petty shit, like what most of the residents with money are complaining about most. In Adams Morgan that can be anything from panhandling to public drunkenness. I know they're not getting into any long-term drug investigations nowadays. That's what Luna complains about most. The department's definition of long-term is anything that'll take more than twenty-four hours. No one works *cases* anymore.

About an hour after I see the kid leave, I notice two men walking up Euclid from the area I saw him biking into. The two men meet up with one of the crew boys on the corner at 17th. The taller, fatter one looks like Cordell Holm, and the short, stout one looks like his muscle. Can't make out his face, but I'm pretty sure it's Little Monster. He was always like Cordell's second shadow unless Cordell had him go off and do something he didn't want to get caught up in, like beatin' some crackhead, or someone else who couldn't pay, senseless. They enter the row house without knocking, like they own it.

I observe a few other men roll in and out throughout the night. At about one thirty, I see the fat one again. He stands on the stoop as if he's surveying his land. That gives me enough time to focus in on him.

It is Cordell.

He's put on a good hundred pounds since I last saw him. All that takeout his boys must be delivering. His hair is nappy, and he's grown himself a goatee, but he still carries himself the same, despite the weight. He walks back down the stairs and then to Euclid, where he heads east, in the direction he came from. He walks like an inmate in control of the prison yard, but only 'cause his boys are nearby. I watch him until he cuts left and out of my line of sight. He's gotta be going into the Ritz complex. There's not much else in that direction and on Mozart except for a smaller apartment building on the east side, across from the rear of the school. But it'd be easier for him to get to that building walking north on 17th, then taking the driveway and cutting across the parking lot.

He's gotta be bedding down in one of the apartments at the Ritz. Probably even has himself a few units there, including a stash house. It's a tough place to hit and even tougher to get a buy out of, so it'd be the perfect spot. Again, nothing I'd chance hitting. All of Cordell's family and crew members would be breaking outta the walls if I got caught walking the stairs or any of the hallways in that building. Still, it's tempting. I gotta remember why I'm here, though, and it ain't to build up my personal stash.

Damn if I don't start feeling a little like a cop again.

Fifty-nine

The clouds are breaking up and daylight's pushing through.
It's Saturday.

Oh-six-twenty hours.

The corner's clear. A couple of lights are still on in the row house. Blinds prevent me from seeing any movement inside.

Playboy's car is still there. He might have his own girl, or maybe he's dreaming of what Tamie might've been like. Who knows what the fuck Little Monster's doing in there. Wouldn't want to be in a room next to his, though.

I don't want to call it yet. I'd like to see who exits in the morning. They might be using a rear door, making this nothing but a waste of time, but I don't want to chance trying to find a new location to set up. I wouldn't be able to find a good parking spot anyway. It's best to stay put.

I've damn near snorted up most of what I brought with me. Flask is empty and I gotta take a mean piss. Fortunately, the Oxys I've been takin' keep me constipated, so I don't have to worry about that. I find an empty Gatorade bottle on the floor behind my seat. It's still got the cap on it. I keep a couple of empties around for this purpose. They serve me well, since they have a big opening.

I straighten up as much as I can, unzip my pants, pull out my dick, and aim the head in the bottle. It doesn't take more than a second before the bottle starts filling up. Luckily, it's a large bottle, 'cause I nearly top it off.

When I'm done, I twist the cap tight so there's no chance of spillage, and then set it back where I got it. I tuck my dick back into a comfortable position, then zip up.

Minutes later, I see the door open wide. A few seconds after that, a girl steps out. She's shouldering a large handbag. I check her out through the binos. She's Latina. Looks young, too, maybe late teens, early twenties. Hard to tell. I see enough that I know it's not the girl I'm looking for.

She lights up a cigarette and walks down the stairs, turns toward the doorway, and says something in Spanish that I can't make out. She continues toward Euclid, then walks in the same direction as Manny and Cordell.

Just as I focus back on the house, two other girls step out; one of them sure as shit looks like Miriam.

I quickly turn the key in my ignition, but don't start the engine. I just want the battery juice so I can raise my seat back up to a driving position and power down the window so I can hear better.

I go back to the binos as the girl who looks like Miriam zips up her puffy black coat and reaches into the right front pocket, pulls out a pack of cigarettes, taps one out, then lights. She waits for her friend to do the same, and then the other girl closes the front door and they both make their way down the front steps.

I wait for them to make that turn onto Euclid just like the first girl. It's a straight shot for me, so I start the car up and ease out.

My heart is slamming. It's only seeing her that I realize I never thought I'd find her; she was already dead.

By the time I reach the girls, they're walking side by side on the sidewalk near the end of the large row house on the corner of 17th and Euclid. The one that seems to be Miriam is on the other girl's left, so I can't get another good look at her face.

The Latina girl beside her turns in my direction to check me out. I pull ahead of them and double-park alongside another car.

I step out of the car and walk across the street at an angle to them, but I don't look in their direction. I can see them enough to know they stopped as if they are expecting me to approach them.

When I get to the sidewalk I turn and shoot them a smile and then look toward the Ritz, which is about a quarter of a block up. I turn back. They're still standing there, about ten feet away.

"Aren't the two of you a little young to be out so early?" I ask.

"Fuck you," the girl who I'm now almost positive is Miriam says.

The Latina girl reaches into her bulky purse like she's trying to scare me with what she's going to pull out.

"Hold on there, girl," I say. "I'm a cop. See?" I pull out my wallet and flash my badge quickly.

"Cops don't drive cars like that," the Latina girl says.

"They do when they're off duty."

"Why you stoppin' us, then, if you're not working?" the Latina girl asks.

"I ain't stopping you," I say, walking closer.

They don't step back, but the Latina girl still has her hand in her purse.

"But I might if you don't take your hand outta that purse."

She does, but reluctantly.

The other one is Miriam. I'm positive. But she's definitely not the same little girl from the photo. She looks used up and a couple years older than she really is.

"We're going home," Miriam says.

"You guys have a sleepover or somethin'?"

They laugh.

"How old are you two?"

"Old enough," Miriam says.

"Neither of you look old enough to be walking around this neighborhood so early in the morning. Give me your names."

They look at each other.

"I ain't playin'. Give me your names."

"My name's Angie," the Latina girl says.

"I'm Justine," Miriam says.

I almost break into a smile.

"No last names? Never mind. It doesn't matter."

I step closer. Miriam looks like she might bolt. I've seen that look enough times to know.

I'm close enough to grab her by the arm. Instead, I look at her. "Justine's a nice name. I have some friends who have a daughter named Justine. They live in Burke."

She looks like she's just been stunned. She drops her cigarette and runs back toward 17th. The Latina girl quickly follows.

It doesn't take much effort to catch up to Miriam. I grab her by the left arm before she can make the turn toward the row house. The Latina girl stops ahead, looks back, and then runs off toward the row house.

Miriam's struggling hard, then starts flailing her free arm, smacking me in the face.

"Let me go! Let me the fuck go!"

"Calm down, Miriam. Calm the fuck down."

"Help!" she screams. "Someone help me!"

"Yeah, you call out like that. Get the police to show up. That'll make it easier on me. Now calm the fuck down."

I grab her other arm and force her to face me.

"I'm a friend of your parents," I lie. "They sent me to find you."

"Let me go. You can't take me."

"Either I take you or we wait for the police cars to show, and they will. That'd be tougher for you, 'cause they'll take you straight to Youth Division. Either way, you'll be going home."

I let go of her left wrist, hold tight to the other, and force her to walk toward my car. She tries to pull away.

"Please, just let me go."

I stop again.

"Why don't you wanna go home? They abuse you?"

"Fuck no."

"Then why?"

Before she can answer I see the other Latina girl at the corner, about twenty feet away. She's pointing at us, looking back, as if she's directing someone. Couple seconds later, I see Little Monster run up, with another Latino boy. A second after that, Playboy makes his appearance.

I grab Miriam with my left hand now and pull her to my side. I pull my jacket back and grip my holstered weapon.

"Don't even fucking think about it," I tell them. "She's going home."

"Don't let him take me, Playboy," she cries.

"Shut the fuck up, girl," Little Monster orders her. He turns to the Latina girl and says, "Get yourself back to the house."

She runs back. Little Monster's smart, but not that smart.

He reaches for his back pocket. I draw my weapon and aim it at him.

"Don't go stupid on me," I tell him.

"Ain't nothin'." He smiles wickedly.

He slowly pulls out a cell phone, holds it out for me to see.

"Just back the fuck down," I order. "There's been enough commotion that the police'll be showing up soon. Might be better if I wait."

Little Monster lifts the cell to his ear.

I look behind me toward the Ritz, then start pulling her back toward my car. I don't know who the fuck he might be calling, but I sure as hell don't wanna see any more of them. Little Monster is speaking to someone on the cell. When he's finished, he slips it in his back pocket.

He shows me that wicked smile again.

"Let me go. Let me fucking go," she demands, but quieter this time.

"Listen to me," I tell her, and squeeze her wrist hard so she grunts. "You'll get hurt much worse if I let you go back to them."

"They're about to hurt you real bad, asshole. You'd better let me the fuck go."

"C'mon, now. Let me take you outta here. I'll even take you to Justine's if you want."

A couple more players show up, and I'm starting to feel like this is going to be a real clusterfuck. I'm hoping whatever good neighbors live on this block have already called the police. I'm sure as hell looking forward to hearing some sirens about now.

"This ain't a joke, Miriam. They don't want you now that I've been here. I know you've seen what they can do."

She might agree, 'cause she doesn't struggle anymore. I get to the driver's side door and open it.

Some of the corner boys start stepping toward me, but not Little Monster or Playboy.

"You're gonna step in first, and I'll follow."

I notice a black Ford Taurus stop at the corner on 17th, behind the crowd. These boys make cars to look like ours, so I'm think-

261

ing this looks like it might be a drive-by. I back up with her so we're on the other side of the open door and she's toward the front of my car.

A few of them, including Little Monster, turn to take notice.

"Get your crew off my fucking corner, Little Monster," a man orders from within the car.

Little Monster spits on the sidewalk toward the car. Stands his ground for a second or two, and calmly walks away. The rest follow and they disappear up 17th.

I notice a red bubble light on the dash. It starts flashing as the cruiser turns onto Euclid and stops about two car lengths behind my vehicle.

The driver's side door opens and a large man steps out. A silver officer's badge hangs around his neck.

Plainclothes. That's all the cavalry I need to see.

SIXTY

"Let me see your hands," the large officer commands.

He's on the other side of his open door, weapon out and pointing at me. His view is obstructed by the open car door we're standing behind, so it allows me to slowly holster my weapon without getting noticed (and possibly shot). I keep my hold on Miriam.

"This girl's a teenager, reported missing by her parents," I tell him.

"I said show me your hands. Now."

He's calm and in control.

He keeps his hair high and tight, like most guys who come on this job straight out of the military. He looks familiar, but too young for me to have known when I was on the job.

"I'm not going to let go of the girl, because she might run."

"I'm not going to run," she says calmly, maybe a bit too calmly given the circumstances.

"I'll slowly step from behind the car so you can see I'm not armed."

"Nice and slow."

I obey and sidestep from behind the car, with Miriam at my side.

"Now let go of the girl until I can establish you're a cop."

Establish I'm a cop? What the fuck's he talking about? Unless he saw everything go down. Was he working an observation post too?

Then it hits me and it's like a mental crash.

He's one of the men I observed entering the row house late last night. It's too early for day shift, so he has to be working midnights; I'll bet that's his little hoochie mama's spot. I'm betting he's the one Little Monster called. He got here quickly enough. He's more than likely taking care of that spot for Cordell and he's dirty as shit.

Fuck.

"Her parents hired me to find her. I'm a retired DC police detective."

"Retired?" Miriam blurts.

"I got her real name and DOB. Go over the air with it. You'll find she's reported missing out of Fairfax County."

"Let her come to me. I'll run her name in my cruiser."

"My name's Frank Marr. I retired two years ago, out of Narcotics Branch. You can raise Detective Scott Davidson over the citywide channel. He's on the case, and should be coming on for daywork about now. He'll come down here and straighten this out."

He steps out from behind his door, weapon still on me. He moves forward a couple of feet like a well-trained tactical officer.

"If you need to go over Detective Davidson, then raise your watch commander to respond. I'll release the girl to your supervisor. I'm responsible for her; that's all I'm saying."

He looks at me like he's running everything through his

head. The situation fucked all around, and the last thing I want is for him to realize he messed up and called me out as a cop. In fact, maybe he already realized that and he's trying to figure out how to get out of this one—I'm hoping he wants to get out of it clean.

"Officer, I know you're all about doing the job right. This isn't your normal run. This girl's gonna bolt if I let her go."

"I told you, I'm not going to run. Just do what he says and let me go."

"So raise your watch commander over the air and you'll be the hero for getting her home."

"Daywork's about to come on. Midnight's already rolled in, so walk her over to me and I'll sit her in the back of the cruiser for the shift change. We'll call my supervisor after."

Somehow I doubt that, but what choice do I have? This is seriously fucked up.

"Just come fucking get me, Tommy," she yells.

"Shut the hell up, girl. Shit."

I grip her wrist tighter.

"Ow," she says.

"Officer, I don't care what you got working here. I just want to get her home. You got a lot of lights coming on in a lot of these homes, and I'm sure a lot of residents watching all this through their windows. Units are probably already on their way. Just let me get her in the car and we'll roll outta here."

"No. Don't let him do that," Miriam cries.

"I said shut up," he orders her again. "Now, you're going to let her go and she'll walk to me, and then you can get in your car and roll out of here."

I let her go, I'll probably find myself kissing the pavement, maybe even kissing my own blood. We got ourselves a standoff here, because he's not going to do anything stupid while I got her close. At least I hope he's not. I sure as hell ain't gonna let her go. I know that much.

A fucked-up-looking hooptie with a loud engine, Virginia dealer tags, and tinted windows eases to the stop sign at 17th.

The officer turns to watch it, his gun still pointing my way, but the hooptie doesn't seem to bother him. He turns back to us.

"This is the last time I ask; then I'll come for her myself. You don't want me to do that, so let her go."

The hooptie turns slowly onto Euclid and moves our way.

I can see Playboy driving. The passenger is leaning back, so I can't make him out.

I start moving back to the front of my car for cover.

"Don't move," he commands.

I notice a barrel of a weapon, like a TEC-9, barely out the passenger's side window of the hooptie.

"They got a gun!" I yell out.

He turns, but it's too late. Bullets spray, cartridges ejecting out of the window.

I push Miriam on the ground in front of my car and yell to her, "Stay down!"

The officer doesn't have time to get a shot off. I see his feet falling out from under him as he takes a hit.

I don't have time to draw my weapon. I hear the bullets whizzing by, too fucking close, hitting my car door, shattering windows. I dive over the hood of my car, sliding belly-first across it. I slam my left shoulder against the front door of a car I'm double-parked beside, and then land on the pavement hard, wedged between the two vehicles.

Breath escapes me for a second.

I turn to grab Miriam and pull her in to me, but she's already crawled around to the other side of another car parked in front of the one I landed against. She's in a fetal position on the curb near the front tire, cradling her head with her hands.

That's a safe place, I think to myself.

Bullets still popping out car windows above me now, and then the windshield. I manage to get my gun out, but can't position myself safely to fire or to get to Miriam.

"Stay down, Miriam! Stay down!"

I tuck down and scoot myself back toward the rear of my vehicle. The hooptie's made its way past my car, so I side crawl around the rear end of it, but by that time the shooting's stopped. Suddenly. All in a matter of seconds.

I poke my head out and see the car making a left turn on Mozart. It's gotta be fifty yards, but I still take aim.

Too many buildings beyond the target.

I don't like the possibility of what a stray bullet can do so I tuck my weapon to a ready position.

I look around the area for any other threats, and then back toward the officer. He's now splayed beside the front end of his cruiser.

Miriam is still hunched down at the curb.

I run back to her.

She turns, and looks up at me. A shocked expression, like she thinks I'm gonna hurt her.

"You okay?"

She nods several times, obviously terrified.

"They might come back around. You stay here where it's safe!" I order her.

I make my way to the officer.

His weapon is on the pavement just under the front bumper of his cruiser, arm's length from his body. The clothing around his chest area is soaked with blood. No head wound. I carefully place my left hand under his head and roll him onto his back.

His eyes are open and he's breathing, heavy labored wheezing breaths, but he's still conscious.

"I'm gonna unbutton your shirt," I tell him.

As I do, I notice his T-shirt is drenched with blood. He's not wearing a vest.

Looks like two or more rounds hit him center mass. Blood bubbling from the right side of his chest.

He mumbles something I can't make out.

"I'm gonna need your radio to call for help," I say.

I grab his radio and key it in. "Officer down. Officer down. Seventeenth and Euclid. Get an ambulance here."

"Keep focused on me, buddy," I tell him.

He nods, but with effort; then his bloodied mouth opens and he struggles to speak.

"Help's on the way," I assure him again.

Then I hear something behind me, in Miriam's direction. When I look up I see her running across the street.

"Motherfuck."

I turn my attention back to the officer but it doesn't take me more than a second to realize he's not my concern.

"Help's on the way," I say again, and then I bolt.

By that time she's across the street and near the front entrance of the Ritz. *All that adrenaline made her fast.* I yell for her to stop, and hope with everything I got the hooptie hasn't rounded the block to finish the job.

"Miriam!" I shout.

She opens the glass front door with a key, runs inside, and quickly closes it behind her.

I get to the door. I see her run across the lobby area and toward an opening on the right that leads to stairs.

I yank at the door. It's strong. I yank it harder, but this time with both hands and all my weight.

All that does is make a loud metallic noise and wrench my fingers.

"Fuck it," I say.

I pull out the Taurus from my backside and think about shooting the lock. I realize how stupid that'd be so instead I smash out the pane of tempered glass with the butt of the gun. I have to jump back to let the large shards fall.

With the gun in a tucked position I run into the lobby and make my way through the opening. It's early enough in the morning that no one is around.

Stairs ahead of me that lead up to the first floor.

To the left, a narrow hallway and another door.

I got here fast enough that I should be able to hear her running if she's taking the stairs.

I can't, so I take a chance that she hit the back door instead.

A metal fire door opens to a furnace room. In the back there's another metal door with an "Exit" sign above it.

I open it and see Miriam at the top of a tall metal gate with a chain wrapped around the middle securing them together with a padlock on the outside.

She's straddling the top, lifting her skinny left leg over. I holster my weapon in my backside. It's not far so I get there quick, but by that time she's jumped to the other side.

I reach my arm through the gate in time and manage to grab the sleeve of her jacket.

"Let go!" she screams. "Let me go!"

"Why the fuck you running like this?"

"Fucking let me go!" And she starts hitting me on the arm with her other hand while trying to strip herself free of the jacket. Then she bends down, mouth open, and before I can react she's sunk her teeth into the exposed skin just above my wrist.

I belt out, "Fucking shit, you bitch!"

I can almost hear her sharp teeth break through my skin. My immediate reaction is to reach my other hand between the bars and knock her silly, but by that time she's already let go. She struggles harder now, hitting the arm she bit me on.

She squirms her way out of her jacket. Shoots north on the sidewalk toward the back of the school, the same direction the hooptie was headed.

I drop her jacket on the other side of the gate, look up the fence to make the climb. Miriam's feet are smaller so she was able to get them through the bars. I grasp high, let my breath go and manage to squeeze my toes in, just enough for purchase, and then take hold of the top of the gate.

I crawl over and slide myself down to the other side. The sleeves of my shirt and jacket have fallen back over my wrists.

I visually search the area where I saw her run.

Can't see her.

It's a long block and I'd see her running along Mozart if that's where she was. She more than likely cut left and through the rear parking lot of the school that faces 17th.

I rush toward the driveway that leads to the back of the school and look across the parking lot. I'm not going to find her this way, it's ridiculous. I need to get in the car. Get the police to hit the area with me. But first, I pull up the sleeve of my jacket to check out my throbbing arm. My shirt sleeve is soaked with blood, but the bite's not so bad I need to give it immediate attention.

I shake my head, feel like I wanna scream. Instead I hightail it back to the gate and grab her jacket. I search the pockets and find a pack of Newports and three clean syringe needles with plastic covers.

I look at the needles and realize this shit alone'll keep her from wanting to go home.

Sixty-one

Sirens in the distance, like angels sounding horns. I remember before the shooting the officer said it was a shift change. That's why it took them longer than normal.

Best thing I can do now is get back to the scene and the fallen officer. Miriam's got to be wandering around somewhere. It's cold and she doesn't have her jacket. If she's on the street, the cops will find her. Hopefully before Cordell's boys do.

No blood that I can see along Miriam's running trail or her hiding spot at the curb. That's a good sign.

Sirens are closer.

There's a cab on Euclid and 17th. I notice the driver on his cell phone. When he sees me over the cop, he makes a quick turn onto 17th and speeds north.

No one else is around. They know enough.

The officer doesn't look so good now. His eyes are glazed over, and with every short breath a deep-throated gurgling sound.

"Miriam got away from me," I say.

"Miriam?" he asks with effort, like what the fuck am I talking about?

"The young girl I was holding on to. The reason you were here. Is there another place she might stay?"

The cruisers are very close. The sound of the sirens seems to fold around us.

"Where would she go, Tommy? Let me get her. Take her home. You know they're gonna kill her."

"University," is all he says.

"What do you mean? What university?"

He mumbles something unintelligible again.

"I don't know what you're saying."

He takes in another short breath then, "Don't tell . . . please," almost like a little kid pleading with a friend.

"Where can I find the girl, Tommy? A safe house?"

"Please," he says one more time.

"I got you, brother. I'm not gonna say shit. What university?"

Cruisers are speeding up Euclid from 16th against the one-way sign.

Loud sirens, the sweetest sound in the world right now for him, but not for me, 'cause he didn't give me shit.

Officers roll onto the scene from all directions, blocking off the whole area around us.

"Your boys are here now. You're gonna be okay."

Sixty-two

I'm sitting on a chair with roller wheels at an empty cubicle in the 3D detectives' office. The only thing I got with me is my backpack. My Volvo's still on the scene. Knowing what I got on me and inside my backpack makes me more than a little paranoid, but I wasn't about to leave it in my car 'cause that'd give them an excuse to search it. I'm not a suspect so unless I do or say something stupid they won't even think about it. A crime-scene tech had to take my weapon, though, see if I shot it.

It's been a while since I've been in here. Last time was when we worked a case with a couple of district detectives and we used the office to stage for a search warrant we were about to execute.

This office still stinks.

The interior was recently remodeled, but even the new carpet, fresh paint, and fancy cubicles can't remove the human depravity this place has managed over the years. You can lose the stains, but the odor still remains. It'll always be preserved in this structure, and now, my sinus membranes. The only thing this renovation has accomplished is to add a sickening sheen to an already foul place.

The two officers who took the report have left. I'm not only a witness, but a victim. I've never been a reported victim of anything before. I've been shot at before, but never reported it. I've been shot at on the job, too, even stabbed once, straight through my love handle on my left side. "Victim" is a term given to someone who never had to take an oath. A soldier can't be a victim, and neither can a cop. Regrettably, I'm no longer a cop, so I'm now a reported victim of assault with intent to kill.

A couple of homicide detectives questioned me afterward. I know one of them. Tim Millhoff. He's a good dude. Almost twenty-five years on the job. He told me they were on it because the officer, Tommy, is at MedStar in critical condition.

I told them exactly how it went down but left out a couple of things. I'm honoring the officer's request and didn't give up how I saw him entering the brothel and not exit for a while, and then how Miriam called him out by first name. I told them about the "university," but made it sound like it was something I learned earlier, from a source on the street.

If Tommy didn't get himself shot, I'm sure he could've argued that he had a complaint on the row house from an anonymous neighbor, and so he had to check it out. No, I didn't go there. I simply said he must've been nearby because he got there quickly. Probably because it was close to checkoff and he was just sitting in his parked vehicle. I said he was doing his job, but it went down so fast he couldn't react quickly enough. He paid the price for his dirty deeds. Why make him pay more?

As far as Miriam calling him out by first name, if I were him I'd simply say that it's my beat and I know all the people on my beat. I know better, though, and maybe he asked me not to tell 'cause he knew I did.

I also advised Millhoff that Little Monster was the shooter, even though I wasn't completely certain. But from what little bit I can remember, I'm confident now that he was.

Millhoff asked me to stand by. He said Davidson and the agents he works with are on their way.

A couple of young plainclothes officers enter to talk to Millhoff and his partner. They're standing a couple of cubicles behind me, near a door that leads to a hallway and the Vice office. The skinny one with red hair says something about the Ritz. Millhoff looks my way and then walks over.

"They're from Vice. The whole unit canvassed the shit out of the Ritz. Knocked on every door and even got a couple of other good witnesses who saw it go down from their apartment windows. Uniformed officers did the same along Seventeenth and Euclid. All in all we got some witnesses who can verify most of your story. There is this thing about you dragging the girl to try to get her in your car and then pulling your weapon out at a crowd that gathered at Seventeenth and Euclid."

"Every retired cop in DC carries a weapon, and as far as that crowd, I told you what they were about to do before the officer showed up."

"I don't have a problem with all that. Those witnesses could only see the action, not what was being said. We talked to the girl's dad, so it's all good that you were hired by him. Sorry to say, though, there's nothing on the girl. One witness saw her run up Mozart, but then out of sight."

"I'll give the father a call after we finish up here. The good news is she was last seen alive."

"Maybe you want to word it differently."

"I got a little tact left," I say without humor. "She used a key to get in the Ritz. I'm confident that's where she was keeping herself."

"I'm sure she's not using her real name, and no judge is going to give us a search warrant for every unit in that complex, so the only thing to do is keep knocking on doors and canvassing the area. I keep wondering, though: Why the hell did she run? You think maybe she was being abused at home?"

"No, nothing like that. It's a good family. Bad drugs just got the best of her, that's all. And we both know how this is probably going to turn out for her," I say. "What about that info I gave you about her possible connection to a university?"

"They're working that."

"Maybe one of the universities has one of those outreach programs for prostitutes."

"That's a good one. I'll be sure to let them know."

"Maybe even some sort of GED class for high school dropouts."

"I'll talk to Davidson about all that. He probably knows. Listen, you've just been through the shit, and you need to take it easy. We're on this."

I've never felt so powerless. This is fucked up.

"Oh, and that row house was cleaned out," Millhoff begins. "The only one there was an old man who said he didn't know shit. It was obvious something illicit was going on there. Illegal rooming house, prostitution, gambling. I don't know. Probably all that and more."

"What about Cordell and his crew?"

"They cleared the fuck out of that area. I'd be surprised to see them back anytime soon."

"Give them a few days. Cordell makes too much money off that corner to just let it go. Most of them will be back, except for Little Monster and the driver. They'll be in the wind for a bit."

"Yeah, I know you're right about that."

"Any word on the officer?"

"Naw, he's still in surgery. I'll let you know."

"What about my car?"

"When they're done processing it, I can have it towed back here for you. I know you don't want it to go to our lot, right?"

"No. I'd appreciate if you'd get it here. If it doesn't drive, I'll get it towed myself."

"Want some of this shit they call coffee?"

"I'm good. Thanks."

"All right, then. I'll get back at you."

Millhoff gets a call on his cell shortly afterward. He and his partner both walk past me and into the office where the detective sergeants have their desks, while he's still talking on the cell.

The only thing I hear when he passes is, "Fuck, I'll hit you back from a landline."

Sixty-three

I'm starting to crash. I get a soda out of the machine in the lobby, but it's no use.

Davidson is carrying a case jacket as he walks in with his partner, whose name I still can't remember. Agent Hernandez follows behind them.

Hernandez is not dressed tactically like she was the last time I saw her. She keeps her tiny FBI badge clipped to her belt and her sidearm in a brown holster on her right side.

"Sorry it took so long," Davidson says. "We were at the branch working some leads with McGuire and Luna. Where are Millhoff and his partner?"

"Sergeant's office over there," I direct him, tilting my head to the left.

"Be right back."

He and Whatshisname walk into the office. Hernandez remains.

"Where's your boy?" I ask.

"You mean Hawkins?"

"You got any other boys?"

"He's the main one."

"You got anything on the Soto murder yet?"

"We're working a few things."

"Don't worry. I get it. I'm not a part of the club anymore."

She gives me a half smile, like she agrees.

I do feel like getting under her skin. Maybe it'll take my mind off the crash I'm facing.

"I bet you're real good in the box," I say.

She furrows her brow.

"I mean the interview room."

"You remember why you're here, right? An officer was shot."

"Yeah, I remember. Not gonna forget it either."

"Maybe you should show some respect."

"He got my respect on the scene when I was holding him."

She turns like she's about to walk away.

"You had me going when we first met. I didn't have a clue what you guys were really up to. You played me well."

"We weren't up to anything."

"If I had anything to confess to, you'd be my first choice."

"I'm glad you feel that way. There's an interview room right there if you want to step in," she says.

"It's not cozy enough. And I think you know I had nothing to do with that kid's death."

Before she can answer, Davidson, Millhoff, and their partners walk back over. Millhoff is carrying a folder.

Millhoff and Davidson roll up a couple of chairs and sit.

"McGuire and Luna put together a couple of photo arrays," Millhoff tells me. "Do I have to go through the whole spiel, or can you just look at the photos?"

"I've given the 'spiel' enough times to still have it. Just lemme see what you got."

He hands me an eight-by-ten printout from Live Scan. It has three rows of nine PDID photos. It doesn't take more than a second before I point to the fourth photo on the second row.

"That's Little Monster. He's the shooter," I say with certainty.

He hands me another sheet with photos that are possibilities for Playboy. I look it over, but don't see him.

"No," I say. "He's young. Maybe there's a juvie photo on file."

"We'll look into that," Davidson says.

"Or maybe he's a lucky one and hasn't been arrested yet," I add. "You find his Lexus and have some good tac officers sit on it, he'll show. That car's his baby."

"We'll look into everything," Millhoff says. "We get something, then we might have some more to show you."

"I'll be around."

I hate to say it, but I'm glad they don't know who he is. I want that little fuck Playboy to myself. He doesn't know that I know about his prized shiny Lexus. Seventeenth and Euclid is hot now, so he'll go to another spot they have. And yet again, I'm in a race with my former colleagues.

SIXTY-FOUR

Millhoff and his partner are back in the sergeant's office, writing up an affidavit in support of an arrest warrant for Rodney Biggs, aka Little Monster. Millhoff's doing a write-up on the computer. Hernandez and Davidson's partner went to pick up pizza. The only reason I'm still here is I'm waiting to hear about the officer and the result of the canvass being done for Miriam Gregory.

My phone battery's burned out.

"What time you got?" I ask Davidson, sitting in the cubicle beside me.

"Almost fifteen thirty," Davidson advises. "How you doing over there?"

"I'm good."

Millhoff and his partner walk in.

"They found the shooter's car," Caine says. "In an alley off Wiltberger, behind the old Howard Theatre. It was still burning when fireboard got there."

"Damn," is all Davidson says.

"Well, you knew that was going to happen, right?" I say.

"Yeah, pretty much," Millhoff says. "Needless to say, we probably won't find shit out of that vehicle."

"You gotta ask why there, though?" Millhoff's partner asks. "They have a bad history with the crew at Seventh and T."

"That's probably why they chose that spot, then," I say.

The rear door opens, and in comes the chief himself, along with his sidekick Wightman. I'm starting to wonder why I didn't get the hell out of here while I still had the chance.

Davidson stands.

Wightman motions with his head for the three of them to come over. They obey and walk behind the last row of cubicles and toward the television that's secured to the corner wall.

The only parts of them I can make out are their heads.

A few minutes later, they all break up. Wightman and the chief both exit the way they came in, not giving me a passing glance.

Millhoff, his partner, and Davidson walk back.

"The officer didn't make it," Millhoff says.

"Damn, I'm really sorry to hear that."

"What's up with you and Wightman? He wants us to charge your ass for the concealed weapon," Millhoff says.

"We got some bad history. Not even worth saying more than that. And what the fuck does he think you can charge me with, anyway? I'm authorized to carry my weapon under HR218. The permits are all up to date. I even got an extra license to carry as a PI, through Security Officer Management. Or maybe you got destruction of property for me having to smash out the windowpane at the Ritz?"

The only thing Wightman might try to screw me on is my right to carry, but I'll worry about that when and if it happens.

"Marr, even though you're working for a defense attorney, I still consider you one of us. But what the fuck's with that? Do some consulting work or something. Why a defense attorney?"

"There's history there, too, but it's good history. My pension's worth shit, so I have to work. And you know I'm not the only re- tired cop doing that kind of work."

"All I'm saying is Wightman's got it out for you, so you need to tread lightly."

"I'm used to walking that way, brother. And I'm really sorry about Tommy."

"You knew his name?" Davidson asks.

"Yeah, we talked a bit after he got shot."

"Anything I need to know?" Millhoff asks.

"Only that he was a good officer."

I know I should be pissed at the officer. He's the reason I lost Miriam. But I still can't give him up, because I don't know the full story. It might be a good story, too. So I'll allow him some honor in death and all the ceremony that'll soon come with it.

I don't think I'll be staying for that pizza, though.

SIXTY-FIVE

My car's a bullet-riddled mess. Both the passenger's and the driver's side windows are blown out. I stopped counting how many bullet holes the body and the front windshield sustained. And then there's the interior. I notified my insurance company and had it towed to the dealership I bought it from. I'm carless, but that's going to have to change, 'cause I need a car to work this case through.

I hoof it back home. It's a straight shot to my house from the Third District, maybe a fifteen-, twenty-minute walk.

First thing I do when I get there is plug my phone in to get a charge. After that, I grab some gauze, antibiotic cream, medical tape, and alcohol out of a medical kit I keep in the kitchen. I return to the living room and turn on the television for the four o'clock news. The shooting is the top item. Every fucking local channel. They got another Amber Alert out for Miriam, something that was already done months ago, but because of the shooting, her photo is all over the place. I'm hoping the cops find her. It'll make it easier on me. I never wanted to work this shit in the first place.

The bite wound bled through my shirt, but fortunately not all the way through the sleeve of my jacket.

I roll up the sleeve. Her teeth cut dents into my skin like red dashes that make an oval shape. Not bad enough for stitches, but it'll still sting like hell. It's not the first time I've been bit, but I still worry about what disease might have creeped into my blood-stream.

I wince after I douse the wound with alcohol. Then I dab it with gauze until it's clean, rub the cream on, and place fresh gauze over the wound and secure it with tape.

I'm seriously craving some blow about now, but I fight it. No amount of coke will keep my body from breaking down real soon.

When my phone has enough juice, I turn it on.

I got messages. Two of them are from Miriam's father, and one is from Leslie.

I listen to her message first.

"It's me. I saw the news and Miriam Gregory's photo, so I'm sure you were involved in that terrible shooting. Just want to make sure you're okay. Call me when you can. Bye."

Damn, it feels good to hear her voice. I'm not ready to call her, though. As hard as it is right now, the way I'm feeling, I need to call Ian Gregory.

He answers the phone immediately. He sounds distraught, tired.

"Frank Marr here, Mr. Gregory."

"Yes, I know."

"I'm sorry I couldn't get back to you sooner."

"I spoke with the police. They filled me in as much as they could. I was hoping you might have something more."

"What did they tell you?"

"That you and a police officer had my daughter, but there was a . . . a shooting and she ran away."

"I'm afraid that's about it. I want you to know that I didn't find any sign that she might have been injured."

"You mean like . . . blood?"

"Yes. Has anyone else contacted you?"

"No."

"I'm sorry I let her go," I tell him, realizing too late that you never apologize. It's something I learned as a cop. Use any other words, but never apologize like it's your fault. But then again, I'm not a cop anymore. "I'm going to find her."

"Mr. Marr, maybe at this point I should leave it to the police. I mean, they seem to be really on top of it now."

"Yes, they are. I can assure you of that, but I'm going to stay on it all the same. It's on my time now, not yours."

"I don't expect you to do that."

"I know, but it was made personal. The police will do what they do, and I'm going to do what I have to do."

No response.

"Mr. Gregory?"

"Yes, I'm here."

"I'm going to find your girl."

I hear him begin to sob.

"We'll talk soon, okay?"

"Yes, okay," he says, a bit broken.

I disconnect, lean back on the sofa, and light a smoke.

What the fuck did I just do, making a promise like that?

SIXTY-SIX

After twenty-four hours missing, especially under these circumstances, the chances of finding Miriam again are slim to
none. So I gotta get up and move.

Despite the fear of crashing, I get a little support from the
white powdery substance.

I'm going to need a car. And I hate to say it, but I know just
where to go.

I put on my new suit, go to my stash, and count out ten
grand. I straighten the bills out as best as I can and fold them
into thousand-dollar wads. I also grab one of my throwaway
guns, a .45-caliber Taurus pistol. It's not my style. I don't
like the shine on the steel. It's too fucking flashy, but maybe I
need a little dazzle for what I might have to do. I also take my
.38, another gun I have licensed, and then I make sure I got
enough powder this time just in case I have to pull another
all-nighter.

I cab it all the way out to the Ethiopian dealership in Maryland, where I took care of Lenny's truck.

I give the cabbie a hefty tip, and he blesses me.

I find the same Ethiopian in the lot's trailer office. He recognizes me and pops from his chair like a Whac-A-Mole.

"I'm here as a customer," I assure him.

"Oh, I see," he replies, with some hesitation.

"I can show myself around."

"Feel free. Feel free. I'll be right here when you need me."

I exit and check the few rows of cars he has on the lot. First one that catches my eye is an older-model silver Toyota Camry. It's got some good tint, but not enough to make it stand out. It's nice enough that it'd look natural sitting in someone's suburban Virginia driveway. That's what I need right there.

The price on the windshield is $8,999. I know that's high for this year and model. We'll see how much I can talk that fool down.

I go to check it out. Looks clean, but I gotta hear the engine. I turn and notice the Ethiopian staring at me through the window. I wave him over.

He responds quickly.

"That's a very excellent car."

"Let's say we dispense with the sales pitch. You got a key so I can hear the engine?"

"Yes, sir, most certainly. Let me start it for you now."

He opens the driver's door, sits, and starts the engine.

"Pop the hood for me," I tell him.

He does. I unlatch it and open it up. Looks clean enough, but a lot of that is probably just superficial. Might be leaking like a sieve, for all I know. I close the hood.

"I can arrange for you to test-drive it if you like."

"That won't be necessary. Let's go in your office and talk."

I brush off the seat in front of his desk, then sit.

After he sits I say, "I'm not going to test-drive it, 'cause if it breaks down on me I'm going to come back and have your license taken away. We clear?"

"The car will not break down, sir. Rest assured."

"Cash for the title, then, but it ain't gonna be anything close to your asking price. The car's got a hundred thousand miles on it."

"You can make an offer. We'll talk."

"I'll give you four thousand cash right now."

"No, sir. I lose money on that. Lowest I will go is eight thousand dollars."

"That's not even close to a deal. Take six-five, or I walk outta here."

He shakes his head, but more like he's thinking hard.

I stand up.

"I'll just go somewhere that wants cash, then."

"Most of my business is cash, sir. Seven thousand and it's yours."

I don't have time for this shit.

"Yeah, okay."

He stretches out his arm to shake hands. I do it, but in disgust. He won.

Sixty-seven

The car drives okay, but it'll never replace my Volvo. I'm sure the insurance company will consider the Volvo totaled. Despite that, I'm not about to hang on to this car for long. I don't like where it came from. It's like a dirty gun you get off a hit, just another throwaway.

I call Davidson on the cell.

"Hello, Frank."

"Scott. Anything new?"

"Just hitting the street like we do, knocking on doors. Chief's got almost every unit working this one. It's really hard to talk right now. Can I get back to you?"

"It'll just be a second. And I need you to stop with all this clandestine bullshit, Scott. You know me. I'm not about all that. You get anywhere with the possible university lead?"

"We're working everything. Just take it easy. I'll let you know."

"Listen, Scott, the girl might already be dead. We both know Cordell Holm can't risk the connection she has to him if she's found. If she's alive, she probably won't be for long."

"I know that, and so does everyone here. We're working it through. That source you have on the street who's giving you all this information, I'd really like to talk to whoever it is."

"That'll be the day, Scott. The source talks to me. I talk to you. It won't happen any other way, so don't ask again."

"Damn, Frankie, for an ex-cop, you're really starting to make a lot of enemies."

"You be safe, Scott," I say, then disconnect.

I make my way toward 16th and Fuller, a couple blocks from where the shooting occurred. I know it's been canvassed and the area's burning hot right now, but I have to see for myself and make sure they didn't miss the Lexus, or maybe even a familiar face.

I gave Playboy's number to the police so that rules out an okeydoke; they'll be working that number, maybe even trying one themselves, so hitting the street is a safer bet for me.

I turn off 16th and onto Fuller and park along the curb just before Mozart. Euclid would be to the left, and 17th is a long block straight ahead. I last saw the hooptie going north on Mozart, so it more than likely hit Columbia Road, which is to the right.

I'm not close enough to the corner to see Euclid. I'm sure marked cruisers are blocking it off. I notice one parked farther up Fuller, at 17th Street. A couple of uniformed officers are standing on the southeast corner.

Aside from a couple of old Latina ladies walking down Fuller from Columbia carrying grocery bags, this area's clear for now. Usually you'll find a couple of boys hanging in front of the apartment building on the corner across Mozart, and even to my left.

I decide to roll out. I hang a right on Mozart and then another right on Columbia Road, see what's going on at 16th and Park.

Sixty-eight

There's a bus stop on 16th, across from the sitting man, a statue of some religious figure near the corner at Park Road. I take a seat on the bench next to an old black homeless man. He doesn't give me a glance, just stares at the ground at his feet, as if he's studying the cracks in the sidewalk. I already smoked up my cigarette, so I pull out another. It's a little weird because I'm wearing my tactical gloves and still have my pack slung over my shoulder.

I offer a cigarette to the old man, holding it out to him even though he isn't looking at me.

"Wanna smoke?"

He lifts his head. It's an old face, probably looks older than it is because of alcohol and the elements. He looks at the cigarette, but not me. He gently takes the cig, puts it in his mouth, and finally acknowledges me with a nod. I flick my lighter and offer him a light. He accepts, then looks back down toward the cracks in the ground.

A lot of the folks across the street are just passing by, but a few are hanging, a couple of them drunks, drinking their cheap liquor from brown paper bags. A couple of them look like crackheads, and one of them I recognize from past ops at this spot. It doesn't take me long to make two of the Latino boys for dealers. They started up on the corner quicker than I thought they would. A lot of clients waiting to be served and a lot of money to be made.

The crackhead I recognize is more than likely holding the stash for them. He's just moving around a small area surrounding the monument, acting like he's got purpose. He was a regular when Angelo and company worked this corner. These boys will often use crackheads like him to hold for them, after they prove themselves as regulars and pay like they should. When it comes to work like that they're usually dependable 'cause they don't want to get the crap beat out of them, or worse, for pinching a bit of rock for themselves. Looks like these two guys who took over after Angelo got locked up work a different system. A crackhead for the stash instead of an empty Dorito bag tossed to the curb. I'll have to walk the curb to make sure.

The old man beside me adjusts himself on the bench, straightens himself up.

"You spare a bit of change?" he asks.

I still have some rolls in my pants pocket, but I don't want to pull out one of those. I reach in the pocket of my jacket for some loose bills. I pull a couple out. Two twenties.

He sees them, and his eyes widen with the possibility of getting even one of them.

"This your spot?" I ask.

"You the police?"

"Fuck no. I'm just a man looking for his runaway daughter. She went to school up the street, and I used to catch her hanging with some of those boys over there. That's what brought me here." I motion my head toward the boys I suspect are dealing.

"And you're trying to work up the courage to go have a chat with them?" he asks.

"Yeah, that's about it. Can I show you a picture of her?"

"I don't see much around here."

"Just the same, if you could just look at a couple of pictures, maybe let me know if you've seen these guys around. I'll make it worth your while."

His eyes are on the bills again.

"You can get yourself hurt bad, messin' with those boys there," he mumbles.

"Let me worry about that. What do you say?"

"A'ight."

I unzip an inner pocket of my hooded jacket and take out the photos. One is a photo of Miriam, and the other two are arrest photos of Angelo and Viktor. I show him the photo of Miriam first.

He studies it long and hard, then says, "Naw, can't say I seen her. Sorry."

"That's all right. I appreciate you taking the time. I got two more. The police gave me these pictures."

I hand both of them to him. He doesn't study them so hard.

"I seen them, but not for a bit. They used to work the corner where those boys are now."

"You ever seen the two in the photos hanging with any of those boys across the street?"

"Just one of them. That little shit over there by the statue."

"You mean the one that looks like he's a drug addict?"

"Yeah, the little skinny fuck. He be holdin' for those boys. He's the only one that's still around. He used to do the same for the two you showed me pictures of. They call him Cookie. But he ain't sweet like that."

He hands the photos back to me and I pocket them.

"He mess with you a lot?"

"You could say that."

I hand him the two twenties, reach into my pocket, and pull out another twenty and two tens. I hand him those, too.

"Damn, thank you."

"Buy yourself a bottle of some of the good stuff. What you've been drinking probably tore a hole in your gut."

"And you think the good shit'd fix that?"

I smile.

"You might wanna go hang somewhere else for a little bit. I think I got some courage now."

Sixty-nine

I zip up my jacket and walk south on 16th, then cross so I can come up to them from behind. When I get to the area where Angelo used to park his car, I scan the gutter along the parked cars, but I don't see the kind of trash I'm looking for.

At the bus stop I turn and walk into the tree-lined area surrounding the statue.

I get closer and the two Latinos see me, but don't seem to mind.

I flash my badge and say, "Roll on outta here."

They obey without hesitation. Cookie starts to slowly walk away in the opposite direction. He could run, but I'd catch him in no time.

When the two Latino boys cross Park to the other corner, they look back to see what I'm doing. I motion for them to keep moving. They continue north on 16th.

I return to Cookie, who's about to hit the sidewalk on 16th and make his way south. I get behind him.

"Hold on there, Cookie."

He turns sideways and looks like he's about to bolt.

"You make me run and I'll fuck you up."

"I ain't done nothin'," he tells me.

I grab a bit of his jacket behind his shoulder.

"What the fuck I do?"

He tries to struggle free, but with hardly any force.

"Keep your hands where I can see them and move on back here."

I escort him back to the statue of the sitting man, and I push him face-first against the large granite base. "James Cardinal Gibbons" is etched on the pink granite. I can't help but look up for a second. The seated figure's right hand is extending out and lifted just above my head as if trying to bless me.

The crackhead smells. It's the kinda smell that sticks to your clothing. Something I don't like taking home with me.

"C'mon, now, Officer Friendly, what's your cause?"

"I don't need probable cause, dopey."

I pat his waist area.

"You got anything that's gonna poke me?" I ask him.

"Naw, man, I don't do that shit."

I search his pockets and pull out a couple of small green empty dime-bag zips and a cell phone. I drop the empty zips on the ground and pocket his cell.

"Aw shit, c'mon now," he says.

When I reach into the pocket of his jacket I pull out a nice-size baggie that contains a shitload of the same small zips—dimes and twenties.

"This has gotta be more than a sixty here. Damn, that'll get you some good time."

"Fuck, you have no cause to reach in my pockets like that."

I ignore him, slip the large baggie in my side coat pocket, and continue my search. I find another baggie that contains several more zips, but these are blue and stuffed with nice powder. It looks like it's about an eight ball's worth of coke. I stick it in the pocket with the crack.

I keep Cookie pushed against the monument with my left hand and reach around to my backside with my right to grab my cuffs.

He struggles when I start to handcuff him, but I twist his wrist so he yelps and changes his mind quick.

"Fuck," he says.

I start marching him to the car, using caution as we walk across 16th. These drivers don't pay attention. We get some stares from the pedestrians, but there's nothing so unusual about someone who looks like me walking a handcuffed man like Cookie, so no worries there. Unless some cop decides to drive by. Then I'll worry.

That doesn't happen. Instead I get him quickly to the car, the passenger's side.

"What in the . . . ?" he spits out. "What kind of car is this?"

"It's an undercover car, dope."

I open the door and help him sit and then, trying to maintain a bit of distance, mostly because of his filth, I buckle him in.

I pop the trunk and grab my pack and hop in the front seat. I set the pack down on the floor behind Cookie and start the car.

"What kind of setup is this shit here? Let me see that badge again."

"I'm not gonna show you shit, Cookie."

"And how the fuck you know me like that?"

"I'm not here to answer your questions either, so you'd better just sit tight and shut the fuck up unless I ask you something."

He looks at me with an amazed, openmouthed kinda look, but without fear, just really bad teeth.

I park the car in the lot between the two trailers where I met up with Tamie. Cookie's been surprisingly quiet. I take him for someone who's been in rougher situations than this. I'm sure he knows if I was gonna beat the fuck outta him, or even kill him, I would have taken him somewhere else.

I keep the car running.

Hard to tell how old some of these guys are. He's probably in his thirties. His clothing stinks, but it's not the kind of clothing a homeless person would wear, just something he doesn't wash regularly. I can't tell, but under the black skullcap it looks like he's got an old-school barber cut.

"So here's where we stand, Cookie."

"These cuffs are kinda tight. You can loosen them up a bit?"

"Shut the fuck up."

I pull out the baggie with the crack and drop it in his lap. His big eyes immediately gravitate toward it.

"That's a lot of crack. Looks like there's a nice rock in there, too, something they shave off for a hit or two, huh?"

"Is this where you think you're going to roll me?" Cookie asks. "'Cause I ain't gonna roll. Your people done tried that before, but I took the time instead."

"No, man. I don't expect that much work from you. Let me lay it out here, 'cause I don't have much time."

I pull out the photos of Angelo and Viktor and set them on the dashboard in front of him. He leans forward as best as he can.

"Before you say anything, Cookie, I wanna make something real clear. You don't answer my questions truthfully—and I'll know if you don't—I'm not gonna take you to jail or sit here and try to convince you with bullshit threats. I'm just gonna kill you."

"What?!" he exclaims.

"Look at me."

He does.

"No bluff. This shit is real."

"You're no cop."

299

"It doesn't matter whether I am or not. It only matters that you believe I'm gonna kill you if you don't cooperate. Tell me you understand that."

"Fucking understand that. Yeah."

"Okay. Then let's get started."

SEVENTY

"Tell me about those two 'migos in the photos."

Cookie bends forward to look.

He motions with his head toward the first one.

"That one there is Angelo. He used to run the corner you got me at, but he got himself locked up. The other 'migo is his running partner, Vik."

"Good, you're being truthful. You ever been to their house?"

"Fuck no. They'd never take me to their house."

I pick up the photos, set them in the center console, and take out the one of Miriam and place it gently on the dashboard.

"You ever seen her before?"

He looks at it, then leans back in his seat and turns to me.

"Who the fuck are you, man?"

"Fucking answer the question."

"I seen her before. She stays in one of them row houses. Up at Seventeenth, Euclid."

"She's my niece. She's only sixteen years old."

"Aw, fuck that shit. I ain't have nothin' to do with her. C'mon, man . . ."

"I'm not accusing you of something like that. I just want to know where I can find her."

"I told you where."

"You know about the cop that just got shot up there, right?"

"Yeah, I heard."

"Then you know they rolled outta that house. I need to know where they're keeping themselves now."

"I'm not in with them like that. They got themselves a lot of spots around there."

"So you know Cordell?"

"Hell yeah. Everyone in this area knows Cordell."

"You know what unit he keeps himself in at the Ritz?"

"His peoples are the only ones that know something like that."

"Little Monster?"

"How the fuck?" He looks at me. "I mean, yeah, he be one of them."

"What about Playboy?"

"There's a lot of boys who like to call themselves that."

"This one's a good-lookin' boy, real short-cut hair. He drives a black Lexus."

"That sound like one of them I know."

"I need to know everywhere they bed down."

"I told you I don't know all that."

"All right, then. I guess we're done here."

"What the fuck you mean by that?"

I put the car in reverse.

"Hold on, man. Just hold the fuck on."

I put it back in park.

"I might know someplace, but I don't know if your niece be there, too."

"I'll drive. You direct me where to go."

"I can just tell you. I can't be seen like that."

I reach over him and pull the latch on the side of his seat. He drops back suddenly; he isn't prepared for it.

"Damn, man, give me some warning."

"There's some good tint on this car. All you gotta do is stay low. They won't see you. I'm not some fucking rookie."

I put it in reverse and back out.

"Which way?"

"You wanna go left, then to University Place. You know where that is, right?"

University Place? Fuckin' A. Is that what the fuck the officer meant?

"Clifton and Euclid, or Fairmont?" I ask.

"Clifton and Euclid."

It's not far from here. I head toward 14th. Cookie goes quiet again. I think he hit the pipe before I snatched him up, and his brain hasn't caught on to the reality of the situation.

I get to the light at 14th and Clifton and turn the blinker on to make a left.

"No, not here." He panics. "That block's too hot. Take that left at Euclid."

I've done this more times than I can count and never had a problem. And as much as I've put up my nose, you'd think I'd be the paranoid one in this car. Yeah, I know this area well. The 1300 block of Clifton Terrace behind us is the real hot spot, and even Garfield Terrace, a couple more blocks east of that. We used to play around there all the time. Problem was, those mopes didn't want to play with us.

I make the turn on Euclid. The next street is University Place.

Before we get there, Cookie says, "Keep on Euclid here. I'll point the house out when we pass. It'll be just to the left on University."

I don't do what he says. Instead I make the left.

"Fuck no! What're you doing? Shit . . ."

On the left side, past the side of an apartment complex that faces Euclid and takes up about a quarter of the block on University Place, is a light green house with a large porch. A couple of boys are hanging out on the front porch.

"Shit. That's the house there. To the left. Don't fucking slow down. Just go. Man, you gonna burn the fuck outta me."

"Relax. You stay low, they can't see shit. You're referring to the house with the two guys on the front porch, right?"

"Yeah, that's it. Fucking get me out of here. I can't be seen in a car with someone like you."

"Now you fucking hurt my feelings."

I prop my left elbow on the edge near the window and cup the left side of my face with my hand so they can't make out my face. I drive at regular speed and pass them.

I make a left on Clifton and head back to 14th.

"Is there another spot you might want to show me?"

"Naw, man. That's the only place I know outside of Seventeenth and Euclid. There be a couple places up there, but like you said, they probably be up outta there right now."

"Did you recognize those two on the porch?"

"I didn't look to see them good enough."

"How do you know about the house?"

"A lot of 'migos be stayin' in there."

"Like the two you been holding for?"

"No. I told you I don't know where they live."

"What do they do outta this house, then?"

"They got some rooms up in there they rent out, but mostly for the 'migos. A lot of drinking and gambling. All that kinda shit."

"What's Cordell's connection to that house?"

"He might keep some girls up in there and a couple of his boys. He's got a piece of it."

"Is it a stash house?"

I can see out of the corner of my eye that he looks at me funny.

"I don't know that kinda shit, but I don't think so. There be too many people in and out of there for him to keep his shit there."

"He got some prostitutes working out of there?"

"Yeah, I said he got some girls in the house."

"You been in there before?"

"Not like that, man."

"You never went in to get your dick sucked?"

"No. No. I can't afford any of them girls."

He looks at me like he might have said the wrong thing.

"I don't mean anything like that about your niece, all right?"

"But you've been in the house before?"

"Yeah."

"Where do the girls stay?"

"I think they keep themselves in the basement. They got a lot of rooms in that house."

I make a right on 14th.

"You still didn't tell me how you know about what goes on in there."

"This is my 'hood. I grew up here, man."

"Where do you live?"

"C'mon, now, why I gotta tell you that?"

"Because I asked."

"My moms and pops have a house on Girard."

"What hundred block?"

"Shit. I told you what you want to know, so why do you need to get personal?"

"What hundred block?"

"Fourteen hundred. Shit."

"You still live there?"

"Yeah, I stay up in there."

"I'll take you home."

"No, you don't gotta do that. Just let me out back where we was parked and I'll walk. Don't be goin' and dropping me off where I live. You trying to get me killed?"

"I can do that myself, fuckwad. Now take me to your house so I can see you walk in. I want to know where to snatch you up if you're lying to me."

When it's safe, I make a U-turn and head north, toward Girard.

"I ain't lying to you."

"Just the same. You're going to show me the house."

"Fuck, you're—" but he doesn't know how to finish the thought.

I know that look he's giving. I know it well. It's the kinda look you have when you recognize your own kind. Or is it?

I quickly let it go 'cause I'm probably reading too much into it.

I turn onto the 1400 block of Girard. It's a whole new crew in this area, and they play just as hard as the boys on Euclid. A lot of them hanging at the apartment building when we make the turn. First dead body I ever saw was on this block. He was on the sidewalk in front of the corner building, his head bent down into the gutter and his blood spurting out like a spout.

"Where's your house?"

"Get past this shit here, man. Drive on."

Before we hit 15th, he points to a row of two-story connected row homes on the right.

"The one right there past the alley."

It's a one-way street, so I park on the other side, near a large community center. I remember when it was a smaller abandoned building with busted-out windows and occupied by squatters. Looks like DC did something right for the neighborhood by replacing it with a community center.

"Your parents still live there?"

"Just my moms. My pops passed on."

"I'm sorry to hear that."

He doesn't respond; he's probably not used to hearing people offer their condolences.

I grab the bag of crack off his lap, reach in, and take five dime bags out of it. I drop the zips in his side coat pocket and then the large baggie back in my coat.

"What the fuck kinda cop are you, man?"

"The broken kind."

I turn the car off, find the handcuff key on the key ring, and reach over to unlock the cuffs.

"Bend forward," I tell him.

When he does, I unbind him.

"You know a kid by the name Edgar?"

"Naw, never heard of him."

"He's Latino, seventeen years old and lives in Virginia, but hung out with Angelo."

"No, man, don't know him."

"You ever hear about any of the boys in Cordell's crew taking a hit out on a kid in Virginia?"

"No, I never heard nothin' like that."

I grab his cell phone out of the pocket of my jacket.

"You got Cordell's number in here? Playboy's or Little Monster's?"

"Fuck no."

I search it anyway. I find Angelo, José, and Viktor, but no one else I recognize.

"I told you I ain't got no numbers like that."

I tap in my cell number to call myself.

"Now what you gotta go and do?"

When my cell rings, I pull it out and look at the number.

"I'll save your number. You're now a Cookie in my phone. You answer if it ever rings. Am I clear?"

"Yeah, you clear."

"Now let me see you walk into your house."

He crosses the street. He takes some keys out of his pocket and walks the short flight of stairs to the porch. He fiddles with the keys, unlocks the door, and enters, shutting the door behind him.

I wait a couple of minutes, then call him from my cell. He answers on the first ring.

"You forgot some of your shit in my car."

Seconds later, the door opens and he returns.

I roll down the window so he can lean in. I take out the large bag of crack and toss it on the seat.

"You keep that shit. Don't be seen for at least three days, and if anyone asks tell them your case got no-papered because it was a bad search. You understand that?"

"Yeah, fuck yeah."

He snatches it right up. "Bad search, no-papered," he repeats, then looks to his right, then to his left, and pockets the shit.

"You better do just what I said 'cause you know what they'll do otherwise. And you fuck with me I'll do worse. I'll bust into your home and kill your mom and then you."

"I got you, man. Shit, you don't gotta worry about shit. But what about that powder you took off me?"

"Don't get greedy."

Seventy-one

I make the turn in the alley behind the 1400 block of Euclid that leads to University Place. Several cars are parked in a small area at the back of an apartment complex. One of the cars is a black Lexus that looks exactly like the one Playboy drives. I get as close to being excited as I possibly can nowadays. And that fucking Cookie's the man.

I'm hoping Playboy doesn't stay in that apartment complex. It'd be a nightmare trying to find his unit. Street-corner mopes generally don't sign leases. None of the spaces are marked with numbers, so more than likely he's just taking the space and calling it his own. I'm guessing he's in the house my new boy Cookie pointed out.

These boys have already proven they don't mess around. I don't have reinforcements. I'm not in the gang anymore. I'm tempted to call Luna—he'll get a surveillance crew on the car and the house, but damn if they don't spend too much time on shit like that. The Lexus parked in the alley doesn't obviously connect Playboy to the house, even though I'm convinced it does.

Police need much more than that before they go in. But I'm not about to go in that house with guns blazing, either, even if I do have a flashy throwaway. This ain't the movies or one of those fucked-up cop shows you watch on TV.

I back into one of the parking spaces at the far end, beside a Dumpster. I'll sit here and see how this plays out. That pretty much sums up what you do in this line of work.

Seventy-two

Throughout the day and into the early evening, a number of people walk by the opening to the alley on University. I can't tell how many of those folks are walking up to the house. The only visual I have on the house is the rear and the small backyard. A six-foot-high bent-up chain-link fence surrounds the yard. The windows are either blacked out or, like my bedroom windows, have thick curtains.

My window is rolled down partway. Cars in the distance sound like gentle waves against sand. I got a bottle of Jameson in the pack, and now, with what I took off Cookie, more blow than I need. Only thing I forgot was my Gatorade bottle, but I'm far enough back that I'll just piss behind the Dumpster if I have to. I'm prepared to sit for as long as it takes.

I usually like the solitude, even the confinement that comes with conducting surveillance. But sometimes, like now, it triggers something in my brain, like a switch with a short, so I can't do anything but yield to whatever my mind conjures up. I'm pretty good at blocking certain things out, but it's getting tougher, especially after what happened with Leslie, and then los-ing Miriam.

In my line of work the most commonplace decision can de-stroy a life, or take it. I don't worry about things like that 'cause it'll cripple you. I do have worries, though, and never talking to Leslie again is one of them. I don't even know what we are . . . or were. Two lonely people who need each other? Or just one lonely man who thinks he needs her?

These thoughts I'm having are more than likely the result of fatigue, too much alcohol, and not enough blow. But what can I do? Stop drinking?

God forbid!

Who the hell am I kidding? I'm too fucking needy sometimes. Maybe I should blame my parents, and growing up in a broken family, like some of these messed-up kids I've been dealing with do. Or maybe just blame my mother, the one responsible for all the destruction. She killed herself when my older brother and I were nothin' but kids.

At least that's what our father told us.

Enough of this shit. I grab my flask out of the center console and take a hard swig, and then another for good measure. As far as the blow, sometimes the knowledge that it's there when I need it is enough. So I control the urge to self-medicate further.

A couple of crackheads walk through the alley, coming up from Euclid, scoping out the garages and the cars on the other side for a quick hit. I tuck down and watch them pass. They slowly make their way to University, and walk right in the oppo-site direction of the house.

The evening fades into night. There's a heavy darkness over this alley. The streetlamps that are here don't work. The only light I get is what filters out of windows.

It's 12:43 when I notice the headlights from a car entering the alley from the direction of Euclid. I lean back as it passes. It's a newer-model Escalade. It drives slowly and then parks near the Lexus. The passenger's side opens and a black man I don't recognize steps out. He walks toward the rear of the vehicle and meets up with the driver. I creep up as best as I can to get a better look. They open the back of the Cadillac and the passenger pulls out a bag of groceries or something. When he steps back to allow the driver to close the hatch I can see the driver.

Fuckin' Little Monster.

They walk toward University Place and then left toward the house.

All the training I went through as a cop tells me not to step out of the car and go after them.

I hit Luna on the cell, but it kicks into message.

I try Davidson and it's the same thing.

"Fuckwads," I say to myself.

As I'm searching for Millhoff's number, my cell rings. It's Luna.

"You'd better not be getting fucking drunk," I say.

"Hell no. I'm still working on the shooting. What do you need?"

"I'm sitting behind a house that your shooter, Little Monster, just walked in."

"Fuck, you are kidding me?"

"I'm pretty sure he's going to be in there for a while, but you might want to get surveillance set up on it ASAP so you can get an emergency search warrant."

"And you're sure about this?"

"Hell yeah, I'm sure. That mope almost killed me, too."

"Where are you?"

"In the alley rear of the fourteen hundred block of Euclid, parked in a four-door Toyota alongside the only Dumpsters in the alley. The house is on the twenty-five hundred block of University Place. I didn't get an address, so I'll have to point it out. Don't drive in the alley. Come on foot from the Euclid side. You know where I'm talking about, right?"

"Yeah, now you fucking stand by and don't go stupid. You hear?"

"Who do you think you're talking to, partner? Now hurry up."

I pull out my flask and take a nice hefty swig of Jameson to calm my nerves.

SEVENTY-THREE

It doesn't take Luna more than a few minutes to show, probably because the area they've been working is only a few blocks away.

He's dressed down for the occasion. Looks like a bum. I roll down my window.

"Hop in," I tell him.

He walks around the rear of my car to the passenger's side and enters.

"See the Escalade and the black Lexus over there?"

"Yeah."

"Little Monster got out of the driver's side of the Escalade along with another subject, who I don't know, and they walked to University Place. The Lexus there belongs to Playboy, the driver of the hooptie."

"Where's the house?"

"Straight ahead. The light green house to the left of the red-brick row house. It has the chain-link fence."

"Got it. I have to ask again, so don't jump down my throat. Are you sure about this?"

"When was the last time I wasn't?"

"I'm just saying, because we bust into that house and you're wrong, it's my ass that's going to get spanked, not yours."

"They're in there, Albino."

"All right, then." He looks around the alley. "I can get an undercover car set up back here no problem. I need you to drive me through University Place to point out the house so I can get the address and a quick look at it."

"Just like old times."

"Hoorah, partner," he says. "Stand by until I get the cars set up back here."

He pulls out his handheld radio, keeps it low and near his lap, and calls the undercover vehicle over the air. After they respond, he advises them to come in and park on the north side of the alley beside my car, and he gives them a description of my car.

Not even a couple minutes later, an old beat-up Honda hatchback drives through from Euclid, pulls ahead of us, and then backs into a thin space on Luna's side, between my car and a small truck.

Luna rolls down the window partway.

"The light green house straight ahead with the chain-link fence. You got it?"

"Yeah," I hear the driver say in a low voice. "We got it."

He rolls up the window and I start the car but don't turn the lights on. I head toward Euclid.

When I make the turn to Euclid, I turn on the lights.

I loop around and point out the house.

It looks hot, maybe five or six guys on the porch drinking and smoking blunts. I drive the speed limit, looking straight ahead, and turn left on Clifton.

"You get what you need?" I ask.

"I got it. Lot of players on that patio. ERT's going to have to come in on this one."

"Where do you want me to drop you off?"

"In the parking lot, rear of twenty-five hundred Fourteenth."

"I'm going back to my spot in the alley."

"Fuck no. You go home."

"No, fuck you, I stay until I hear from you and you tell me whether you have the girl or not. You get that Little Monster and hopefully I get the missing girl. You got no say."

"You just stay out of the way. And I only say that because I'm looking out for you."

"I can take care of myself."

"I'm not talking about that. I'm talking about a certain assistant chief that wants your head."

"Don't worry yourself, I won't go near the scene."

He picks up my flask from the center console.

"Is this fresh water?"

"Yeah, but it might have a little bite."

He tilts it up and takes a good swig.

SEVENTY-FOUR

I have enough tint on the side windows that I don't worry about the prying eyes in the UC vehicle parked next to me. Even though, I still try to be discreet.

This was the part of the job I always liked, just sitting and watching. There's no action to watch here, though, just the back of the house and the occasional drunk or crackhead pissing in the alley.

Before I know it, the daylight's breaking through.

Just before the clock hits 0600, I notice four officers quietly exiting the undercover vehicle. They shut the doors without a sound. The driver taps on my passenger's side window. I roll it halfway down.

I recognize him from the branch, but forget his name.

"What's up, Marr?" he almost whispers.

"You guys sleep well?"

"I wish," he says, and then: "Luna wanted me to remind you not to get out of your car and he'll hit you on your cell when they clear the scene."

"I got ya."

"All right, then."

They move to cover the rear of the house. I roll the windows down all the way so I can hear. When they get where they're supposed to be, they draw their weapons and tuck them to their sides.

Two more unmarked detective cruisers drive past me and stop at the end of the alley, on University Place. Plainclothes officers step out and all but one of them move toward the front of the house.

The ERT wagon drives by quickly on University Place, followed by a line of marked and unmarked units, and then seconds later I hear what sounds like the front door getting bashed open by a ram—two quick hits. Obviously no knock-and-announce for this one.

Then I hear them hollering out commands.

"Get down!"

". . . Hands!"

I hear what sounds like a window being smashed out.

A flashbang, followed by a bright white light, like lightning, through a second-story window at the rear of the house.

That same window squawks open; someone crawls out and hangs, and then drops down. Someone else jumps after him.

Three of the officers at the rear of the house holster their weapons while the other one covers them and they climb the fence to the backyard. By that time, two more subjects have dropped down.

It's hard to tell from here, but I know they're fighting. The sounds of huffing and whacking. They all seemed to fall to the ground.

The cover officer holsters his weapon and climbs the fence, and just as he's getting over and dropping to the other side, I see a black male in nothing but his boxer shorts start to scale the fence to get out. The cover officer leaps for him and grabs a leg. The guy in the boxers kicks at him with his bare foot.

Two shots ring out from the backyard, and the officer lets go of the guy's leg, draws his weapon, and turns. I'm thinking it's about the time I should jump out and assist, but I see the flash from the cover officer's muzzle as he fires two times, and then the boxer-shorts boy getting over the fence and running in my direction. No one is paying attention because of the shooting, and maybe they're still fighting, 'cause I don't see the cover officer anymore.

The running boy in the boxers is Playboy. He's approaching fast, about to run past me toward the cut that leads to Euclid.

I step out of the car just before he's about to pass. He doesn't get a chance to outmaneuver me. I send him one solid punch, square on the left side of his jaw, and he can do nothin' but drop to the ground.

I look around, thinking some of the officers will be running my way, but they're too busy both inside and outside the house. I grab Playboy by the hand, drag him to the rear of my vehicle, and roll him onto his stomach. I look back up and toward the house, but there are still no cops approaching me. I'm sure it's a cluster-fuck back in there.

I look at Playboy. He's starting to groan. I look around, trying to see if anyone is looking out windows. No one that I can see, but then again it really wouldn't matter, because they'll just think I'm a cop.

I open the rear door of my car and grab zip ties out of my pack. I use them on Playboy's hands and feet, so he's hogtied like we used to do to fighting prisoners. I grab him from under his armpits and hoist him up. He's limp as shit, but starting to come to. I half drag him to the back of the car and drop him face-first on the backseat. I have to bend up his legs to shut the door.

I hop in the driver's side, grab my pack from the backseat near Playboy's feet, and place it on the front seat.

I sit and wait for Playboy to wake up and Luna to call. Last thing I'm gonna do is walk him over there now.

SEVENTY-FIVE

The unmarked cruisers are blocking the entrance to the alley from University Place, so the ambulance has to park in the middle of the street. The EMTs squeeze by the parked cars, carrying a portable stretcher. They run to the rear of the house. A couple of firemen run to the scene shortly thereafter. One of them is carrying a Halligan bar and the other one has bolt cutters.

I look back at Playboy. I had to duct-tape his mouth so he'd shut up. He's conscious and obviously scared. He's positioned so he's sideways and his back is against the backseat. He's got a nice knot where I punched him, and the soles of his feet were cut up from the run, but it shouldn't be much of a cleanup.

"Shouldn't be that much longer, Playboy."

He mumbles something unintelligible.

"And shut the fuck up."

It looks like they had to snip a lock that secured the gate to the backyard.

They carry out a body secured to the stretcher with straps. I can't make out if it's a cop. They run him back to the ambulance, and seconds later they pull out with lights and sirens.

It's been almost two hours, and I'm wondering when Luna will call. I'm actually thinking I should call him and tell him I got his runaway in the backseat of my car. More than that, I need to know if he has Miriam.

I call him.

He answers on the fourth ring with "It's really fucked up in here, Frank. Gotta call you back."

"Just tell me if you have the girl."

He doesn't answer right away.

"I'm sorry, partner. She's not here."

"Fuck!"

"I'll call you back. I promise. Just stand by."

I disconnect.

"Fuck," I say again. "Why'd I get involved with this fuckin' shit? Fuckin' . . ."

I wanna hit something—the dashboard, or bust out my window with my fist.

"Fuck."

I look back at Playboy.

"It looks like you might be Miriam's last hope, and for your sake, she'd better be alive."

He's blinking tears out of his eyes and mumbling something I could care less about.

Seventy-six

I know the spot, and it's not far from here.

It's still early, with only a little traffic.

That's what I love about DC. You can find a pocket spot like this when you need one. It's an alley with a dead end that stretches one block. It's nice and secluded. There's an old working car garage along the north side and a large abandoned warehouse on the south. The warehouse is boarded up, so I don't have to worry about waking up whoever might be calling it home. And it's too early for the crackhead prostitutes, junkies, and all the other filth to be hanging there doing their shit.

I drive to the far end of the street and park alongside the warehouse.

I exit, open the rear door, pull sobbing Playboy out of the car, and drop him on his bare back on the dirty, broken pavement. His feet are bound together tightly with the zips, maybe a bit too tightly, 'cause there are thin areas of dried-up blood around the edges of the zip ties.

Empty dime-size ziplocks, used needles, and condoms are scattered around. Playboy didn't cry out through the duct tape when I dropped him, so I'm sure he didn't get a needle through his back.

It's then that he starts rolling back and forth on his back, trying to break free. I slap his face.

"Stay."

I lean into the back of the car and grab the stun gun, but then decide to put it back because I want him conscious. I grab my tactical folding knife instead. I take my gloves off, toss them on the front seat, pull out two latex surgical gloves from the pack, and put them on.

I step out, pull Miriam's photo out of my jacket, and then take the jacket off so he can see my holstered .38 and the throwaway semiauto wedged in the back of my pants, where I keep the cuffs. I reach in the back of the car, drop the jacket onto the passenger seat, and then return to him.

"Stop fucking mumbling. I don't understand a word you're saying. All you gotta do is listen up, and then I'll give you a chance. All right?"

He gives several quick nods.

"Okay, then. Here's the bottom line. I ain't the police anymore, so I don't have to follow those rules. That's why you need to be afraid. I'm prepared to do whatever I gotta do to you to get the answers I need. We clear on that part?"

Several more nods.

"I'm going to show you a photograph and then I'll take part of the tape off so you can answer my questions."

I squat down, but before I peel part of the tape off I say, "You fucking scream out or some shit like that, it goes back on and I'll fuck you sideways."

I peel it halfway off. I show him the photograph of Miriam.

"Where is she?"

"Aw, fuck, fuck, I . . ."

"Tell me."

"I don't know who that is. Please, man . . ."

"You fucking know who it is. I had her in my hand at Seventeenth and Euclid when you and Little Monster called up your cop friend. Remember, the one you shot?"

"I didn't do that shit, man. Shit. C'mon, now . . ."

"One more time and then I'm gonna cut your dick off."

"Aww, c'mon, now."

"Where is she?"

He pulls in his lips over his teeth like he needs to bite down to prevent himself from talking.

"I don't have time for this shit. Don't think I won't follow through, little man. She's my niece. I love her."

One thing I've always been good at is knowing people. And I know if you have a man hogtied in an alley in nothin' but his drawers, he'll be feeling so vulnerable he'll more than likely do just about anything to get out of that position.

I press the tape back over his mouth and flick the knife open with my thumb.

He's shaking his head back and forth on the ground, whimpering, so the tape puffs out and then sucks in.

I pull the front of his shorts down. He flails like a fish on dry land.

His knees are pressed together, so I press my left knee over them and give him all my weight.

I look at his crotch.

"I can see why they call you Playboy. This might take more than one cut."

I grab his dick with my left hand and stretch it out, then I hold the knife up so hc can see it.

"You're gonna make this worse if you keep jumping around like that."

I pull the knife back. Look in his eyes hard.

"You want one more chance?"

Frantic nods.

"This is your last chance," I tell him, and pull the tape back.

"Fuck! Fuck!" he yells.

"I'm not playing. I will cut your dick off, then dump your ass in the river, so you talk."

"Apartment on Fuller, man! Sixteenth and Fuller."

"Is she alive?"

"Last I saw she was alive, but I got nothing to do with what they do. You gotta believe."

"Give me the address and the unit number."

Seventy-seven

Damn, the things I gotta fucking do.

I put Playboy's shorts back on, put fresh duct tape on his mouth, and dropped him in the trunk.

Now I'm heading to 16th and Fuller. It's the complex I was looking at yesterday. She's probably been there all this time. I don't know how long after the shooting she got there. I'm sure Little Monster didn't stop to drop her off. They had to get her back there somehow, but I don't know how, with all the cops that were rolling through that day.

I park right at the corner and run to the front door. It's still too early for most of the boys to be hanging, but then it's also still hot 'cause of all the recent action.

The glass front door is locked. I try to jimmy the lock with the tip of my knife, but it's got a solid bolt.

Not again, I think, after remembering having to smash the glass door out at the Ritz.

I'm surprised by someone approaching me from behind. I

328

turn to see an old Latina lady carrying two grocery bags. She obviously wants to enter, but seems hesitant to approach.

"Policía," I advise her calmly.

I pull out my wallet and show her my badge. She smiles kindly and hands me one of her grocery bags, then unlocks the door for me.

I hold it open for her to enter and once inside I hand her grocery bag back.

"Gracias," I say.

She smiles kindly and walks toward the elevators.

I decide on the stairs, taking two steps at a time to the second floor.

When I get to the apartment door, I unholster my .38 and pound on it with a closed fist. When no one answers, I pound harder.

I'm about to kick the door in when I hear, *"¡Espera un momento! ¡Un momento!"* from a lady on the other side of it.

The door opens. She's old and wearing an apron. I smell something good from the kitchen. It's a small unit—open door to the kitchen, a living room area that opens up to a little dining area, and a small hall with two doors that I can see.

She's startled at the sight of the gun and backs up, murmuring something that sounds like a prayer. I start to think that Playboy either gave me the wrong unit number or just made up some shit. A young Latina girl wearing men's boxer shorts and a white T-shirt enters from another room. It takes a second, but then I recognize her as the girl who was walking with Miriam and had her hand in her purse like she was threatening me with something.

"¡No, Abuela! No!" she screams, and runs over to try to shut the door on me, but I shove it open, throwing the girl back and almost on her ass.

I aim the gun at her.

Grandma shrieks.

"Anyone else here I should worry about?" I ask.

She doesn't answer.

"I'm not playing, girl. Do something stupid and I'll shoot." And then I say, a little louder, "And anyone else who's in the apartment."

"There's no one else here," the girl says.

Grandma's hands are across her chest.

"Have your grandma take a seat before she keels over."

"*Sentarse, Abuela,*" she says softly, and helps her to sit on the couch, then puts her arm around her shoulder to comfort her. "*No te preocupes, Abuela.*"

"Where's Miriam?"

"I don't know," she says.

"Fucking don't move," I say, and then go to search the apartment.

"I told you, she's not here."

I tuck my gun and sidestep so I can see in the kitchen. It's clear.

"Please go. Please, mister," she pleads.

"Get up," I tell her.

"Please."

"Get the fuck up," I demand.

She stands. I grab her by the left arm and tug her toward me. Grandma stands like she's going to defend her.

"Tell her to sit the fuck down before she gets hurt."

"*Siéntase. Siéntase, Abuela. Está bien.*"

Grandma hesitates, but sits.

"*Por favor, señor,*" Grandma begs.

"*Cálmarse, Abuela,*" I say.

I push the girl in front of me and walk toward the hall.

"Miriam," I call.

No answer.

I pass one open door. It's a bathroom. There's another door to the right of that. It's partially open, so I kick it softly with my foot to open it all the way. I look in. It looks like Grandma's room. The sliding door for the closet is open and the bed is neatly made, but the covers hang all the way to the floor.

"You go in there and lift the covers so I can see under the bed."

She obeys. I look down, but there are just a bunch of shoe boxes.

"Get the fuck back here."

I grab her arm again and start moving toward the bedroom.

"You're going to get us killed," she says. "Please, mister."

I walk to the other room. It has two single beds. On one of them is a girl on her side, tucked under the covers.

SEVENTY-EIGHT

I have the Latina girl sit on the other bed, and then I walk over to the side of the bed where the other girl is facing.

I know it's Miriam, but her face is pale and sickly. There's caked vomit on the pillow by her mouth and on the sheet.

I gently nudge her by the shoulder.

"Miriam. Wake up, girl."

She doesn't move.

"What'd they do to her?" I ask, pulling the covers back. She's in a nightgown. I gently pull the gown up to expose her upper right thigh. She has a birthmark that looks like Australia.

"They gave her some heroin, said that it would calm her down, but she's doesn't do that stuff. I think she's OD'ing."

"No fucking shit."

I keep a hand on my gun just in case, but I lean down, and with my free hand I brush her hair from her face and lift her eyelid. After that, I check for a pulse. She still has one, but barely.

"Why didn't you call a fucking ambulance?"

"I can't. They said I can't. She just needs to sleep it off."

Man, drugs make people stupid as shit. I should know because I'm tempted to search her apartment to find her stash and take it for myself.

"You don't let someone OD'ing sleep it off, you dumb twat."

She's not gurgling, but I still open her mouth to make sure she's not drowning in her own vomit. It's clear.

I don't know if the girl put her on her side or she just fell that way, but it's the best position for her to be in. I've seen this more times than I care to remember. Most of those ODs were already dead by the time I got to the scene.

I get my cell out to call an ambulance. I can't just throw her in the backseat and drive. I can get her to MedStar in less than ten minutes if I take her, but still, I can't have her in the backseat alone and I can't trust this girl enough to help. If she dies back there, it's on me.

I call 911 and advise the dispatcher that I have the teenage girl, Miriam Gregory, who has the recent Amber Alert out on her.

"She's unconscious. Possible OD," I say.

The dispatcher tries to keep me on the phone, but after I give the address, I say the girl needs attention and disconnect.

I put my hand on Miriam's shoulder and nudge her again a few times.

"Help's on the way," I whisper. "You'll be okay, Miriam. You'll be okay. You'll be okay."

Seventy-nine

The police got here before I can follow the ambulance.

I walk up the ramp to the hospital, I find another two officers standing by the lobby entrance.

After the officers take my information, I have them notify Davidson to respond. I also give them Miriam's parents' info, because she's in their hands now. They should be the ones to call the parents. Fact is, I'm not feeling up to making the call myself.

I enter and talk to the receptionist at the counter. He advises me that the doctors are with her now and they'll have information soon.

I go and find a seat near the window, next to a fake plant.

It doesn't take long for Davidson to show up. He's with Hawkins and Hernandez. When he's done talking to one of the officers, they walk over. He shakes my hand and takes a seat beside me.

"How the hell did you find her?"

"Pounding the pavement, knocking on doors; one lead led to another."

"What's with the girl she was staying with?" Davidson asks.

"All I know is that's where Miriam was staying, nothing else."

"Good job," Hawkins says.

"Goes without saying, Frankie," Davidson adds.

I even get a smile from Hernandez.

Hawkins returns to the officers. I'm assuming to get more information from them.

"We need to head back, see how she's doing, and talk to the doctors," Davidson says.

"Let me know as soon as you can," I say.

"Of course," he says, and they walk back and through the double doors.

Detective Caine walks in about an hour later with Miriam's mom and dad. Caine sees me and stops, but the mom and the dad are led back to the ICU by one of the other officers.

Caine approaches me.

"Davidson called me to let me know. I picked up the parents."

"Hopefully she'll be all right," I say.

"I'm hopin' that too. Mind if I sit and wait with you?"

"I'm tired, so don't expect much."

"I'd like to say that I read you wrong, and I apologize."

"Cops should never apologize."

"It's okay if it's to another cop." He smiles.

That's a nice compliment, but I don't tell him. We sit quietly and wait together.

Officials start showing up, one after another. Even the chief and then, a few minutes after him, Wightman. Caine and I are sitting off to the side beside a few other people who are waiting around for their loved ones, so they don't notice me. I'm thankful for that.

I'm starting to fade fast. Davidson and his two cohorts return. They brief the white shirts. A lot of eyes have probably been on

Davidson for this one, including those of the chief himself. I never liked working under those conditions. The politics of the job can wear you down faster than the actual work. I'm grateful to not be a part of that anymore. Caine looks at me and offers his hand. I accept.

"I should probably see what's going on," he says, and after a hearty handshake he joins the team.

Miriam's parents come out of the back. The chiefs, along with Wightman, walk up to greet them. They shake hands like good politicians should, and I take it that means she'll be fine.

Davidson returns to me and confirms it.

"They're going to admit her, but she should pull through," he advises.

"Damn good to hear. Now, is there any way I can sneak outta here without those fucks seeing me?"

"They've already seen you, but they're busy taking all the credit so I don't see why not."

"They got their job to do."

"We know better, though, and we're the ones who matter, right?"

"Whatever it takes to keep them off my ass. That's all I care about."

"Well, you certainly accomplished that."

"I meant to ask, do you know about the search warrant they executed this morning?"

"Yeah, we were there."

"Did someone get shot? I hope not an officer."

"No, just the one they called Little Monster. He thought he could make a last stand in the backyard."

"He dead?"

"Howard Hospital. On arrival."

"Everything balanced itself out, then."

"I guess you could say that," Davidson replies.

I manage to sneak out and return to the car.

I tap on the trunk as I walk by, and then enter.

Before I start it up, I turn toward the rear and say, "Don't worry, Playboy, I didn't forget about ya."

EIGHTY

It's a cloudless day and getting chillier. It's a good time of year. The Anacostia is still a filthy river, though.

I power my cell phone off 'cause I know the calls will start flooding in soon, and I don't want to be disturbed right now. I open the trunk, and I'm temporarily taken aback by the smell. He shit and pissed in his boxer shorts. They used to be white. Now they look like he rolled in mud, and there's a bit of blood mixed in. Much of it worked its way into the fabric in the trunk of my car. That's a difficult smell to get rid of, and something I hate cleaning up.

He's fucked up, with teary, red, puffy eyes, and the swollen left side of his face has now turned a purplish red. I don't think he's got any more struggle left in him, just some moans and groans.

"She's alive," I tell him.

He nods his head up and down quickly, and what looks like a smile is trying to work its way out of the duct tape.

He's struggling to say something through it. I pull it halfway so he can talk.

"Oh, thank you, God. Thank you. I did what you told me, right?"

"Yeah, I suppose. You're responsible for a lot of people getting hurt, too."

"No, man, I told you I ain't about that. That's not me. That be them."

"No, that be you, too, little man. I want you to tell me something, though. Why didn't you take that girl Justine to work the brothel like the others?"

"Justine?"

"The high school girl in Virginia. You know who I'm talking about. The one you got fucked up on crack."

"Oh yeah."

"So why didn't you get her to work at the brothel?"

"'Cause . . . I don't know. I just didn't like her for that."

"You just liked to fuck her, then?"

"Fuck no. I don't mean like that."

"Well, it doesn't matter now."

I pull him out by the arms, careful not to soil my gloves. I let him fall over the bumper and to the ground. His feet are hogtied to his hands so he falls to his side.

He sees the river. By the look he's got, I know he knows what's up.

"Aw fuck no, c'mon, now. Fuck this."

I lean down to grab him.

"Wait, wait . . . I can give you something else. I got somethin' good you need to know. Maybe we can work this shit out, huh?"

"What do you got?"

It takes him a moment to catch his breath.

"I can tell you who shot that officer."

"Didn't we go over that shit already?"

"Naw, man, naw."

"I must be tired, then."

"Little Monster did that shit."

"That's old news, Playboy. He got himself killed by the police in the back of the house you ran out of."

"What?"

"No shit. No more Little Monster. You can tell me one other thing, though."

"Yeah, man. Anything. What you need?"

"Why did he have to go and kill the cop? I thought it was just me he was after."

"He crazy like that. He got himself all worked up when Officer Tommy rolled up and called it his."

"That's some shit."

"Yeah, man, sure is, but he crazy like that."

"All those dippers he smokes, huh?"

"Yeah, must be."

"But still, you were the driver."

"Fuck, man, shit . . . I had to drive. I told you he fucking crazy. But wait, I got somethin' else for you. Something much better. You need to hear this shit, man."

"Make it good."

"That officer who got shot, he wasn't all you think."

"Yeah?"

"He got himself a girl at the brothel. This young Latina girl. He be up there almost every night with her. He never pay, either."

"He's dead, so what the fuck do I care for?"

"Instead of paying he worked it off in trade, with Cordell. Just a couple days ago he did somethin' big for him."

"What was that?"

"He shot some fucking kid in Virginia. Tapped him in the back of his head in his own bedroom."

"Fuck you," I say.

"No, man, this is for real. I'm like a witness to that shit. I heard it get set up through Monster and Cordell and Officer Tommy."

"Police will need more than you as a witness. You ain't that credible."

"There is more witnesses. The hit came through one of the 'migos that got himself locked up. His name be Angelo, and then one of his other boys was with Cordell and Officer Tommy. A boy named José. He be Angelo's brother, and the one that knew where the boy lived and shit."

"José gave the officer the address for the boy who got shot?"

"Yeah, shit yeah. Cordell okayed it, but the request came through Angelo 'cause of some shit the boy got himself involved with."

"What shit?"

"I don't know about all that, but that's good information, right?"

"Yeah, that's fucking good information, and I'll pass it on."

"So you'll let me go?"

"Fuck no. You're nothin' but a piece of shit."

I tape up his mouth before he can talk, and give him a shove so he rolls down the slope. It's an awkward tumble, like a quadruple amputee with a back deformity who is desperately trying but can't stop himself. He lands on his side and gets caught up on some trash along the riverbank. I slide myself down. He's jerking and trying to kick himself free.

I give his body a good push off the bank with my foot and send him into the river so the current'll slowly take him. His body naturally rolls upward, like a fishing bobber made for great white sharks. He sucks in air through his nose and his chest expands like he thinks that'll keep him afloat.

I pull out the Taurus and take aim at his chest. His eyes widen and nostrils flare. He struggles to break free, but all that does is take his head under. It quickly pops up again and he blows water out of his nose and almost pops the duct tape from his mouth.

He stretches his neck out, trying to keep his head up. His eyes are glazed by the cold water. They fix on me, but only for a second. It's an odd look.

I put my finger on the trigger, and then his eyes turn away from me and toward the sky. It's sudden. I know he realizes I'm not the one to give him grace, and so he doesn't want to see it coming.

I think about leaving him to the filthy river and let it do the job instead. Just turn around and walk away. But I can't imagine drowning in that foul place, pulled under, or maybe I can.

So why can't I pull the trigger?

I lower the gun and watch the light on the surface of the water, then toss the gun out, as far as I can, and I know Playboy sees it swooping over him, 'cause his black eyes follow it. It splashes into the river about ten feet past his floating body.

I look toward my feet and the river's edge. The dark water slaps at the muddy bank. It's not even a foot deep at the edge and you still can't see the bottom.

I take my suit coat off, survey the ground above me, looking for a clean spot, but there ain't one.

"Shit," I mumble.

I gently fold the suit coat and set it on a small strip of dead grass.

I step in the river. My feet sink into the mud, the cold water just below my knees. Playboy's a couple of feet out. I pull my foot out of the mud to take another step and it's like a mouth holding me in place.

Now that it's got me it doesn't wanna let me go.

I pull my right foot out of the mud and lose my shoe.

"Fuckin' hell..."

The next step is a plunge and the water's at my belly. The cold hits me with a sudden surge and I gasp and then belt out what was supposed to be "Fucking shit," but sounds like, "Foggin-shh."

I step on something I hope is a log and almost fall forward, but I reach for a small branch above my head to steady myself. I think about turning back 'cause I get a strong feeling this is it for me. This is how I'm supposed to go—in the worst possible way.

Playboy is right there in front of me. His head's now just barely out of the water, but I know he sees me. I'm chest deep in this murk and ankle deep in muddy decay. The current is strong, but not so strong to take my feet out from under me. I feel for the next step and then reach for Playboy's head. He goes under, but I manage to get my hand under his chin and pull him toward me.

When his head is at my chest I secure his chin between my forearm and bicep and slowly sidestep back to the bank, careful not to trip over any sunken debris, like a fucking suitcase.

I struggle to the bank and push him halfway up so he's on his side. His breathing is labored and snot bubbles out his nostrils. He's scratched up pretty bad and his left kneecap is swollen to the size of a softball like it's been dislocated.

I rip the duct tape off his mouth. He spits water, but not far enough to hit me.

"Don't move or I'll leave you where you are," I tell him.

"Plea..." he struggles to say.

"And shut up."

I kneel down so one knee is on the bank. I pull out my knife and fold it open. I cut the zip tie that binds his ankles to his wrists. He belts out a painful cry as his legs drop like he's lost all muscle control, and his feet splash toes-first into the water. I grab his left ankle and pull it up and cut the zips from his ankles. His hands are still bound behind his back, but I don't cut them free. I fold the knife back in place and slip it in my pants pocket.

I crawl on my hands and knees out of the water and onto the river's nasty edge. The mud's so thick it's still caked on my socks and pants legs below my knees.

I grab him under the armpit and pull him out so he's in a safer position on the bank. The heels of his feet are scraping the edge of the water.

"The rest is up to you," I tell him, and then grab my suit coat to make my way back up to the car.

"I don't think I can walk," he snivels.

I turn to look down at him.

"That look you had out there, when you turned from me to the sky and you realized it was over—what was the first thought that came to you?"

He looks up at me, not quite sure how to answer.

I don't expect him to, so I say, "You keep that thought with you. Don't forget it 'cause if there's ever a next time I'll let you sink."

He's smart enough to keep his mouth shut.

I turn away and walk back to the car.

EIGHTY-ONE

I wash out the interior of the Toyota and then I park it about a block south of my house. I never expected to keep this car; I knew that when I bought it. Good thing about Toyotas is they are among the top ten most stolen vehicles in the District.

I strip off my suit in the laundry room and let it fall to the ground. It'll never be the same. Doesn't matter how good the dry cleaner is. They'll never clean out what can't be seen. I'll let it dry on the ground and then watch it burn.

I don't draw any lines, or drink scotch, or drop Klonopin. Just shower and sleep.

The first thing I do in the morning is take another long, hot shower. Then I dress comfortably—khakis and an old faded blue T-shirt.

I make some strong coffee and sit at the kitchen table to have a cigarette with it. I remember my cell is powered off, so I turn it on.

A few messages. A few calls. Some of the numbers I don't recognize.

Leslie called again, but didn't leave a message. Luna called, asking me to call back when I can, "Nothing urgent." Davidson called, but didn't leave a message. Miriam's dad, Ian Gregory, left a message: "I don't know what to say except how thankful we are for what you did. Miriam is in a recovery room, resting now. The doctors say she'll be fine. I look forward to your call."

I'll call him, but not now.

I haven't had much time to think about Leslie. I definitely want to talk to her. I fucking miss talking to her, seeing her on a regular basis, even if it is mostly at her office.

My cell rings, startling me. I look at the display. It's Luna again.

"What the fuck you keep calling me for?"

"Damn, Frankie, you're a hero," he says.

"It's too damn early for me to talk shop."

"It's a working man's time."

"Call me later. I'm not working."

"Seriously, though, you're a fucking hero around here."

"You fucks got it all wrong. I'm just good at breaking the rules."

"Keep doing what you're doing, then."

That's so good I almost spit out my coffee.

"Davidson said he talked to you at the hospital, so you know about Little Monster?" he asks.

"Yeah, good job. Happy it wasn't a cop."

"Me too, but this one was all you, brother."

"Shut the fuck up already."

"I'm just saying."

"Well, enough said, then. Tell me how the warrant went otherwise."

"Damn, I haven't been home yet. That's how good it was."

"Happy it's you, not me," I say. "Was it one of his stash houses?"

"No big quantity of narcotics, but some PCP that looked like it was more for personal use so I don't think it was a stash house. Lot of guns though. Lots. We're thinking it was a safe house. A crash pad. You'd probably like to know: we got Cordell Holm in there."

"No shit."

"Yeah, in bed with a minor."

"Girl or boy?"

"A little girl. She was reported missing out of DC more than four months ago."

"They'll like him in prison," I say, and have a fleeting thought about how Lenny Claypole might be able to work off the title to his truck. Just putting the word out to the right prisoners is all that would take.

"You get a boy named José in there? I don't know the last name, but he's Angelo's brother."

"Yeah, we got him, too. He had a gun on him. Lot of the main crew was being held up there. More than likely because of the shooting. Why?"

"I know him from sitting on the house I got that girl Amanda out of. He's one that got away from you all. That's all."

"He'll be visiting his brother soon enough. Let's do drinks later this week."

"Sounds good."

"I'll call you."

"All right, partner, you stay safe," I say, and then disconnect.

Eighty-two

I've been thinking a lot about what Playboy told me and how I should handle it. I'm confident he won't be walking into a district station to give up what he knows about Officer Tommy, including his story about a crazy uncle who almost killed him at the Anacostia River. I'm also sure he's in the wind about now, and if and when he does get caught, whatever story he has won't matter as much as the officer he had a part in killing.

Officer Tommy's death wish was that I "don't tell," but that had nothing to do with murder. I might do dirt, but I'd never hunt some punk down, let alone kill him because someone like Cordell Holm ordered me too. Tommy crossed the line with that alone.

It doesn't take me long to figure out that the Feds are more equipped to handle something like this than Internal Affairs. Not that IA wouldn't. They just have a tendency to drag their feet. But for my own selfish reasons, I don't want to have to talk to anyone there.

After a nice long line, I call the FBI's Washington Field Office and ask to be connected to Special Agent Donna Hernandez.

They put me through, but it goes to her voicemail. I don't want to call Davidson, so I call the WFO again and advise the operator it's an emergency and pertains to the search warrant Hernandez is probably still working.

I get put on hold.

The operator comes back on and asks, "Do you have a number she can call you on?"

I give it.

Not even a minute later my cell rings.

"Frank Marr," I answer.

"Agent Hernandez, Mr. Marr. How are you?"

"Thanks for calling back so soon."

"I was told you have some urgent information?"

"Not so urgent, but important enough. Scott Davidson with you?"

"He's in the office, yes."

"Does he know you're talking to me?"

"No, why?"

"Nothing at all having to do with him. It's just something I feel should go directly through you guys."

"Okay. Stand by for a sec," she says, and then I hear scuffling, like she's moving somewhere else.

I hear a door shut.

"What do you have?"

"You already know that I gave the location where you got Cordell Holm, so don't try to pull all that top secret shit and not share anything with me. If you're going to be like that, then I'll give the information to someone else that'll want it."

"Understood," she says politely.

"I know Cordell Holm got arrested in the house and so did one of his mopes, a kid named José. He's the brother of Angelo. You remember Angelo, right?"

"Yes, of course."

"I got this information from a very reliable source, and don't ask who it is, because the source will not make itself available to you or, for that matter, to me anymore. According to the source, Angelo called in the hit on Edgar Soto through his brother José, and it was cleared through Cordell."

"But without a source——"

"Let me finish. Cordell approved the hit, but used someone outside to do it. The officer who got shot. They called him Officer Tommy."

"What?"

"It's good information. You can trust that. The officer was a frequent guest at the brothel. He had himself a Latina girl there. I'm sure if you talk to some of the girls, put together an array, and convince them it's in their best interest, they'll identify him. Another thing I know well, because despite what you might think, I was good at my job——"

"I never meant to give you the impression——"

"You can apologize later. Listen now. You got Angelo and Viktor in jail, Cordell Holm on good charges, and this boy José, who was involved in Amanda Meyer's abduction and probably rape. I'm sure you all got some other good stuff out of that house, and those boys are facing serious time. You set up debriefings with them through the U.S. Attorney's Office, one after the other, and it'll only be a matter of time before they all start rolling on each other."

"This is incredible, Frank, but I really need your source of information."

"Don't ask that again, because it's not going to happen. You have to work for this one. It might take a little time, but it'll pay off, because everyone rolls."

"Will you be available to give a statement?"

"Donna, close the fucking Edgar Soto case with some good legwork. I've seen your legs. They can work. I've given you everything you need to know, so be the hero and do it all yourself."

I disconnect.

We'll see how she plays it. I have a feeling she likes the idea of making a name for herself.

EIGHTY-THREE

I've got a nice chunk of coke on the glass table to chop up. I can't think of anything better to do today.

The doorbell rings and I nearly fall out of my seat.

I peek through the curtain.

Fuck. It's Leslie.

I run toward the door, but remember the coke.

"Who is it?" I ask like an idiot.

"Frankie, it's Leslie."

I look back in the living room. I can't let her in yet.

"Leslie, just a minute. I'm not decent. Just wait a second."

"Okay, then," she says.

I run back to the living room, look at the chunk I've been cutting up. It's gotta be more than an eight ball. I look around the living room and see the *Washington City Paper* on the coffee table.

I grab it.

"Be right there," I call out.

I open up the paper and put it on the floor near the glass table. I tip the table over it and scrape the coke into the newspaper with the razor, drop the razor in, too, fold up the paper, and slip it under the sofa cushion. I move a couple of pillows from the other side of the sofa to the cushion that covers the paper.

The glass table still has white powder residue on it, so I brush it with the palm of my hand and lick it off. I look at the palm of my hand. No powder. I wipe the saliva on my pants and check my nose in a hallway mirror.

I open the door.

"I'm sorry," I say. "Come in."

"I can't right now, but thanks."

"I have coffee."

"Maybe another time. I took a detour on the way to the office. I just thought I'd try you at home, since I haven't been able to get you over the phone."

"I meant to call back, but it's been a little crazy."

"I can imagine. I've seen the news, and Ian Gregory called me. He told me everything. Damn, you really got her back."

"And you doubted I could?"

"No, of course not, but you know this world. You know the odds."

"Yeah . . ."

"You did good, Frankie. That's all I wanted to say. And despite all the shit you recently put me through, I'm really proud of you."

Her smile might just feel better than the drugs.

"Does that mean I'm forgiven?" I say.

"You're forgiven, but on probation."

"I'll take that, then, 'cause I like the idea of having you as my parole officer."

"Don't think that I won't step you back if I have to."

"I'll do my best to be good. Can we have dinner sometime soon?"

"That would be nice," she says.

"There are a couple of new spots I've been wanting to check out."

"Me, too. Maybe the end of the week. Give me a call."

"I will."

She reaches up and kisses me lightly on the cheek. I want to make a turn for her lips, but don't. It'll just fuck up the moment.

"It's getting cold. Winter will be here soon," she says. "Then, before we know it, Christmas and a new year."

She turns and walks toward her car.

I step out on the porch.

"I'll call you at the end of the week," I say.

She turns to me and says, "Okay."

I watch her get into her car and drive. She makes a left on W and disappears.

The holiday season is right around the corner. Thanksgiving, Christmas, and especially New Year's Eve are the only holidays I don't like spending alone, and I'm thinking she doesn't either. She's got a family like mine—pretty much nonexistent. Maybe she threw me a hint that we'd be spending this one together, too.

So I feel damn good, and it's not because I'm high or because of the nice stash I have tucked away. I have more than enough so I don't have to worry for a while, but still, where's the hope in that?

ABOUT THE AUTHOR

David Swinson is a retired police detective, having served sixteen years with the Washington, DC, Metropolitan Police Department. Before joining the DC police, Swinson was a record store owner in Seal Beach, California, a punk rock/alternative concert promoter in Long Beach, California, and a music video producer and independent filmmaker in Los Angeles, California. Swinson currently lives in Northern Virginia with his wife, daughter, bull mastiff, and bearded dragon.

MULHOLLAND BOOKS

You won't be able to put down these Mulholland Books.

CLOSE YOUR EYES *by Michael Robotham*

THE EXILED *by Christopher Charles*

UNDERGROUND AIRLINES *by Ben H. Winters*

SEAL TEAM SIX: HUNT THE DRAGON *by Don Mann and Ralph Pezzullo*

THE SECOND GIRL *by David Swinson*

WE WERE KINGS *by Thomas O'Malley and Douglas Graham Purdy*

THE AMATEUR'S HOUR *by Christopher Reich*

REVOLVER *by Duane Swierczynski*

SERPENTS IN THE COLD *by Thomas O'Malley and Douglas Graham Purdy*

WHEN WE WERE ANIMALS *by Joshua Gaylord*

THE INSECT FARM *by Stuart Prebble*

CROOKED *by Austin Grossman*

ZOO CITY *by Lauren Beukes*

MOXYLAND *by Lauren Beukes*

Visit mulhollandbooks.com for
your daily suspense fix.

Download the FREE Mulholland Books app.